I0611007

After Wife

By David Farrell

Other available works by David Farrell:

The Last Resort

The Glove

Twelve

Dropping the Belt

Twelve More

Portals

2 for 1

Printed in Australia

First Printing 2023

ISBN: 978-1-64999-452-3

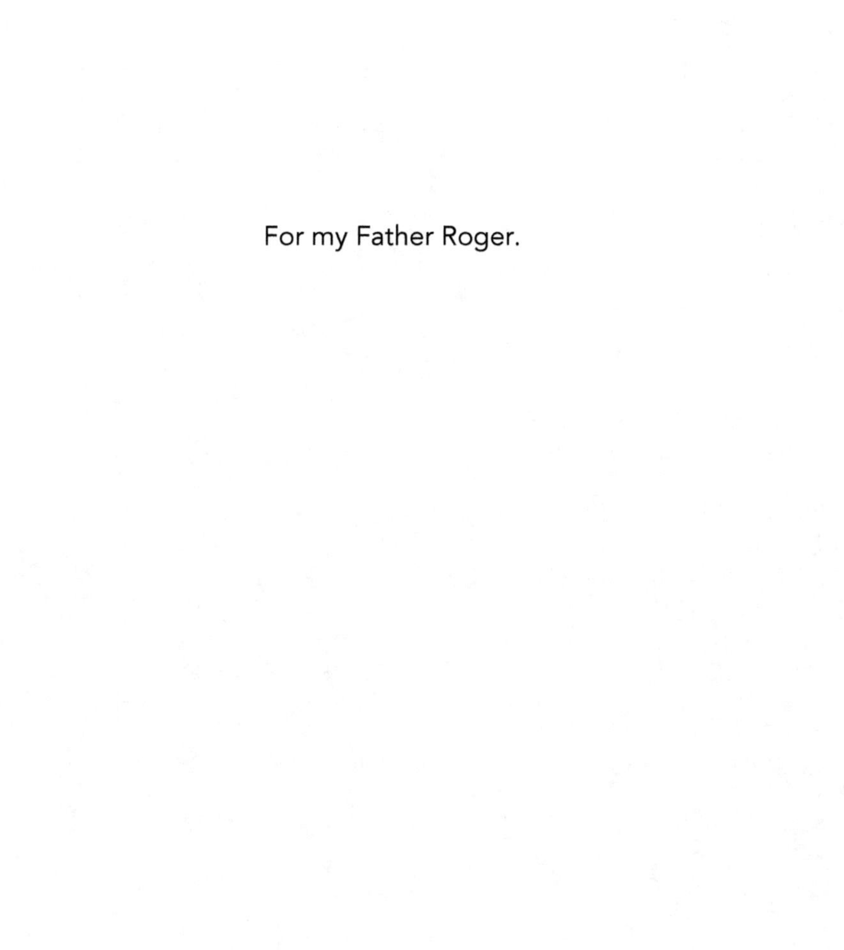

For my Father Roger.

Chapter One

<u>Suspicious Minds</u>

Richie was holding one of The King's original vinyl recordings in his hands. The priceless artefact contained audio from Sun Studios in Memphis, recorded at a time when a young Elvis Presley was on the precipice of a musical career. Richie turned the disc over, tested its weight, and then snapped it aggressively over his knee.

'Do you feel better now?'

'No,' replied Richie as he discarded the broken halves.

'I understand this was a very rare and expensive record.'

'Yeah. I love vinyl,' said Richie. 'I love vinyl records and I snapped it in two without a second thought.'

'Fascinating.'

In life, whenever he'd needed to make small talk Richie had steered the conversation toward music. It was a subject he could ruminate on for hours, making him seem intelligent and worldly. In death, it seemed that nothing had changed. Looking at the two pieces of ruined vinyl had prompted a musical thought, which Richie instinctively wove into their dialogue. 'Did you know that Elvis had a twin?'

'No, I did not know that.'

'Most people don't. Or they forget about him. When I went to Graceland I stood at their gravesites. They're both buried there, next to their mother and father. It's so strange that people line up and take photos of his final resting place. It's like… *disrespectful*. I mean… I definitely felt weird about it. I tried to stand as far back as I could. I didn't want to walk anywhere near him, but they lead you around on this little path and you don't really get a choice. You move along with the group like a conveyor belt. I felt like I was treading on his memory or something. Anyway, Elvis had a twin brother who was stillborn. It makes you wonder, you know?'

'Wonder about what, Richie?' came the measured reply.

'Like… if Elvis's brother *had* been born, would he have still been *The King*? Like… if Elvis had grown up with a brother… with that fraternal influence… maybe he would have made more allowances,' Richie offered with a shrug.

'Allowances. That is an interesting word.'

'Yeah. Maybe he wouldn't have tried as hard, or maybe his brother would have led him towards something else entirely. Maybe they would have paired up and started rowing every Saturday morning. Maybe neither would have been particularly interested in music. Maybe Elvis's brother would have become *The King* instead.'

'But that is not what happened. What is the sense in thinking about the many billions of alternatives to the way things actually unfolded?'

Richie contemplated this for a moment but continued to control the conversation. 'I read that his mother used to make him sing to the moon. She told Elvis that when he sang to the moon he was singing to his brother.'

'Interesting.'

'I guess… I guess I like thinking about it because… well… Elvis Presley was the greatest, right?'

'Yes, he is a highly regarded musician…'

'So, think about how many things had to go right for him to become The King of Rock and Roll,' said Richie. 'By the same logic a million things could have stopped him from achieving that.'

'But they did not stop him.'

'No. He became a huge phenomenon.' Richie looked a little forlorn, prompting his companion to speak.

'What are you thinking about now?'

Richie shrugged for a second time. 'I guess a lot of things would've needed to have gone differently in *my* life for me to achieve one tenth of his fame and fortune.'

'Is that what you wanted? Fame and fortune? You never picked up a guitar, despite your ongoing fascination with music. You are not a singer or a performer as far as I know. Did you *seek* fame? Honestly?'

'I suppose not. I'm just thinking out loud, you know?' replied Richie. 'Isn't that what we're doing here? Rehashing things?'

'Richie, you cannot change what has been and gone. Things happened the way they happened.'

'Yeah. It's wishful thinking. Like what if I'd won the lotto, you know?'

'Again, that did not happen. Elvis did not grow up with a brother and you did *not* win the lottery.'

'No,' said Richie.

'You did have some obstacles though. Would you like to *think out loud* about any? You are quite right, by the way. That is one of the primary reasons for our sessions-'

'Hey, did you ever think about how there isn't a Queen of Rock and Roll?' asked Richie, interrupting and sitting up even straighter in his seat. 'There isn't really one woman who is as revered as Elvis was.'

'I guess there is truth to that statement, but once again you seem to be changing the subject.'

'Madonna maybe? Cher?'

'Richie...'

'Men and women... that's the great divide right there. In my opinion there's a disparity between the genders that only really evens out in your late twenties,' announced Richie, as he shifted in his faux-leather chair. He'd been moving intentionally at various intervals but had been unable to make the leather squeak. The silent piece of furniture was starting to annoy him.

'Tell me what you mean by that please.'

'Well... when I was a teenager, I looked young and scrawny. I had bouts of acne and no idea what to say to the girls at my school. It was as if they were planets and I was a moon, trapped in their orbit and never able to move any closer. I was just nervous. I didn't want to get hurt. I didn't want to be embarrassed. I wasn't... comfortable being me.'

Richie studied his new acquaintance. The figure in the brown jacket sat patiently, notepad in hand. He was the picture of professionalism and patience. He was as human as anyone Richie had ever met.

'You have had love in your life. You do not need to analyse it.'

'I've never been in any kind of therapy before,' confessed Richie.

'I know.'

'Do you think that I should have tried therapy? Maybe after May died?'

'They say it helps to talk about it.'

'I guess.'

'You are doing well. Please continue.'

'What was I saying?' asked Richie.

'You were offering your insight into the disparity between genders.'

'Right… so the male sex drive is at its peak throughout a man's younger years, while a woman's is later in life. So, surely as the male's desire for sex slows down and the woman's picks up there must be a point where they even out. It's the same for physical attractiveness.'

'Go on.'

'See, I wasn't attractive to the opposite sex as a teenager because I was scrawny, but I grew into an attractive man. You don't have to agree. Generally speaking men age better than women in most cases. I think I was one of the lucky ones. I had a career. I was stable. I just had to wait around for the disparity to even out. It's all timing.'

'This argument does not leave much room for emotion, or an emotional connection between people.'

'Well, things always start in a physical way, don't they? You don't usually start a relationship as pen pals and then fall in love. You *see* a person and decide you have to meet them. You have to know them somehow.'

'Richie you are implying that there is a moment where everything lines up, and both parties are at their equal peaks?'

'Yes.'

'So, staying with that theory… was there a moment where you stopped being attracted to your wife?'

Richie sighed. 'For me to be attracted to someone… I guess it's a formula. They need to be physically attractive to me, like I was saying, but I need a person to be aloof as well.'

'*Aloof.* An interesting way of putting it.'

'Being aloof is a kind of mystery,' stated Richie. 'I want to feel as though they don't need me to be happy. I want them to be happy on their own and for our relationship to be… *extra*. Icing on the cake, you know?'

'I understand. And your wife was sufficiently aloof?'

'My first wife was. May and I were University sweethearts. She didn't need me at all, which only made me want her more. She oozed happiness at every moment of the day. I wanted to be near her. She was fun. She had plans. I was always very attracted to May. It probably helped that we were young and naïve.'

'It sounds like the timing was right.'

'Well, good things come to those who wait. At the time I felt like I'd waited just to be with May. I'd been through so much teenage self-loathing and disappointment that I probably didn't know how lucky I was. The odds were so slim, you know? If you find a rare vinyl in great condition the first time you go to market you figure that it will always be that way. There are a lot of markets, and most of them are stocked with average records. May was one of a kind. I only truly realised what I had after she died.'

'It is never easy to be separated from someone you love.'

'It's horrible,' said Richie, his head feeling suddenly heavier.

'How was that sensation? Being suddenly alone?'

'I was broken. Looking back, I can see that it was the lowest point in my life. And I never thought I would recover. It would have helped to talk about it, wouldn't it?'

'I could only guess.'

'I mean, I got my head straight eventually,' continued Richie. 'It took almost ten years, but I managed to stop wallowing for long enough to enjoy my life again.'

There was a pause in the interrogation that made Richie look up. In that moment he recognised what was missing from their interaction. No notes had been taken, just earnest engagement in his words. Richie had fully expected to hear a soundtrack of scrawling as he unearthed his soul, but the room had remained as silent and respectful as the leather chair. The situation felt artificial, like they were just going through the motions, which made him strangely sad.

'Is everything okay Richie?'

'Yeah.'

'You were given a second chance at love. You married Janice. Do you want to tell me about her?'

'Honestly I never thought I'd get married again. It's such a hassle,' confessed Richie.

'Are you referring to the ceremony? The ordeal of it?'

'Not just the ceremony,' said Richie as he shook his head, 'I mean all of it. You have to stand there, in front of everyone and pledge to love this person *forever*.'

'That is the ritual of marriage.'

'Well I'd *already* gathered everyone that was important to me and I'd *already* pledged that with May, hadn't I? To me it felt sort of ridiculous to do it all again.'

'You loved May. You loved her for her entire life. You were committed to those vows and only parted by death. Your family and friends were aware of the situation.'

'Yeah.'

'So, were you having second thoughts about Janice?'

'No. I just couldn't believe I had to do it all again.'

'But you *were* happy together?'

'Yes. For a time at least.'

'And Janice was happy? To be marrying you?'

'I guess,' mumbled Richie. 'I thought so anyway. I thought I was doing the right thing by her. Who knows? We had our issues. I think all married couples do. It's normal to disagree here and there. I suppose I could have had an even better marriage if I hadn't died so abruptly.'

'As I said, you cannot change what has already transpired. You all have to come to terms with death in your own way.'

Richie paused suddenly. 'Wait, are you talking to them as well?'

'Talking to-'

'To May and Janice. You're having these reflective sessions with both of my wives, right?'

'Yes, naturally.'

'And?'

'What are you asking me Richie?'

With the truth now out in the open Richie was genuinely nervous. May and Janice knew everything about him. *What dirt were they now spilling?* He had to know.

'What are they saying about me?' he demanded.

'Whatever they like. I am not policing their thoughts of you. I let them speak in the same way I am letting you speak.'

'Fuck.'

'You are clearly displeased with this arrangement. May and Janice have the same right to unpack the emotional baggage of their lives. To understand the experience and achieve a more enlightened state.'

'I just don't want the mess of our lives to ruin things here,' stated Richie. 'Things were complicated when we were alive.'

'And you think the odds of them ruining heaven are… *likely*?'

'Absolutely.'

Chapter Two

<u>Can't Help Falling in Love</u>

Richie Walsh was on display before his friends and family, dressed to the nines. His curly black hair had been gelled and tamed for the occasion of his second wedding. Every moment of the day had been tinged with déjà vu, but thankfully the ceremony was over. The eyes of the room now relaxed on their over-priced meals. His new bride Janice sat before him, wearing a custom-made wedding dress. It had been bequeathed to her after a similarly shaped cousin caught her fiancée with their shift supervisor. Even though the dress was a perfect fit his new bride had stressed about the more mystical connotations of wearing another woman's dress on such an important day.

Janice Walsh (nee Norman) was something of a believer. She considered signs to be important, and always re-read her daily horoscope at the start and end of the day. Richie had assured her that the garment was free from any bad energy, which hadn't stopped Janice from browsing eBay for alternatives.

Richie had realised that due to superstition he wouldn't see her dress, cursed or otherwise until the day of the wedding. 'I'm sure whatever you wear will be perfect,' he'd offered. In a marriage you have to pick your battles.

Earlier that afternoon when he'd been checking his appearance in the bathroom, Richie had accidently overheard a bridesmaid, who was likely outside the adjacent female toilets, talking to Janice's cousin about the ongoing dress saga.

'She's wearing your dress Minka.'

'Shit, really?'

'I know. It's a bad omen, right?'

'I don't know. It's Richie's *second* wedding. That's always a bad sign if you ask me.'

'You're right, this whole thing is doomed.'

When Richie had finally seen his bride he'd refused to acknowledge that a wedding dress could have any power over their union. He'd told Janice that she looked beautiful, which she certainly did. Just because her cousin Minka hadn't used it, didn't mean they shouldn't. Richie told himself that it was fine. Everything would be fine. People got married in used wedding dresses all the time.

The event had been exceptional, as excruciatingly planned by the bride. With the ceremony behind them Janice seemed able to relax. She'd had some white wine and removed her high heels beneath the table. Richie tapped on his glass and stood. He beamed at the assembled room, which was packed with their nearest and dearest. His ageing parents Stephen and Helen, who'd been married for over thirty years, smiled back at the newlyweds. Richie thought perhaps they'd view a second marriage as a failure, but they'd warmed to Janice quickly, and to the idea that maybe this was the avenue through which they'd gain additional grandchildren. Out of the corner of his eye Richie could see his sister Dawn juggling his overzealous nephew Mikey, and succeeding to calm him down. She'd been happily married to a bartender named Derek for almost two years, much to the delight of their parents. Their only qualm had been that Mikey was not short for Michael, which had been a source of heated debate.

The room was now blanketed in silence with the exception of Janice's field hockey girlfriends. Richie and the other guests waited patiently for the group as they gradually realised the groom's call for calm.

'I didn't think I'd ever be up here again,' Richie said into the microphone. The room became solemn as the groom's side recalled the last time Richie had worn his blue velvet tuxedo. He forced a smile, knowing he had to continue his speech.

'After May died I didn't see this… marriage… in my future. Janice honey, you brought me back from a nightmare and showed me that there was still good in the world. You brought my smile back. Today I'm so happy to affirm my love for you, my lovely new wife, in front of all of our family and friends. In the words of the great Elvis Presley… wise men say… only fools rush in. But I can't help falling in love with you. I love you Janice.'

Even though Richie spoke the words instead of singing them, the room still burst into pleasant applause. Janice's mother started chanting for an embrace. Her enthusiasm for their union had been endless, as Janice was her only child. The field hockey team, whom Richie had confused the names of all night, started wooing wildly from their table.

'Kiss! Kiss!' Janice's mother called through cupped hands.

Janice stood up and succumbed to the pressure, planting her lips against Richie's. She looked resplendent in cousin Minka's eggshell coloured wedding dress, her blonde hair flowing effortlessly like a shampoo commercial. In the early days of their relationship Janice had confessed to Richie that she didn't need to get married and was completely fine with being monogamous de facto partners for the rest of their lives. The look on her face now said otherwise. Janice delighted in being the centre of attention.

The venue was a simple, white room at the local yacht club. It had become a sanctuary from the intense heat of the day. The guests had sweated through Richie and Janice's vows, the only shade of the afternoon electing to land on the happy couple. Richie hadn't really noticed the crowd's discomfort, given his extreme nervousness. With the exception of a heckler on a boat jokingly shouting 'Don't do it!' they'd married without a hitch.

For Richie the idea of taking the leap for a second time had seemed impossible until recently.

It had felt that way because of May.

While Janice left the table to powder her nose, Richie tuned out the sound around him and let his mind drift back to his lost love. While he missed May and thought of her often, their marriage now felt like a lifetime ago. Richie wondered whether it was as good as he remembered, or whether his recall had become selective over time.

No. It had meant everything to Richie.

They had been infatuated with one another at a time when they were ruled by their hormones. Richie and May had tumbled into a romance where nothing else mattered. After University they'd moved into a loft with slanted walls like a Toblerone bar. They hadn't been able to stand up unless they did so directly in the centre of the room, where the ceiling was thankfully flat. The windows in their one bedroom were at a sixty-degree angle and wouldn't open all the way, but it didn't matter. Nothing mattered. It was all they could afford and they were bubbling with youthful exuberance. The loft had been a wonderful starting point for them, each agreeing that things could only get better.

They'd adopted a cat and named him Fitty. He was like their child, a small life force that linked them. Fitty was scrawny but more reliable and affectionate than the average feline.

May and Richie had worked hard and saved even harder, sacrificing nights out and holidays for their future. The two eventually bought a home in a fairly derelict suburb. It was a plain house brimming with potential, and certainly a step up from their first abode. Richie had loved staying in, avoiding both the gardening and the neighbours. Fitty would dutifully roam the perimeter, slinking across the fence line keeping them both safe. It was their sanctuary, their own little piece of the world.

Their time together had been brief, about three years in total. Richie enjoyed only nine months of wedded bliss before a traffic accident claimed May's life. He'd later learned that she was in the early stages of a pregnancy, which crushed his already fragile state to smithereens.

May's mother had been combative in the wake of the loss. She'd insisted on commemorating her daughter's life by holding special traditional Malaysian meals at various intervals. Richie had been invited to all, but attended none. Richie and Fitty mourned in their own way. His lack of contact isolated him from her family.

Richie couldn't stay in their little home after that. Each room had held so much promise. *Their* bedroom. *Their* laundry room. *Their* would-be nursery. May was everywhere and nowhere all at once. Richie couldn't bear it. He'd rented their house out and moved in with his sister Dawn. When they'd driven away Fitty had mewed endlessly.

Richie's new space had been small but liveable. Before Dawn had met Derek the bartender she was working full time as a flight attendant. His sister was never around, leaving Richie to wallow for as long as he liked.

Back then solitude became the new normal. Fitty seemed less affectionate. They missed May. Richie held onto the small black ball of fluff and cried. He would take care of Fitty for as long as he could, loving the feline on behalf of them both.

Richie had stopped eating at the recommended times, lost weight and found his friendships fading. All of the smiling faces from his wedding to May had reappeared solemnly for her funeral but vanished just as promptly. Life was moving on for everyone else. Richie couldn't bring himself to watch their wedding video and the entire experience now seemed caked in negativity. He'd boxed his life with May and shut out the world.

Richie met Janice almost a decade later in his thirties, when his heart had mended itself. He hadn't known that he was ready to fall in love again, or that he was even capable of it. Oddly, the catalyst for change was an eye test.

Janice was an optometrist and Richie had been dodging the appointment. Each time the reminder slip landed in his mailbox he'd promptly relocated it to the recycling bin. Nine years after May's death he was clear-headed and trying to get things back on track. During a very productive January, after he'd endured a filling and a lecture about flossing from the dentist, he finally got his vision checked.

Richie hadn't really noticed Janice during that first eye test, despite their proximity. He'd obediently read off the required letters one by one and selected some plain black frames that were almost the same as his current pair. Richie then paid for them and left without ever really looking at the woman who would become his second wife.

The manner in which he'd eventually noticed her had been like something out of a movie. Following the initial eye examination Janice had ordered his frames. Two weeks passed. When Richie had come in to collect them, he'd tried them on and suddenly his future had become clear. In an extremely uncharacteristic move, he'd asked Janice out on the spot, without caring about her marital status, or even checking for a ring on her left hand. She'd appreciated his boldness and accepted immediately in spite of the disapproving look from her manager.

And now, almost eighteen months later they were married.

It was a happy ending to their story. Janice had rescued Richie from his loneliness and they could now build a future together. The twenty-two thousand dollar wedding was a large sum but a small price to pay in the scheme of things, considered

Richie. It had taken so long to move on. Richie now realised how important it was to commemorate the *good* milestones, and not just the bad ones. He'd never forget his first love, but May was gone and she wasn't ever coming back. Richie considered himself extremely lucky to have found a second chance with Janice.

'I'm so proud of you,' said Richie's father Stephen.

'We both are! Of you both, of course,' added his mother Helen. She'd had a few champagnes and was looking a bit flushed.

Richie's parents had offered him the same unwavering support and enthusiasm at his first wedding. They weren't a very close-knit family but they were always amicable. Richie was sure they preferred his sister Dawn, even if she had named their grandchild Mikey instead of Michael. While they hadn't offered to contribute anything monetarily towards Richie and Janice's wedding, his father had made available a large number of romantic records from his personal collection. Helen had suggested she might be able to assist with some baking, however Janice had tactfully declined. She'd had her heart set on a two-tier chocolate cake that she'd tried years before at the wedding of a co-worker. The larger bottom section was chocolate marble, while the top layer was mortal sin. The dessert had been a home run by all accounts.

'How are you feeling?' asked Janice as they strolled away from his parents.

'Pretty good. Yeah. How about you?'

'Amazing. Everything was perfect.'

'Even the heat?' Richie asked with a smirk.

'I like the heat.' Janice smiled. 'Can you drive?'

'Of course.' Richie had avoided alcohol all night, favouring orange juice during his toast.

'We should get out of here then,' Janice whispered, before wrapping her arms around her husband. 'Ready for our big exit?'

'Okay, sure.'

Richie was happy to go. The day had been a success and he'd obliged Janice's every desire. Now it was time for her to reciprocate.

Chapter Three
Moody Blue

Richie woke to the familiar sound of crying babies. Their twins Brody and Charlie were eleven months old and neither child would accept that their days of breastfeeding were coming to an end. Janice was trying desperately to wean them, in the hopes that she could return to her full-time job, but the boys were stubborn and demanding. She'd been forced to apply smears of nipple butter to soothe the assaults from her sons and their unrelenting appetites.

Richie wandered into the second bedroom to find Janice nursing Charlie. He'd worried about having twins and was thrilled when he'd learned they weren't identical. He could always identify Charlie from his light red hair.

'You gave in,' said Richie.

'I had to. He was so insistent.'

Richie picked up Brody and jostled him about playfully. Brody giggled happily, his mop of dark curls bouncing along for the ride.

'He's just had a feed. Don't make him throw up!' chided Janice.

Richie obeyed and returned the infant to the plastic mat below. Both boys were quiet now and seemed pleased to have the company of their parents. Richie stared at Charlie's head as he quietly suckled at his wife's breast. Janice's eyes were closed, which allowed Richie to study her. She had such perfectly symmetrical features, sometimes resembling a porcelain doll.

It had been hard adjusting to parenthood, but they were both doing their best to bond with the boys. Janice would point to Charlie's nose or Brody's ears, citing a resemblance. Richie didn't see it. They just looked like babies to him. He'd had the same disassociation with their ultrasound picture. They'd just looked like a couple of blobs.

It wasn't until Brody's hair became curly that something clicked for Richie. As a child he'd hated his curls, which had made him the target of teasing. Richie felt instantly protective of this boy, a feeling that then spread organically to Charlie. Imagining these two helpless figures being bullied for a genetic trait he'd given them stirred something from within. Richie would do *anything* for his twins.

'How did you manage to sleep through their crying?' asked Janice, who looked exhausted in the soft morning light.

Almost anything…

'I woke up a few times,' said Richie defensively.

'Well, next time you wake up in the night how about a hand?'

'Okay.'

Richie had been cautioned that children were a lot of work, but none of them knew what it was like to have twins. Everything was chaos and mess, from their sleep schedule to their mealtimes. The addition of Brody and Charlie had changed everything. His relationship with Janice had morphed into a shadow of its former glory. Her days as a hockey goalkeeper had been excellent practice, as she now stopped Richie from scoring on a regular basis.

Janice's previously loving nature had now completely shifted focus to their dependants, with Richie taking a distant backseat. He was now tasked with all of the domestic duties, from scrubbing the toilet to making their meals. Janice was in a perpetual state of 'too tired' thanks to their demanding boys. Richie had started to prefer it that way. Cleaning was something he could control, unlike the needs of two growing children.

They'd stopped planning outings and activities in the wake of parenthood. Brody and Charlie were unpredictable and prone to embarrassing tantrums, a lesson they'd learnt the hard way.

'Do you want a coffee or something?' asked Richie.

'I've had two already,' she replied. 'But thanks.'

Richie had moved Janice into the property that he'd purchased with May. The years had been kind, both gentrifying the area and increasing the value of the house. Moving had been an adjustment for Janice.

The latest of his wife's list of gripes was that she was growing tired of the décor. Janice seemed to crave change, an endeavour that posed a substantial cost to Richie. Her ideas, while not without merit, would alter the structure of the residence.

'We need a second bathroom!' she'd declared.

Janice's greater vision involved the removal of walls to create open spaces, as well as an extension into the backyard. It was an overwhelming and expensive concept for Richie, and his reluctance was obvious. He and May hadn't lived there for very long before her accident, but she was an unseen presence. His new wife's agenda was equally obvious. Janice was trying to personalise the space and purge the past.

One of the walls she wanted to remove held a lasting memory for Richie. When he and May had first moved in, she had ceremoniously hammered a nail into it. This was to prove that they could do whatever they liked, a fact that had not been the case in the Toblerone loft. That nail currently held a motivational poster that said 'Life is beautiful.' Whether it was intentional or not Janice was erasing May.

'Can you clean up in the kitchen?' Janice asked. Charlie was now dozing against her breast, wheezing slightly.

'Sure.'

During the week Richie was happy to escape to work. He'd been employed at the Bureau of Statistics for several years and found the compilation of data and facts to be soothing and controllable. Statistics just made sense. Richie enjoyed the freedom of his workweek as much as Janice despised it. She saw Richie's face light up on his way out the door and in retaliation ceased any and all manner of affection beyond perfunctory greetings.

Richie had been filling the silences in their marriage by dipping into his recently deceased father's record collection on the weekends. His mother had downsized and he'd acquired the vinyl albums without a contest. Unsurprisingly, his sister Dawn had declared she'd had 'no interest whatsoever' in the artefacts. She'd selected some smaller items and novelties to remember him by, citing that her place wasn't big enough for a collection of that magnitude. Richie's wife had also taken issue with the imposition of his inheritance.

'You've got to get rid of some of these albums Richie,' Janice had complained. 'There's way too many.'

'This is my father's legacy. You can't ask me to do that!'

'I get that but this is *our* home. You can keep it all it a storage locker if you want, but it's everywhere.'

'You can't store vinyl records in a storage locker Janice. They'll get ruined. You have to keep them in a specific way or they'll deteriorate and they won't play properly.'

'Haven't you been playing them enough lately?'

'Yes and no. Music is meant to be played,' Richie had argued.

Janice left the room in a huff.

It was an impressive assortment of vinyl and Richie didn't want to see it given away to charity or sold to a stranger. It had been his father's hobby to trawl markets and vintage fairs in search of each piece. To discard them felt unkind, as though dismissing a vital part of the late Stephen Walsh. Each album had clues to its origins: a sticker indicating a price or the name of a former owner. Listening to the crackling sounds of the past made Richie feel something that he couldn't explain to Janice. He'd found that each collected record seemed to speak to him, verbalising another piece of a puzzle. Although he'd shared no interest in the music while his father had been alive, in his absence the hobby now held a renewed importance.

Richie loved Elvis Presley the most, but lately he'd been favouring long deceased artists like Jim Croce, Buddy Holly and Jeff Buckley. His father had saved a number of Croce records, and Richie could understand the appeal. He would engage as intently as he could, trying to decipher the lyrics like a message from beyond the grave. That morning he'd elected to put on the 1972 album *You Don't Mess Around With Jim* while busying himself with domestic chores.

Since his father's death Richie had been consuming music at an abnormal rate. He'd increased his intake in order to justify the collection living in their home. Richie would try to play albums during dinner, while he cleaned and instead of putting on the television on weekends.

While he was enjoying *Time in a Bottle* by Jim Croce there was a knock on the door. Richie was hesitant, hoping that it wasn't a devout religious group seeking his membership. As a lifelong atheist it was a commitment he would never make. Religion was for small towns and housewives in need of community. He turned a dial, freezing the music mid-song, and got up out of his chair. His father had always insisted that you should let a record play all the way through before lifting the needle, a habit that Richie had adopted.

On the doorstep stood his next-door neighbour Dan, dressed in a dirt-stained checked shirt and gloves. He'd confidently decided to keep the top four buttons of his shirt undone, drawing Richie's reluctant eyes to his chest hair.

'Morning neighbour,' said Dan, in a deep voice.

'Morning,' replied Richie, immediately regretting his decision to remain in pyjamas bottoms and an old T-shirt from his trip to Memphis.

'How's the family?' asked Dan.

'Fine.' The sound of Charlie crying could be heard behind him but Richie refused to acknowledge it.

'It's a great day Richie. Beautiful wife, two kids and a house in *this* neighbourhood. You're living the dream,' stated Dan.

'You're in this neighbourhood too,' countered Richie.

When he'd first invested in the property with May they'd appreciated having Dan as a neighbour. He had been welcoming and then left them alone. Since Richie moved back in with Janice, Dan's interruptions were much more regular.

'I visited May's grave last week,' said Dan, seemingly reading Richie's mind. This man was the biggest link to May and everything he'd lost, because Dan had actually met her. He appeared determined to ensure that Richie didn't supress her from his everyday thoughts, that he should think of his deceased first love frequently.

'So did I.' It wasn't true, but Richie wanted to prove he was equally noble. 'Why were *you* there?'

'I just think about her sometimes,' replied Dan, looking a little sheepish. 'I miss her, you know? Huh… of course *you* know. Look who I'm talking to.' Dan slipped his hand into his shirt, toying with his chest hair.

Richie wondered whether his neighbour was trying to make him feel guilty. Whatever he was up to Richie didn't appreciate it.

'Is there something I can help you with Dan?'

'Well,' started Dan, 'I've been working on retiling my roof. Perhaps you've seen me up there?'

Richie shook his head. He had no desire to watch his neighbourhood. It was hard enough keeping track of his two sons and the messes they made hourly without concerning himself with the world outside his front door.

'Anyway, from up on the roof I can see that *your* roof could use some repairs. Maybe a pressure wash too. I wanted to ask… do you have any leaks?' Richie noticed Dan's jawline as he spoke, cursing himself for admiring it. This man's jaw was an enviable feature, masculine in its definition.

'No leaks,' stated Richie, before quickly adding, 'not that I'm aware of.'

'Okay… I was thinking that you might like to come up and help me finish tiling, then maybe I could give you a hand on your place next?'

Janice wandered over from the living room to investigate. Upon seeing their neighbour she smiled.

'Oh, hi Dan!'

'Hi Janice. You're looking lovely as always.'

Richie didn't like the inviting nature of his wife's robe or the opening it seemed to create from his angle. *Was she wearing that lip-gloss earlier?*

Janice sauntered away and Dan reiterated his request for assistance.

'I'd like to help… I would, but the twins are being a handful at the moment. You understand.' Richie's excuse seemed to placate the man.

'Sure, sure, no worries.' Dan retreated across the lawn to his house. Richie watched from the doorway as he climbed a ladder and disappeared from view, presumably to continue his retiling. Richie shook his head and wondered what time Dan had woken up that morning. Probably the same obscene hour as Brody and Charlie.

Before he went inside Richie scanned his front yard properly for the first time in months. The house had been built on a slight hill, with the garden up higher towards the road. This created the illusion of a sunken residence, held hostage by vegetation. Richie hated gardening. The way the weeds would present themselves over and over again, the repetition of removing them just to keep things presentable. Weeds would always bide their time and fester out again. Due to the incline it always looked like nature was trying to reclaim the sunken house.

The landscaping seemed random to Richie. Alongside their driveway was a collection of yucca trees that had been planted at Janice's request. They were growing even faster than Charlie and Brody were. Their sharp green daggers had stretched out to the point that they were intruding into one another's space, jostling for their lives. In time they would be bound in endless conflict, each pressing out as far as possible until they crashed into the fencing at the side of the property. The rest of the yard housed smaller plants and the yuccas seemed too dominant. Richie thought they were quite ugly and refused to water them. It didn't matter. They kept growing on their own despite his neglect, deepening their roots. There was a small dead bird near the mailbox.

Richie couldn't go back to his record as Janice was settling the boys down for a nap. During the day they still slept side by side in a makeshift cot in the lounge room. It took up far too much real estate for a second sleep location, but Richie was now an expert at picking his battles. He waited in the dining room, knowing that once the kids were resting his wife would find him. Richie swallowed two Aspirin tablets while he waited, having heard that doing so daily could prevent heart attacks. *Or did they thin the blood?* Uncertainty aside he'd repeated the ritual almost every day since his father's sudden death.

Richie wondered what menial domestic task Janice would insist he complete next. He didn't have the strength to complain. He knew that she'd been just as unprepared for their family's expansion, and that they were both dealing with it as best they could.

There was a light at the end of the tunnel though, and Richie was looking forward to it. As the boys grew they would become more independent, and spend less time monopolising his house. He was counting down the years. He'd tracked the timeline onto a piece of toilet paper the other day before flushing away the evidence. Once Janice went back to work, they'd go to childcare. As time passed Brody and Charlie would go to school, and then one day in the future his marriage to Janice would be free to return to its former temperature. Their friction would once again be the fun kind.

'What are you smiling about?' demanded Janice, in her quietest voice. Richie hadn't noticed her come into the dining room.

'Nothing much. Did the boys fall asleep?' he whispered, matching her volume.

'Yes. They're down.'

Richie braced himself as Janice sat. She pulled her fair hair into a ponytail and tied it using a black elastic band from her wrist. There was no such thing as downtime anymore. *Was Janice about to highlight that the gutters needed cleaning, or that the microwave could use a scrub?*

'I've been thinking…'

'Hmmm?'

'I want to have another baby.'

'What?' Richie was momentarily dumbfounded. 'I thought you wanted to go back to work?'

'Well, I did… but now I don't. I've changed my mind,' offered Janice.

'Just like that?'

'Yes.'

'But… the boys are such a… *handful*,' he said, trying to find the right word.

'They wouldn't be if you helped out more often,' said Janice calmly.

'You want to do *this* again?' Richie's voice rose slightly. 'I thought the twins might've put you off having any more children.'

During their arrival the boys had done significant damage to his wife's body, which Janice appeared to have forgotten. Richie, who was not under the influence of any drugs during their birth, remembered their traumatic entrance more vividly.

'That was a year ago. I'm ready to try again.'

In life Richie wanted to believe that when something bad happened, there was an equal karmic correction of good coming to balance the scales. With each piece of good comes a piece of bad, and vice versa. Since the boys had been born he'd purchased a lottery ticket every week. He'd manage to lose on each and every one of those tickets. Forty-seven times he'd failed to secure even a minor prize, which felt like an amazingly bad run of luck. The revelation that Janice wanted to get pregnant again was too much for Richie. He couldn't fathom the karmic correction that would be required to balance out such circumstances.

'I don't… I don't know…' he said, mostly just to fill the silence.

'Will you think about it?'

'I can do that.' Richie knew his feelings on the matter wouldn't change. The only advantage of accepting such a proposal would be the supposed increase of intimacy, which he'd been missing. They would never be able to replicate the intensity that had existed at the start of their relationship, and Richie feared it would be short lived. *But a child?* It was too much.

He had a sudden and overwhelming urge to flee the scene before Janice could add anything, and he could only think of one viable excuse.

'Listen, Dan wanted me to help him with the tiling. Maybe I should take him up on that. He reckons if I help him out then we can work on our roof next.'

'Oh.' Janice looked surprised. 'If you think you can help him…sure…'

'Yeah, should be pretty straightforward,' claimed Richie, who hadn't considered the magnitude of this commitment.

'Can you water the garden afterwards?' asked Janice.

Fucking yucca trees.

'Sure.'

A shell-shocked Richie gave his wife a quick kiss on the cheek and walked out the door. The idea of bringing another child into the world wasn't one he'd considered before now. *What if they had twins again?* That would certainly break him. The house could barely contain its current residents.

Years ago Richie and May had spoken of having a single child. It seemed so simple. By comparison the twins were all consuming. The residence was a three bedroom dwelling, meaning that right now Brody and Charlie could have their own bedrooms when they were older. A third child would mean they'd have to entertain the idea of moving house, or pulling the trigger on the extension that Janice wanted. *Was that what this was about?* Another little person would mean they'd need a new car, not to mention the delay it would put on returning Janice to her job as an optometrist. Money was already starting to become an issue. Richie needed to work out the best way to tell his wife that this was a bad idea without sounding like a heartless monster. An additional mouth to feed could only put more strain on him as the sole breadwinner. Richie couldn't handle it.

He looked at their front garden again. Janice was right: everything needed watering. The once vibrant kangaroo paws she'd planted had started fading. Everything except the yuccas was slowly dying. *Had he neglected his duties that much?* Richie had never had a green thumb but had done his best to keep everything alive at Janice's request. She'd been insistent that if they were to keep the trees - and not just concrete everything - they needed to tend to them. Resale value was important to her.

Richie was failing. The garden, much like everything else in his life, was decaying before his eyes.

He approached Dan's ladder, which had been positioned perfectly to line up with the front door of the house. His neighbour had a neat, green lawn with freshly trimmed edges. At the top of the property Dan had used a hedge to create privacy from passing traffic.

'Dan?'

No response. Richie was feeling a little annoyed that his Sunday was about to be wasted in service of this task. Ultimately he preferred this labour to an uncomfortable conversation with Janice.

'Dan? It's Richie from next door,' he called again and folded his arms in front of him.

Just at that moment Richie's legs buckled and he collapsed to the ground below. His glasses fell off and landed on the welcome mat. He felt faint and unable to form a cohesive thought.

Was that blood?

Richie struggled to move, then found it impossible to keep his eyes open. Before long he'd succumbed to a very sudden, but surprisingly painless death.

Chapter Four

Heartbreak Hotel

'Mummy!'

The door opened slowly and Janice sighed. It was the second time Brody had woken up that night. Thankfully Charlie had remained undisturbed. *Who knew twins could be so different?*

'Brody… honey it's the middle of the night,' she said, hearing the croakiness in her voice.

'I'm scared,' the little boy replied.

'Of what?'

'Ghosts.'

'There's no such thing as ghosts bub. You're here in your room with Charlie. There's no ghost. You're safe, okay?'

'But there *is* a ghost.'

'Where's the ghost? You show me where you think you saw him.'

'Over there.' Brody pointed at the cupboard door, which was slightly ajar.

Janice pushed herself off the bed. She walked over, opened the wooden door and gestured inside. 'See? There's nothing there.'

'Are you sure?'

'Yes. It's just clothes… hanging up for tomorrow.' Janice glanced at the cupboard and spotted two jackets that had belonged to Richie, hanging at one end of the closet.

She crept back over and re-tucked Brody into his bed. She kissed him on the head and said goodnight.

'Mummy?'

'Yeah?'

'Tomorrow can I pick one of the old records to play at breakfast?' asked Brody.

'Of course you can,' she replied.

Richie's record collection had been a recent point of interest for the twins. It was hard to ignore the four hundred or so twelve-inch albums that occupied a custom made shelf in their hallway. The boys had to pass the behemoth daily. Once enlightened about vinyl Brody had asked to hear some of the songs, and they'd started listening during their meals. The boys had been dismissive of James Taylor, Cat Stevens and Judy Garland forcing Janice to refine her choices. A little Miles Davis at lunch, some Beatles songs over dinner. She had no personal interest in the collection but when Charlie and Brody made a request she was happy to select something suitable to accompany a meal. While Charlie had always seemed more interested in the food, Brody had become inquisitive about album covers, artists and then inevitably Richie himself.

'How did Richie die?'

This line of questioning, while expected, took Janice off guard. Brody was going through a phase of calling grownups by their first names. She was the only exception, as Brody insisted that she was just *Mummy*. Janice looked at the clock, noting it was a little after two a.m.

'It's late. And that was a long time ago. Don't worry about things like that.'

'But sometimes I *do* worry.'

'Why don't you let me do the worrying for both of us, okay?'

Brody paused for a moment before continuing his inquiry. 'But what happened though?'

'It was an accident.'

'Why won't you just tell me?' pressed Brody.

'Because Mummy doesn't like to think about it, especially at two a.m.'

Brody furrowed his brow in thought. He had the same worried wrinkles as his mother. 'Do you miss Richie?'

'Yes. Of course.'

'Every day?'

'Yes. Every day.'

'Me too. I think about him sometimes.'

'What kind of things do you think?' asked Janice. She was more awake now, and genuinely interested to learn what Brody felt about her late husband. 'Do you remember much about him?'

'Not really. But I looked at the photographs you showed us.'

In the wake of the tragedy Janice had compiled two identical books of pictures that the boys could have to remember Richie. Charlie - in his own little world - didn't seem interested in the gesture, but it appeared that Brody had appreciated the gift.

Janice spread her fingers widely and found the small photo book hiding in the sheet. 'Do you think it's a good idea to look at this right before bed?'

'No.'

'No. It's not.'

'Do… do you think that if he could come back as a ghost… that he would visit me and Charlie?'

'We've talked about this. Ghosts aren't real,' stated Janice.

'I know… but if they *were* real, would he come and visit?' Brody's eyes were wide, pleading.

Janice smiled reassuringly. 'Of course. Even though he didn't get to spend much time with you, Richie loved you both so much. If ghosts were real then he'd visit. But they're not, okay?'

'Okay.'

'Now try and sleep for Mumma. We've got a busy day tomorrow.'

'I will.'

She smoothed down his blanket. 'Love you.'

'Love you Mum.'

Janice kissed him, his hair tickling her nose as she did. He needed a bath, but that could wait. She'd learned to roll with the punches over the last five years.

On her way out of the room she closed the cupboard door. She'd completely forgotten about those jackets. *Had Brody spotted them and known they were Richie's?* He had such an active imagination. She was sure he'd be a fantastic storyteller.

As she scooted into her own bed Janice was met by the warmth of a second body. A firm hand slid around her waist and pulled her close. She smiled.

'That was Brody. I think he had a bad dream,' she said in a whisper.

'Huh.'

'Oh, before I forget there are a couple of jackets in the cupboard in their room. They used to belong to Richie.'

'Yeah?'

'Uhuh. They won't fit you but I need you to drop them off at the op shop or something. And I need to put those photo books away for a while.'

'Sure babe,' came the tired reply.

'And we should probably do something about his record collection too… maybe thin it right out…'

'Can we talk about this in the morning?'

'Oh… sure. Sorry…'

'Night. Love you.'

'Love you too.'

Chapter Five

<u>It's Now or Never</u>

Richie Walsh was now dead.

Despite his lack of belief in any kind of afterlife he found himself sitting on a white cube in a setting that felt angelic and heavenly. *It felt impossible but where else could he be?* All around him was cloudless blue sky, and beneath the cube was a plain white platform that stretched out in all directions. The vastness of this horizon seemed endless. There were no other clues as to his location, and things felt undecorated and vague, like the edges of his vision were blurry. He remembered dying, even though he couldn't recall how exactly it had happened. Richie felt no great animosity about it either way. It was done, like finishing a meal. No peaceful calm washed over him. The only amazing revelation was the fact that he was still conscious, that he existed somehow. It was a statistical anomaly.

I think therefore I am. Richie felt smug as he remembered University level Philosophy. He was still thinking, which was more than he'd ever expected. Richie had surmised that when he died his mind would be black, and that would be it. Worm food. He'd never been so pleased to be so uneducated.

He tried his legs and found that he could stand quite easily. Richie walked around a little and stared off into the distance. He wasn't sure if he should wait here or attempt a journey into the unknown. There wasn't a clear path, the cube behind him appearing to be the only physical marker in sight. Richie tried to push it, but it wouldn't budge. As he was contemplating what to do next a figure materialised in front of him. There was no special effect or noise. It was binary. Richie was alone and then he wasn't.

'Hello?' Richie was suddenly nervous.

The man before him was dressed in a classic grey suit that was buttoned up at the front. His hair was brown, and he had a familiar smile. The figure did not appear to pose a threat and looked genuinely human. The thing that stood out about his ensemble was that he was inexplicably barefoot.

'Hello,' he replied. 'Nice to meet you Richie. I am Angel.'

'Angel?'

'It is something of a nickname,' he continued, 'as in guardian angel. I am in charge of this pocket of heaven.'

'So… you're saying…'

Angel smiled, remaining stoic.

'This is heaven?' asked Richie.

'That is the terminology that humans seem most accepting of. This is the place where you will experience your afterlife.'

'And you're saying I'm dead? I didn't imagine it?'

'Death comes indiscriminately for us all.'

'I don't feel dead,' exclaimed Richie.

'You are.'

'Are you sure?'

'Do you remember dying?' asked Angel.

'Yes. Sort of…'

'Then why do you doubt that you are now dead?'

'It just doesn't feel like I am.'

'Have you died before?'

'I don't know. Have I?'

'Not to my knowledge,' replied Angel. 'If you have not died before, how would you know what death *should* feel like?'

'Okay… fair point. So, I'm dead… this is heaven. Great. Now what?'

'This is a pocket of heaven, yes. There are many pockets, as I shall explain. Let me start by welcoming you.'

Richie looked at the blank canvas before him, stretching out into nothingness. 'Where's the rest of it?'

Angel smiled warmly. 'It is a vast place. The idea of heaven differs from person to person.'

Richie studied the man before him. This angel had no wings or heavenly glow. There was nothing outstanding about him. They were even the same height, which was average.

'I can't believe I'm here,' said Richie.

'Because of your atheist beliefs? It does not matter what you believed on Earth so long as your actions reflected the values of a good man, which they did.'

Richie was satisfied with the explanation. He'd have to be willing to accept things as they developed, his immediate world now being what it was.

'So, what happens now?'

'I wanted to meet you here so that you could get your bearings. A lot of people have mixed feelings about being dead. Passing on can be difficult.'

'I don't know. I don't really think I'm feeling anything.'

'You were young. This was entirely unexpected,' pressed Angel.

'I guess so.'

'Tell me how you are feeling about dying.'

Richie took a deliberate breath and exhaled. It was an action he'd performed millions of times without thinking, though now it served no purpose.

'I feel… relieved.'

'Relieved?'

'Yes.'

'Why is that?'

'I think it's sad, don't get me wrong. I'm sad thinking about Janice and I'm annoyed that I won't get to see my kids grow up, but I'm also feeling relieved. The last thing my wife said to me was that she wanted to have another baby. I was stressing out about it. I was stressing out about everything in the end… money, the future and the house. When I died… I was almost *happy* to. I was glad that those things that stressed me out… wouldn't anymore, you know? I don't know. Does that make any sense?'

'Everyone processes this transition differently. You should let these feelings wash over you. I will be your guide. You will have ample opportunity to talk to me during your time here. About anything, alright?'

'Okay.'

'You might feel fine now, but if that changes I will help.'

'Sure thing.' Richie nodded agreeably; keen to move through this obligatory seminar. He knew all about bureaucracy from his years of public service. Angel had to go through the terms and conditions of heaven, with all its disclaimers, before Richie would be allowed to enjoy it.

'Heaven will be an adjustment and there are things you will need to know,' said Angel.

'Such as?' Richie noticed that Angel's arms had remained by his sides for the duration of their interaction. His grey suit remained crisp and immaculate.

'The first thing to know is that time works differently up here. Years can go by in moments while moments can feel like months. You are no longer bound to the constraints that you had in life. All of that is behind you.'

'That's… great. So, I'll have time for everything that I want to do?' asked Richie. 'Is that what you're telling me?'

'Yes. You will be free to explore heaven and make it your own. You can customise your world as you choose at the speed of thought. You are welcome to stay here as long as you need to.'

'As long as I need to?' repeated Richie. 'Where else would I go?'

'Heaven might not always be as you imagined… or in your case, did *not* imagine,' said Angel.

'Do people actually *leave*? Why would they?'

'Eternity can be a long time for some.'

'Right, but if you don't like something you can change it?'

'Yes.'

'Well, that sounds perfect to me,' reported Richie with a grin.

'I am glad to hear it,' said Angel.

'So, where are these other people? Will I be able to see my loved ones again?' Richie's thoughts were suddenly of May and the nine years he'd spent without her.

'Of course. This place has been designed to pair you up with the person you loved most in life. Are you familiar with the concept of soul mates?'

'Yes.'

'Good.'

'And you're bound to them for all eternity?'

'Well, we have found that happiness is nothing without someone to share it with. I know that it must be challenging Richie, but I would like you to consider who makes you happiest. Who would you like to be with forever?'

Angel paused dramatically, which gave Richie time to think. He now realised that if an outsider was to analyse his life on Earth it could be divided into two significant chapters: May and Janice. This guardian angel was allowing Richie to choose between them.

'Are you saying I have to pick between my first and my second wife? Is May here?'

'May has been here since her death, yes.'

'And Janice is still alive?'

'Yes. At this time Janice is still alive.'

Richie imagined Janice learning about his death, perhaps finding his body outside Dan's front door. He knew that she would be suitably distraught. It was so sudden; just as losing May had been for him. The difference this time was Charlie and Brody. Janice would now be stuck raising their two boys alone, which he considered an overwhelming task. Richie felt sorrow as he mourned the moments he would never have, the assistance he could no longer provide.

'I don't feel that sense of relief anymore.'

'No?'

'No.'

'It is still a fresh wound. You are going to continue to experience all manner of emotion about your life. I am here to help with that. Consider this to be the beginning of a journey.'

'Dying is a *fresh* wound?'

'What I mean to say is that change is hard.'

'Being dead is a pretty big change,' exclaimed Richie.

'Perhaps some good news then? May has nominated you as her soul mate,' Angel continued, getting on with the formalities at hand. 'The question is whether you would like to accept that nomination. Ultimately only you can decide what you want.'

Richie thought about his darling May and how terrible death must have been for her. She'd spent the better part of a decade waiting around for him, clinging onto the love that they'd shared in life.

'If I accept May, and choose her... I can't choose Janice?'

'No. Once you have chosen to pair your souls that will be it. You will share the experience of heaven with either May *or* Janice. Unless there is another figure from your life that you would like to consider?'

Richie knew there was no other choice. Each woman had been the love of his life, albeit at different times. May represented a defining love, one of youth, discovery and joy. Janice had proven that lightning could strike twice, reigniting something mature and warm within Richie and changing him forevermore.

'There's no one else. It's either May or Janice. They spent the most time with me... they each loved me.'

He paused, prompting Angel to ask, 'Are you okay?'

'Why is it so hard to choose?' demanded Richie, suddenly feeling anxious about everything. He'd contorted his face, straining it unnaturally.

'Perhaps I can help you decide,' said Angel. 'There is a way.'

'What is it?'

'In heaven you are allowed to view any moment from your life. You can look back upon anything before making a decision.'

'How?'

Angel stood side by side with Richie, demonstrating the required movements.

'Place your hand onto your wrist and visualise the moment that you want to see. You will then re-live that moment.'

'Just like that, huh?'

'Correct.'

'And I can see anything from my life?'

Angel nodded. 'If you can remember it, you can be transported to it.'

Richie placed his right hand onto his left wrist, his thumb unable to find a pulse. It was strange to think of the vessel that he'd inhabited for his entire life being buried somewhere. Richie was free of his body, now conscious as some kind of spirit, some force of energy. He didn't feel changed, even though he wasn't alive anymore. Richie felt odd, like an imposter. He looked up at Angel, who nodded his encouragement.

What memory do I want to see?

There were a plethora of moments Richie wanted to revisit. He decided to choose one of the biggest days they'd shared. Richie felt a little bit silly as he thought back to the day he'd married May. It was like suddenly believing in Santa Claus and expecting presents again. Nevertheless he did as Angel had asked and visualised his first wedding in his mind's eye.

Without warning Richie was there. He'd been projected into his past at the speed of a blink. Once again it was binary.

The room smelt like lavender. He was standing at the altar, wearing his blue velvet suit and watching May approach him. She looked breathtaking. May was dressed in a wedding gown that she'd found in the window of an op shop. Richie hadn't been allowed to see it until this moment, as she'd hidden it in a box beneath their bed. It had taken a concentrated effort not to peek, and the resistance had been worth it. May had surprised him in the best way.

Richie started to compare his wives. It was a strange phenomenon but he knew that that was the purpose of this exercise. May, who was of Malaysian descent, was a lot more practical than Janice. She wasn't superstitious at all and hadn't given a thought to the former owner of her dress, or whether it was cursed in some unseen way. Richie thought about how carefree she was, and how they'd leapt forward together into marriage.

While inside this memory Richie occupied the same space that he had on that morning in October. He made eye contact with May through the same eyes, with the same vantage point and felt like he was back *in* that moment. It was impossible not to. It felt instantly immersive from Richie's point of view. Her black fringe looked perfectly cropped and Richie remembered that she'd told him afterwards how difficult her hair had been that day. It was so bittersweet to see May so clearly, with such optimism in her coffee-coloured eyes, and know so surely that their love would end in tragedy.

'Hi handsome,' said May as she squared off in front of him.

'You look beautiful.' The words were spoken by the Richie of the past. The script for these memories was set in stone. Whatever happened happened. He was just a mental tourist, a lucky visitor gifted with the insight to enjoy these moments again. May beamed at him and Richie was overcome.

He watched the vows and stayed for their first kiss as husband and wife. It was painful that he couldn't experience any corporeal sensation when May kissed him. He could smell the lavender, but he couldn't touch anything. It felt unfair.

Then, just as he was becoming accustomed to his surroundings, Angel placed his hand gently onto Richie's wrist. It was jarring, as Angel was suddenly sharing the vision, standing beside him at the wedding as if in a magical dream. Evidently he was able to connect with Richie's memory by holding his wrist too.

'I hope you do not mind,' said Angel.

'Not at all,' he replied politely. 'You can see this too?'

'Here most things are possible.'

'Amazing,' exclaimed Richie. 'It's so real.' He had a sudden sensation to scream at the top of his lungs, so he did. The intrusion of sound did not startle Angel, nor did it attract the attention of anyone in the living memory.

'They cannot hear you,' confirmed Angel, 'no matter how much you scream.'

'I thought as much. Just wanted to check.'

May was embracing her friends in the congregation. The gathering was limited to fifty people for financial reasons, and most of them were animated schoolmates. She gracefully navigated her way through the room, making getting married look effortless.

'I really loved her,' stated Richie to Angel.

'You must have been well suited. May still carries you in her heart. She nominated you as her soul mate after all. Do you feel the same way?' asked Angel.

'I loved May with such an intensity that when she died it destroyed me. I don't ever want to lose her again.'

'Then continue the story. Be with her again.'

'If I don't choose May… if I decide to wait for…'

'Janice?'

'Yeah. What will happen to May if I don't choose her now?'

'May will be placed in limbo. She will wait for as long as it takes to find an appropriate partner. May might nominate someone else from her life. She might not. It is like the principle of the yin and the yang. May must find her opposite and equal. Sometimes it is someone new.'

'That sounds like it could take a long time.'

'Eons, sometimes. We place souls together and hope for a lasting partnership. It is always better when the souls knew each other during their life. They grow a bond much more easily.'

'Can I watch more? From my time with May or Janice?' asked Richie.

'You can visit any moment in your life if it will help you make this decision. You can see these memories at any time in heaven. They are yours,' stated Angel.

At that moment the vision of May in her wedding dress walked up to them and threw her arms around his neck.

'I love you Rich,' said May.

'I love you too.'

She smelled sweet, like berries. Richie wished he could feel her touch. May had been his salvation; representing everything he'd wanted from life. Richie thought about rejecting May and in doing so found his answer.

He and May were entwined.

Richie couldn't bring himself to send her to limbo, dooming her to wonder why he'd chosen another. May would be left without any explanation and for all of time. It felt cruel. Angel was right; Richie needed to continue the story that had been cut so tragically short. May meant too much to him.

'I don't need any more time. I know who to choose.'

Chapter Six

Mystery Train

'Let me see the ring?'

May obliged, holding her left hand out for her friend to examine. Violet took her hand and squealed.

'It's so pretty,' stated May, glancing at the beautiful object and finding that it still felt foreign on her finger. It was a simple and understated ring, definitely reflecting Richie's financial position. While May knew they were heading towards this kind of commitment, she had hoped that the proposal would have occurred after graduation.

'So when's the wedding?' demanded Violet.

'Um… not totally sure.'

May was a planner, and this significant little rock had thrown itself into the gears of her life, stopping all momentum.

'Are you ready for that? One guy for the rest of your life?' asked Violet, eyes playful.

'Yeah. I love Richie.'

'Sure, but like…' Violet raised her hand so that none of the other café patrons could read her lips. 'One penis *forever*?'

May chuckled at her friend. Violet was nowhere near settling down and they both knew it.

'Depends on the penis!' joked May, loudly enough to turn heads. Violet almost knocked over her herbal tea as she flushed with laughter.

'But seriously…' said Violet as she recovered, 'this is a big deal.'

'It's huge!' offered May.

'Lucky you then!' Violet winked, still channelling her immature side.

'I'm ready,' said May confidently. 'It's all in the plan.'

'Oh, May. You're always doing this. Planning every step of your life out. You have to just let it happen!'

'Like you do?'

Violet had been on six dates in the past four days and taken three of them home with her. Sure, there was an untethered attractiveness to her friend's current lifestyle, but May knew it wasn't sustainable.

'At least let me plan your hen's party? Oooh! Can I be your maid of honour?'

'Violet...'

'*Please*? Oh my God it will be so much fun! I promise.' Violet was practically salivating at the idea. Her enthusiasm was infectious and May couldn't deny her.

'Like I have a choice. You're my best friend.'

'Damn straight! If you absolutely *have* to get married then I insist on sending you out in style,' vowed Violet.

'Well, if it doesn't work out I can always get divorced.'

'Of course you can!'

'To be clear, I do *want* it to work out with Richie,' insisted May.

'Sure! I get it.'

'Do you?'

'Well...' Violet offered a shrug, 'I get that *you* think this is a good thing.'

May's phone interrupted them and she answered it promptly, cutting off the lyrics of 50 Cent's *In da club*.

'Hi Mum, I was just thinking about you-'

'May? May... can you come over to... our place... please?' There was something strange about her mother's voice that made her immediately wary.

'What's going on?'

'It's your father. He's... he's dead.'

There was a decent police presence at the apartment. Three officers lingered in the doorway chatting, which had brought out a number of stickybeaks. The onlookers feigned concern as they paired off in the hallway of the complex and waited for answers. May hadn't acknowledged them as she'd brushed past. She'd felt numb since the phone call. Violet had offered to accompany her but May, ever the practical person, had declined seeing as they'd driven two cars to lunch.

Nobody stopped her as she entered the doorway. She thought that one of the policemen should have, but perhaps they recognised her from the photos inside. Maybe they'd been alerted to her impending arrival. May didn't want to believe, but the moment she saw her mother she knew it was true.

Her father was dead.

'May?'

'I'm here Mum.'

The two hugged and May was able to hold back her tears. Fatimah, her remaining parent was reserved, wearing the mask she'd perfected as a semi-professional poker player. Her winnings had never been consistent, yet they had resulted in some outlandish and memorable purchases. Fatimah was keeping it together.

'Are you okay?' she asked her mother.

'I'm okay.'

May looked over to the jade dragon that was prominently displayed on the coffee table. It was almost certainly a fake, yet her mother loved it as if it were an ancient and valuable antique. It stood out against an assortment of silver knick-knacks that littered the home. While the residence was modern, the décor was less so, cobbled together like a patchwork of past lives. They'd had the same dragon as long as May could remember. It had been one of the first things her parents had bought to furnish their home after migrating from Malaysia. She couldn't believe that the piece, which she had always considered quite an eyesore, had outlived her father. She had been so sure that reason and good taste would have prevailed.

'You have to sit down with me.' Her mother's insistence took her by surprise.

'I want to talk to the police Mum,' pleaded May. She craved answers. Two officers, a man and a woman, were in the kitchen speaking in hushed tones.

'Sit May.' The command was accompanied by a forceful push in the direction of a small living room table.

May was tiny and she didn't appreciate being led around the room. 'You don't have to push me, I'll sit with you.' Fatimah released her grip and they settled down together. 'Are you going to tell me what happened?'

'He jumped.'

'What?'

'He jumped off the balcony.'

May had arrived at the apartment complex via the rear side and parked in the underground car park. She'd ridden the elevator up to the nineteenth floor without seeing anything unusual.

'Why? Why did he do that?'

May hopped up and started walking towards the glass balcony doors. The female officer stopped her.

'Ma'am, you can't go out there right now, okay?'

'My father-'

'Yes, I know. Please. We'll be over to talk to you momentarily. Could you keep your mother company for now?'

There was compassion in this woman's eyes and May trusted that. 'Sure,' she replied absentmindedly. The whole exchange felt so surreal.

May sat down, this time next to her mother instead of opposite her.

'I was boiling the kettle when he must have jumped,' said Fatimah.

'Do they think Dad could have fallen?' asked May.

'I don't know.'

'What were you talking about? Right before he died what were you two saying?'

'I had pulled my old wedding dress out of storage. I wanted to use some of the old material and make you something to wear on the day. Like some lace ties that you could put around the bouquets. I thought maybe…' She trailed off.

'Maybe what Mum?'

'I thought maybe my wedding dress could be your something old.'

'So you were talking about wedding dresses and you boiled the kettle and Dad committed suicide?' May was angry and her words were sharp. Her mother started to cry. 'Sorry. I know this isn't easy but I spoke to Dad two days ago when Richie proposed. He sounded fine.'

'I thought so too.'

'Why did he do this? We talked about him walking me down the aisle…' May could feel a shift, a pressure building. 'You don't make plans with your daughter and then kill yourself!'

'This isn't your fault May. It's nobody's fault.'

'It's just so fucking selfish.'

'I know he really liked Richie,' offered Fatimah. 'He didn't do this because you're getting married. This feels like it was a long time coming. Something snapped in his head and I think he'd just had enough.' She placed her face in her hands and cried.

May scrambled for an answer. Her father was retired and a little bored, but that didn't feel like an explanation. She took a breath. There was nothing she could do now. He'd made his choice.

'He did this to both of us,' stated May.

Her mother nodded in agreement. Sadness swelled so tremendously within May that she could no longer prolong the tears from escaping her eyes. She cried onto her mother's shoulder, feeling overwhelmed that she would never see someone she loved so much ever again. The most troubling and unspoken truth was that May's father wasn't the first member of their family to commit suicide. But she refused to bring up her brother Arthur. May knew that he was already a permanent fixture in her mother's mind, and she didn't need a reminder.

Chapter Seven

<u>Always on my Mind</u>

'I choose May.'

In the same instant that he spoke the three words out loud the entire setting altered. Angel had transported Richie to what looked like a suburban neighbourhood. It felt like they were back on Earth, and yet it was something more. Everything had an aura. Richie could see that every garden was perfectly manicured and each house had the same modern design. Angel's bare feet stood on a gravel road. Richie reached down and touched the nearest hedge, which was coarse against his palm.

'I can feel it,' he exclaimed.

'Of course you can. The vision of May at your wedding was from your memory. That had already happened. This is your present. This is happening now. So, of course you can feel it.'

'Where's May?'

'She is waiting for you inside your home.'

'I have a home here? In this neighbourhood?'

'Yes. For it to feel comfortable this place is modelled from your memories on Earth. In your life you had a home with May, and that will also be the case here.'

'Can we go inside?'

Angel nodded. He gestured towards the closest residence. It felt familiar, even though Richie had no direct memory of it.

Richie stepped towards the door and exhaled a pointless breath. Angel followed a step behind. Richie didn't know what to expect. The diamond-shaped glass before him was frosted but he could identify a figure moving around inside. He turned the doorknob.

May.

She looked exactly the same as she had on their wedding day, with a smile that was so full it seemed to attack the real estate that her eye's held.

'Richie?' she squealed with delight. 'You're here!'

It felt too good to be true, and Richie was overcome with suspicion. 'Is this real?'

'Yes, of course,' replied Angel.

'Am I in a coma or something? Is this just like… my last synapses firing?'

'I'm real. I'm really here,' said May.

'I don't know what to believe anymore.'

'Believe *me*,' she said. 'There is life after death.'

'That sounds impossible.' Richie looked from May to Angel, searching for answers.

'I don't know how I can prove it to you,' muttered May. She turned to Angel, 'Richie used to work with statistics, so he always relied heavily on facts.'

'Of course,' said Angel.

'When you want to form conclusions you need verified information or else the data is useless.' Richie's eyes darted around. 'You can look at my memories, so you'll know everything I know. I can't ask May to tell me something that only she and I know because you know it too,' he said, indicating towards Angel. 'So there's no way to know for sure that this isn't some cruel trick.'

'Richie…' May looked hurt.

'I have no desire to trick you,' said Angel.

'Well we've only just met. I don't know you that well.'

'May I tell you something factual Richie?'

'Yes.'

'I am not a liar,' stated Angel. 'There is no need for duplicity. A place like this relies on honesty to function.'

'Ok.'

'This *is* May. You have my word.'

Richie looked into her patient eyes.

'Kiss me you idiot,' said May. The suddenness of this request took him off guard, and before he knew it they were connected at the lips, just like old times.

'Oh May!'

The two embraced again causing Richie to involuntarily shed a tear. They were together again, and he was so instantaneously happy that he knew somewhere deep inside himself that it *was* real. It was as real as he wanted it to be.

'Oh, go fuck yourself!' came a voice, just to Richie's left.

'Fuck you Austin! *Fuck* you!'

Richie was taken aback by the verbal assault. *Who the heck was Austin?* As he was standing in the doorway of his new home he determined that the commotion was coming from next door.

'Looks like I have some business to take care of,' said Angel. 'I will be with you both soon. Please, go ahead without me.'

'Thanks.'

Angel walked away, leaving the couple alone with their thoughts.

'I can't believe I'm holding your hand,' said May.

'I know. It's incredible.'

'Oh… look at your *dimples*!' exclaimed May. She'd always loved seeing them, and they only appeared when Richie's smile was at it's fullest. 'This is really real, isn't it?'

'It has to be,' replied Richie. He could feel tears building in the corners of his eyes. As one dashed down his cheek May cleared it with her thumb. 'There's so much… I don't know where to begin.'

'We've got time,' said May.

'I've missed you. I thought I'd never see you again.'

'You can't get rid of me that easily.'

'Oh May. I love you so much,' said Richie as he pulled her towards him.

'I love you too. So much.'

They kissed without regard for time. Richie and May were alone again, with eternity before them. May felt exactly the same. For Richie everything felt right in the universe.

'Have you been waiting here long?' he asked.

'Just long enough to check out the house.'

'Cool.'

'Let me show you something,' said May, taking his hand. She led Richie up a short flight of stairs and into an attic. It was shaped like a Toblerone, with the windows at the same sixty-degree angles that he remembered.

'Incredible,' he said, scarcely able to believe the level of detail before him. It was exactly the same as it was when they'd first moved in together.

'I know, right? I'll bet you feel pretty stupid for not believing in God now!'

'I feel a little… embarrassed. Yeah.'

'Is that all?' laughed May.

'Seeing all of this firsthand makes me feel like an idiot,' confessed Richie. 'Happy?'

'Very. I can't tell you how much I've missed you… *idiot.*' said May playfully.

'I've missed you so much. You look incredible.'

'Why thank you! So do you.'

'Do I look older?' asked Richie, conscious of the fact that he'd aged since her death.

'No. You look the same. How long were you alive?' she asked.

'I made it to thirty-five.'

'That's so young!' exclaimed May.

'It's really weird that you don't know about my death. I mean, obviously I died because I'm *here*… You know what I mean?'

'Yeah.'

'In a way it's like no time has passed but I had twelve more years of life without you.' Richie was still getting his head around this new reality.

'Tell me about your life. Tell me what I've missed,' said May.

Richie started to try and explain everything that had happened in the twelve years between her demise and his, but it felt like an impossible task. He was nervous about telling May that he'd spent the last three years of his life with Janice. Richie felt like without the context of his heartbreak and the years between events, that May might not understand how he could have married again.

'Maybe I can show you,' offered Richie.

'What do you mean?'

Richie told her about the process that he'd been through with Angel and the way he'd been able to play back his memories.

'He never showed me how to do that,' grumbled May, who didn't like to miss out on things.

'He didn't?'

'No. We spoke for a time and he explained that I was dead.'

'And then he asked you to pick a soul mate, right?' asked Richie.

'Yeah. And I picked you.'

'Right away?'

'Yes. Right away.'

'That's so nice.'

'Well of course I picked you Richie. You were the love of my life, you big lug.' May planted a kiss onto his pillowy lips.

'You're the best,' he replied.

'So, do you think that would work for us? That I could see *your* memories, I mean?' asked May.

'Angel could see them, so it should work for you. He told me that I could revisit any moment from my life just by thinking about it and holding my wrist. Do you want to try?'

'For sure!'

Richie placed his right hand over his left wrist once again. He thought about May's funeral. He remembered sitting on a cheap black chair in the front row of a congregation of people and watching as her coffin was lowered into the ground. Suddenly he was transported there, and May had vanished.

'Take my wrist,' he called out, not knowing whether she could hear him. He felt her fingers coil around his forearm and May reappeared at his side.

'Whoa.'

'I know.'

'This is trippy!'

May looked at all of the faces around her, weeping as she was lowered into the earth. She spotted Violet, her blonde hair tied modestly into a ponytail. She was weeping loudly, pausing only to blow her nose with a tissue. Violet looked like she hadn't been sleeping. Almost all of their school friends had come out for the service. May's passing had been tragic, and nobody was quite sure how to process it. The sky was full of clouds, each threatening to dampen the occasion even more. Richie remembered that sky, and knew that despite its ominous appearance, the rain would stay away.

Suddenly he felt himself stand, compelled by the actions of his former self. May, still holding his wrist floated forward to the grave. Then, in a private move Richie reached into the pocket of his trousers and took out a handful of salt and pepper packets. It looked as if he'd pilfered them from the tables of many restaurants over the years, only to collect them for this moment. Richie threw the assortment into the grave like one might toss a handful of dirt, before returning to his seat.

'So you have to move around the way you did when you were alive?' asked May.

'Yeah. I'm stuck repeating the same actions. I guess since you're holding my wrist you get dragged along for the ride,' he replied.

'This is so peculiar,' said May. 'Seeing the world from your perspective, I mean. But it's a bit morbid. I don't really need to see everyone mourning over me.'

'You don't?' I would have loved to have seen my funeral.'

'Why? It's sad.'

'I suppose so.'

Richie didn't have a will, or any specifications about what to do in the event of his death. He wondered whether Janice would have selected some music, or perhaps read a loving poem. It annoyed him a little that he would never know.

It seemed unusual to be able to speak during such a solemn procession. Richie still felt obliged to behave as if he really was at a funeral, but May seemed to have accepted that this wasn't actually happening. It made sense. Richie had experienced this event once before, while May was more detached from this particularly horrid day.

'Show me something else?' May had stopped paying attention to the scene around them and was missing her mother Fatimah's antics. Richie looked past May and watched his mother in law collapsing to the ground in dramatic sorrow. Richie could see that May was right: this was kind of depressing. They had the power to jump to any moment in their shared lives. There were certainly other things he could show her. There would be time for everything.

Without considering it too much Richie's mind wandered back to a moment several years later. He and May watched as the living incarnation of Richie sat in a car outside the house that they'd purchased together. Richie occupied the driver's seat and May was beside him, travelling along for the ride. In the window of the residence was an old Vietnamese couple.

'Oh, you sold it?' May seemed disappointed at the revelation.

'I rented it out. I never sold it,' said Richie.

'Did you ever live in our house again?'

The time to tell the truth had arrived. Richie hoped that transparency about his life with Janice wouldn't upset May too much.

'Yeah… I… I got remarried,' declared Richie.

'You did?'

'Yes. I'm sorry. I wasn't sure how to bring this up. About ten years after you…'

'Died? You can say it. I *died*. I was there,' said May. 'I'm dead.' She slumped back into her car seat for dramatic effect.

'We both are,' said Richie, feeling the calm sensation returning. He no longer had to worry about his house, or the kids, or bills, or work, or stress, or Janice, or his parents, or his annoying neighbour Dan, or the yuccas in the garden, or the ailing kangaroo paw plants, or the roof tiles that may or may not have needed replacing. Richie didn't have to worry about anything ever again.

He was free. They were both free.

The scene in front of them continued. Richie watched as Dan introduced himself to the Vietnamese couple. They nodded and bowed and seemed very happy to make his acquaintance. Richie rolled his eyes.

'Any kids?' May asked nonchalantly.

'Uh...'

'You had kids?'

'Two.'

'Wow. You *were* busy!'

'It's not like that... I mean... they were twins.' He struggled to organise his jumbled thoughts.

'It's okay Rich. Let's get past it, okay? Let's get everything out in the open. Tell me what happened.'

'Right,' said Richie. 'Thanks.'

'No problem,' replied May.

'So, ten years after you died, I married a woman named Janice Norman.'

'Was she Malaysian too?'

'No. Janice Norman. Does that sound Malaysian?'

'Not really, no.'

'She was Caucasian. She was a blonde.'

'Aw! I was sure you had a type,' teased May.

'Whatever.'

'So, why did you remarry?'

'Well, I didn't think I'd ever see you again. I was an atheist, remember? I didn't think I'd wind up spending eternity with you. I was lonely and broken for a long time. Eventually it just sort of… happened,' said Richie.

'Marriages don't just sort of happen. I can see you moving on… wanting companionship. But you *married* her. You must have loved this woman.'

'Yes. In a different way… but yes. I loved Janice.'

'Oh my God.' May seemed suddenly startled. She let go of Richie's wrist, prompting him to do the same. In a blink they were back in the upstairs attic of their heavenly abode.

'What?' Richie was confused with the outburst.

'She's going to die! And then she's going to turn up here and you're already with me!'

'Well… possibly.'

'Possibly? Do you think she might *not* die?'

'No… I mean… everybody dies.'

'She was your *wife* Richie.'

'Right, but so were you…'

'Oh I feel awful!' shouted May, staring out of the window into a sky full of postcard perfect clouds.

'No, listen. *You* shouldn't feel awful. We should feel happy.'

'Don't get me wrong, I'm glad you chose me. I love you Richie and I want to be with you forever. But I stole you from Janice. She married you last.'

'We were only married for a couple of years. Three years!'

'We were only together for three years too!' said May.

She was right. Neither of Richie's marriages had lasted very long. May shook her head and walked downstairs. Richie followed, a half step behind. She sat down at the kitchen table and put her head in her hands. May was faced with a new crisis, and much like the rest of heaven, it was uncharted territory. Instead of comforting her Richie decided to look in the fridge. He wasn't hungry per se, but considered that if this were heaven the fridge would have his favourite kind of apricot chutney inside. He opened the door to find a wall of glass jars, each filled with exactly that. Richie closed the door, visualised leftover Thai food and then pulled it open. Staring back at him was Chicken pad Thai and massaman beef curry, each in the plastic takeaway containers that he and May used to get. The fridge seemed capable of meeting their every wish.

'Look at this,' he said, closing the fridge.

May watched as Richie opened and closed the appliance a dozen times. With each reveal he'd changed the contents to a different novelty food item.

'Isn't that amazing?'

'Richie...'

'Sorry. What were you saying?'

'What if Janice shows up?' asked May, unimpressed with Richie's fridge experiment.

'We'll deal with that *if* it happens,' he replied.

'You might see her, and then you'll remember how great it was to be with her. Then you'll-'

'I wont,' announced Richie, interrupting her. 'May, I never thought things would unfold this way. If I had known there was even a chance that we could have had this... heaven... together. I would have waited for you. Truly. I love you,' said Richie.

'I know you do. This is just such an unusual situation. I'm having trouble taking it all in.'

'Me too.'

'There's so much that happened to you over those twelve years. I guess I just feel like some of your life is in the shadows, hidden from me. It's never been like that before,' said May. 'I used to know everything about you.'

'Then let me show you. Let me help you understand what you missed. Then maybe we can move forward together.'

'Okay.'

Richie sat down beside her at their kitchen table. He started by remembering the years after May. The heartache and struggles that he'd suffered after her death. Moments into moments stretched into forever as they looped their lives before them like mental time travellers with complete control of their destinations. He'd forgotten a lot of the details. It was hard to ignore how badly he'd managed his emotions, and how introverted he'd become. May watched Richie grow up, clawing his way out of a depression and putting his life back together.

'You were starting to get a little bit of grey in your beard,' observed May.

'Was I?'

'Yeah. I liked it.'

Soon May was introduced to Janice at the optometrist. She watched their interactions and saw a change in him. By experiencing it through his eyes May was starting to comprehend how much she'd meant to Richie. For years he'd been like a bird with broken wings. May had seen it for herself. When Richie met Janice she could tell he was ready to fly again.

'You look good in glasses,' she determined.

'Thanks. I keep reaching up to adjust them, but I don't need them here. I keep thinking that my phone is vibrating in my pocket too, but obviously I don't have a phone.'

'You can keep wearing the glasses if you want.'

'But I don't have them anymore.'

'Yeah but we can change anything here with a thought. So think about your glasses.'

Richie reached into his pants pocket. Sure enough his glasses were exactly where he imagined they would be. He put them on and suddenly felt better, more present somehow.

'Was it love at first sight?' asked May.

'With Janice?'

'Yeah.'

'I was so tired of being alone,' confessed Richie.

'I know. If the situation were reversed, I might have done the same thing,' she offered.

May didn't want to fight with Richie. It was clear how much Janice had meant to him. Even now, when asked to choose between them in a union for all eternity, Richie had wanted her. They could move past this and enjoy all that heaven had to offer. May softened, comfortable in the knowledge that she was his true love, his soul mate.

'It's okay,' said May.

'Thanks.'

They stayed up for a long time revisiting the moments that highlighted their lives. Richie and May felt no desire to sleep or eat and so they simply existed together. Time must have passed, but it wasn't clear to either of them how much. It didn't matter.

Soon they were discussing their deaths.

'I'm not really sure how I died,' said Richie.

'How can that be?'

'Well, I was alive and then my body collapsed. Like I had a brain aneurysm or something. It's a bit embarrassing but I don't exactly know what happened.'

'Let's not share anything that might make us sad,' said May, noting the change on Richie's face. 'I don't want to watch you die. I only want to see you live.'

'I don't want to watch you die either. It's the only thing I don't really want to see,' he said, agreeing to the plan.

Richie thought back to their wedding night, and the hotel room where he'd undressed his new bride. 'I might like to review the night of our wedding, if you're interested?'

'Oh my. That might be fun. Although now that you mention it, there are a few other nights I might like to… *review*.'

He and May reminisced about their most memorable sexual encounters until May questioned whether they were still capable of repeating them.

'I'm not sure. But there's really only one way to find out,' he said with a cheeky grin.

May led them to the bedroom of their new home. They disrobed quickly and clumsily as if it was their first time. It was a different experience than it had been on Earth. While the mechanics remained the same the sensation was magnified, as if with each movement they were pleasuring each other's souls.

When it was over Richie felt an overwhelming peace, as if he'd found his purpose and was now centred and balanced.

'That was something else, wasn't it?' sighed May, who was obviously equally sated.

'Yeah. Let's do that again.'

'Your dimples are back,' chuckled May.

'Oh yeah? I'm smiling, am I?'

'Uh huh.'

As Richie started kissing May their peaceful environment was pierced with nearby screams.

'You are such a lying piece of shit, aren't you?' came a female voice.

'Oh, because you're so honest with me!' came the rebuttal, a male voice this time. Their accents were American.

'Do you hear that?' asked Richie.

'It's hard not to,' said May.

The couple peered out the window cautiously and saw their next-door neighbours arguing in their front yard. The man was wearing a singlet of red, white and blue. On top of his head was an off white cowboy hat. His companion had light brown hair and was skinny to the point of anorexia. The simple blue dress that she wore was loose fitting, but her thin figure was clearly outlined underneath. As if to compliment her partner's outfit she wore red cowboy boots.

'Sounds like we live next door to a couple of rowdy Texans,' chuckled May.

'We've lived next door to worse!' replied Richie.

'Do you mean Mrs Winters? She wasn't so bad. She used to feed Fitty sometimes.'

Richie had meant Dan, but he quickly realised that May hadn't lived long enough to share his distaste for the man. He dismissed the thought and fumbled through a response.

'Yeah… I suppose you're right. Mrs Winters never shouted curse words in her front garden.'

'She did sing to the daffodils though, thinking it would help them grow.'

'It didn't work. They seemed like regular old daffodils to me,' shrugged Richie.

They watched the domestic argument continue for a time before Angel arrived, and ushered the Americans back through their front door.

Chapter Eight

Lawdy, Miss Clawdy

'Do you go on many dates?'

'I mean… a normal amount. Are you asking if I'm a slut?'

'God, no! Sorry, I was just trying to make conversation.'

Janice shook her head, wondering why she'd bothered. The restaurant was extremely elegant, with candles illuminating their meals. It was a proper grown up outing. There weren't any children present, which only made her miss her own. Charlie and Brody weren't quite old enough to look after themselves, which had led Janice to source a babysitter from a local service. The teenager that they'd sent had seemed competent enough, but leaving her boys in the company of a strange girl was creating some unwanted anxiety. Janice had ordered fish and regretted it immediately.

'It's okay. I'm just… not used to this I guess,' she said earnestly.

'I'm not either. I was engaged for a long time. We separated six months ago.'

'That must have been hard,' said Janice.

'It was.'

Her date's name was Dominic. Janice guessed from the creases on his face that he was probably approaching fifty. He wore it well. Dominic had made an effort with his appearance, electing to wear shiny black shoes. Janice had the feeling that they might have once been part of a wedding ensemble.

'Do you still talk to your ex?' she asked.

'Yeah, we email a little here and there. I think she feels guilty,' replied Dominic.

'And why is that?'

'She cheated on me.'

'Oh. I'm sorry. Is she a Taurus?'

'What?'

'Do you know her astrological sign?'

'Um… I think she's a Gemini. Born in June?' replied Dominic with uncertainty.

'Geminis can be very two-faced,' said Janice. 'Not always, but sometimes.'

'Anyway… she's still with the guy. The one she left me for. I think she wants to make sure I'm okay. Ease her guilt a little bit.'

'It sounds like it was a rough breakup.'

'Smashing glassware, yelling til the neighbours called the police. The whole nine yards,' admitted Dominic.

He didn't strike Janice as violent, although when backed into a corner or hurt, people were capable of being less than rational.

'It sounds like, at the very least, that you're a passionate person.' She smiled politely as she cut up a piece of sweet potato.

Dominic changed the subject. 'What do you do for work Janice?'

'I'm an optometrist.'

'Ah, that's good. Do you like it?' asked Dominic.

'I do.'

'I haven't been for an eye test in years. Twenty-twenty vision they tell me!'

'These things do change… deteriorate I mean. You should have a check up.'

'Maybe I will.'

'And you're in finance, right?'

'Good memory. Hedge funds mostly. Trying to turn money into more money. That sort of thing.'

Janice popped a vegetable into her mouth and chewed slowly.

'Look… I don't want this to be awkward, so let me just say that you are by far the prettiest blind date that I've ever had the pleasure of being set up on,' stated Dominic.

'Is that right?'

'Definitely. I hope you're enjoying yourself as much as I am.'

Janice paused. 'Do you have any kids?'

'No, no kids.'

'I have two. Charlie and Brody. What do you think about that?' she asked.

'Well, I'm not opposed to kids. As long as their father's not in the picture anymore, romantically speaking. I mean… how old are they?'

'Thirteen. They're twins.'

'And what do thirteen year olds like these days?' asked Dominic.

'Charlie's into sports, soccer mostly. Brody likes to write, but he's sensitive. He won't share his poetry with me. He keeps a diary and I took a peek at that though.'

'Any good?'

'It's your typical teenage angst. He's figuring things out,' said Janice with a smile. 'I just wanted to make sure he wasn't plotting anything sinister.'

'They sound great.'

'They are. I can't complain too much. I guess they could put their dirty washing in the laundry basket once in a while, but that's not the end of the world.'

Dominic chuckled, 'That sounds about right.'

'I've just been wearing the Mum hat for so long. I think it's time that I focus on myself. Does that make sense?'

'Yes, it does.'

'I'm reaching a point in my life where I'm starting to think about what I want. My needs.'

Dominic nodded along, cutting up his steak.

'It's like… have you ever thought about a complete lifestyle change? Doing something you've never done before?'

'Are you about to tell me you're a vegan?'

'Funny… but no. I'm trying to decide whether or not to go home with you.'

'Well, I might be a little biased on the subject but I vote that you do.'

'And what would we do? If I came over tonight…' asked Janice, her voice intentionally lowered.

'I'd do my best to show you a good time.'

'I think I'd like to have a good time.'

'I might be shooting myself in the foot here,' started Dominic, 'but all that stuff about your boys…'

'Charlie and Brody.'

'Yeah. Did you tell me about them because you're looking for something serious? Because I can be serious. I know I said my fiancée left me, and I know it was only six months ago, but I-'

'Relax Dominic… I'm not looking for a father for my boys. They've already got one.'

'So, this would be something more… *casual*?'

'I think casual is all I'm capable of right now,' said Janice.

'I don't want to pry too much on our first date,' he said wiping his mouth, 'but you've got a pretty pronounced tan line on your ring finger. Did your marriage end recently?'

'No.'

'Okay, good.'

'I'm still married,' declared Janice.

'Huh? If you're still married then that kind of makes me wonder what you're doing here with me,' said Dominic.

'Like I said, I'm considering a lifestyle change. I'm thinking about myself for once.'

Dominic's expression changed. His food now sat untouched on the plate. 'I'm not really looking to break up a happy home. Like I told you, I've been cheated on and it hurts.'

'So have I, and I know it does.'

'Your husband cheated on you?'

'Still does.'

'Why don't you leave him then?'

'I love him,' stated Janice.

'But surely you can see how unhealthy it is? He's using you,' declared Dominic.

'That's kind of why I agreed to go on this date with you. I wanted to even up the playing field. Tit for tat so to speak.'

'An eye for an eye makes the whole world blind.'

'Don't you ever feel like your ex-fiancée won? That she's happy, even if she's feeling a little bit guilty?'

'I don't know… I guess deep down I want her to be happy,' replied Dominic.

'We only get one life. This is it,' said Janice. 'Why shouldn't we do what we want?'

'Because that would be chaos. Rules exist for a reason.'

'Look,' started Janice, 'you like going to restaurants, right?'

'Sure, who doesn't?'

'Okay, so when you go to a restaurant you might have a favourite dish…'

'Steak, usually,' said Dominic.

'Perfect… *steak*… so, you love steak and every time you go to a restaurant you order steak. Eventually, aren't you getting tired of the same thing, over and over again?'

'No, I'd love to have steak every night. I probably shouldn't though.'

'Alright, but if I force fed you steak every night for a *year*… you'd be sick of steak.'

'But with the right sauce, spices or garnish it would take an extremely long time…'

'Steak is still steak, no matter how you cook it and no matter how you dress it up.'

'Perhaps.'

'Well, that's what I'm trying to avoid,' said Janice. 'I don't want either of us to wonder what else is on the menu. If we're hungry, we should be able to eat.'

Dominic studied her face. 'Who are you trying to convince? Me… or yourself?'

'It's not like that. I've just come to this a lot more cautiously, but it feels like the right way to go,' said Janice.

'Do you think Chucky and Brody-'

'*Charlie* and Brody,' she said, interrupting him.

'Right, sorry,' said Dominic. 'Do you think Charlie and Brody would approve of this behaviour?'

'They're never going to know. Think about it… how much do you know about your mother's love life?' asked Janice.

'Nothing.'

'See? It's none of their business.'

'Sounds to me like you've made up your mind about that lifestyle change. But you can count me out.' Dominic folded his napkin over.

'Come on, don't be like that,' she pleaded.

'You might think it's all fun and games right now, but there are consequences to your actions. People get hurt.'

'Take me home Dom. Do your best to show me a good time. Please?'

'No,' he replied firmly. 'And don't call me Dom. My ex used to call me Dom. Go home to your husband.'

'He's not home. He's off with another girl.' Janice bit her lip.

'Then he's a shitty husband.'

'I can't go home. I don't want to be alone.'

'Who's watching your boys?'

'Babysitter.'

'Look… I don't want to be harsh. You're very beautiful and part of me would love to have some no strings attached fun with you tonight. I mean that.'

'Thank you.'

'But this… pile of emotional baggage that you're carrying around… it's too much. I don't want to mess around with a married woman whose looking to get back at her husband.'

'Can I be honest?' asked Janice.

'I think you're doing a fine job of that so far…'

'My husband cheats on me, and I let him. Maybe I don't mind it as much as I ought to, but it's a fact. Now I'm looking to even things up, that's true. Its just sex. I think maybe you need this as much as I do. I've realised that I can have sex with other people, just like he does… and still be a wife and a mother. It's not conventional, I know. But if I don't sleep with you, honestly I'm just going to find someone else to sleep with.'

'Well, heaven help him,' said Dominic, and he stood up and walked away.

Janice shook her head. Dominic's nobility had surprised her. She stood up, not wanting to linger at the site of her rejection, when her legs gave way and she lost her balance.

'Are you alright?' asked one of the restaurant staff.

'Oh, that's... I'm fine. I just got dizzy. That's all,' replied Janice. She steadied herself using her chair.

'Do you need me to help you up?'

Janice exhaled. She no longer felt faint and waved away the offer of assistance. When she was safely back in her seat the server slipped back into work mode.

'Can I get you some water or anything else?'

'No, thank you. I'm okay.'

'Sure. When you're ready I'll get you the bill.'

'Thanks. I'm ready now.'

The waiter nodded and left Janice alone. Dominic had left without paying. Perhaps he wasn't so noble after all.

Chapter Nine

<u>I Just Can't Help Believin'</u>

Angel had diffused whatever domestic squabble the Texans had inflamed and now re-joined Richie and May in the living room.

'I am so pleased that you two have been reunited,' he said. 'I hope I am not interrupting you now.'

'No, I think you left us to get reacquainted for just long enough,' said May, a knowing smile on her face. She looped her arm around Richie's and her head leaned organically onto his shoulder.

'Thank you Angel,' said Richie. 'I'm not sure I've had the chance to say that yet. This is more special to me than you could imagine.'

'You are most welcome,' said Angel. 'While you should find your new abode both familiar and comfortable there is one other aspect that warrants further explanation.'

'I've walked through the whole place Richie. It's got some of the same rooms as our house,' stated May excitedly. 'The details are crazy. It's exactly the same.'

'Did you happen to notice a door that you could not open?' asked Angel.

'Yes! It's in the nursery. Well, in the room that we *were* going to use as a nursery.'

The trio soon found themselves at the mysterious door. It was wooden, and seemed ordinary except for its odd placement. The door had been installed at the rear of the house. If a person walked through it there was no room to access, just the garden outside. Yucca trees could be seen through the windows on either side.

'That's different,' stated Richie.

'I tried it. It didn't open,' said May.

'Every resident in heaven has a doorway like this in their home. This will allow you to see your loved ones… friends and family… anyone you lost in your lives.'

Richie and May fell silent.

'The reason that the door did not open for you May, was because you did not yet know how to use it properly,' explained Angel.

'Can we use it now?' she asked.

'As you wish. When you hold the door handle you must visualise the person that you want to see. They will have a sudden sensation when you are thinking about them. If they want to see you too, then the pathway between you will open. From this pocket of heaven to theirs.'

'And if they don't want to see you?' asked Richie.

'Then the door will not budge.' Angel's arms stayed by his side throughout the explanation. He made no accompanying gestures at all. His grey suit was still crease free and his feet were still inexplicably bare, but they both appreciated his candour.

'Angel, I have kind of a weird question,' said May.

'I am here to answer it,' replied Angel.

'Who decides what people look like in heaven?'

'What do you mean?'

'Well, when we were watching Richie's memories earlier I noticed that he had some grey hair in his beard, but he doesn't have that now. He looks like he did when he was married to me.'

'The truth is that everyone in heaven appears through the prism of their beholder. You see Richie as you saw him in life. He sees you as he remembers you. It is different for everyone, but ultimately an idealised version of yourself,' said Angel.

'Right, because I couldn't see any mirrors in the bathroom,' said May.

'You look perfect to me,' said Richie with a smile.

'You have to say that, you're my soul mate.'

'Well, I must attend to some of the other residents,' declared Angel.

'Oh, yeah. We might have seen you with the folks next door,' said Richie, pointing in the direction of their neighbours.

'Some gardens require more tending than others.' Angel spoke very eloquently, and both May and Richie found him to be a very calming presence.

'Are there many people in this pocket of heaven?' asked Richie.

'Not a lot. Certainly enough to keep things interesting. You will see more of me. We will have regular sessions together, in order for me to help with your transitions.'

'Like, *therapy* sessions?' asked Richie.

'Private conversations.'

'So, a bit like therapy,' stated May.

Angel stared blankly at them, then carried on with his farewell. 'As always, this is your home and your neighbourhood. Enjoy it. It is whatever you make it. If you need me, I will be around.'

'Thank you Angel,' said May.

He departed, leaving the happy couple to ponder their next move. The wooden door was beckoning them to test it.

'Who do you want to see first?' asked Richie.

'I mean… my parents, my brother Arthur, Violet. I don't know. How about you?'

'My Dad.'

'Oh… I didn't know he'd died.'

'Heart attack. It was pretty sudden,' said Richie.

'I'm sorry.'

'Thanks.'

'So, do you want to go first?' asked May.

'Oh, no… after you. I'll come with you… if you like?'

May smiled appreciatively. She placed her hand on the handle and closed her eyes. When she tried to press the wooden door forward it remained in place.

'Who did you think of?'

'Arthur.'

'Try thinking of someone else,' offered Richie.

May thought of her mother and then her father without success. 'It's not working. Do you want to try?'

'Yeah, I'll have a go. Maybe it's defective…'

Richie approached the door and held the handle. He pictured his father's face, earnest and kind. The doorway opened and they glided through.

They were carried away to a living room filled with music. Richie recognised it as Bob Dylan's *Blonde on Blonde*. Sitting in a brown chair that faced a record player was Richie's father Stephen. He was grinning from ear to ear, looking healthy with unruly black hair. The length reminded Richie of the time his father took a sabbatical and grew it out intentionally.

'Dad?'

'Richie my boy! My ears were burning… or my mind, or something. I'm still new to these heavenly visits, but I sensed you!'

'Do you remember May?' he asked, wrapping an arm around her waist.

'Oh, you're with May? That's nice… lovely to see you dear.'

'You too.'

Richie's father didn't get up. The many cubes in front of Stephen were filled with twelve-inch records, bulging from end to end. It was a much larger assortment than Richie had expected.

'You have a record collection in heaven? Is it any good?'

'It's incredible! I just have to think about an artist, reach into the pile and I pull out their album! They're all in perfect condition too. Check this out…'

He demonstrated, pulling out a copy of David Bowie's *The Man Who Sold the World*.

'That's so wild,' said Richie, admiring the rare album cover on which Bowie wore a dress.

'Got any Elvis?' asked May. 'Richie *always* played Elvis albums.'

'Not *always*,' said Richie defensively. He realised that May was unaware that he'd broadened his musical horizons since they'd been married.

'You've got good taste. He is The King,' said Stephen, pulling out another record. 'How about this one?'

Richie recognised the album straight away. Elvis, half-smiling on the cover, wearing a Hawaiian shirt and lei.

'Oooh, *Can't Help Falling in Love*,' stated May. 'I love that song.'

Stephen finally got up from his chosen spot, set up the player and expertly placed the needle at the start of the track. As they listened to the familiar chords, Richie held the album in his hands. It was unnaturally crisp. In the collection that he'd inherited from his father the records had character. There were stickers from their original sales, worn rings where the records had pressed against the cardboard over time, even the occasional name of a former owner. This album didn't *feel* right. It didn't feel the way Richie thought it should, like it had been held and loved by someone.

'I've got time for everything up here. I can listen to everything I've ever wanted. Even some of the artists I never really appreciated while I was alive.'

Stephen sat back down in his recliner. Richie knew the chair well, as it looked exactly like the one his father had occupied when he was alive.

'Dad?'

'Yeah?'

'The chair...'

'What about it?'

'Dad, it's the chair you died in.'

'Not exactly.'

On that fateful day Richie's mother had found Stephen collapsed in his chair, a record still rotating in the player.

'But it looks exactly the same,' said Richie. 'Do you really want that kind of reminder around?'

'I don't see it that way. That's not the chair I died in. That's the chair I lived in.'

'So, you're just puttering around your house and listening to old records?' asked May bluntly.

'Yeah, at the moment I am,' replied Stephen, a little defensively.

'But don't you want to get out there and see some more of heaven?' asked May.

'Not really. There's still a lot of music I want to listen to.'

A voice called out from the kitchen, 'Stephen?'

Richie recognised it immediately. 'Mum?'

Helen Walsh wandered into the room with a mixing bowl nestled in her arm, wooden spoon whirring in the other. 'Hello son, hello May.'

'What are *you* doing here?'

'I live here honey.'

'But...'

'She died Richie,' whispered May, although not quietly enough.

'Yes, I died,' confirmed Helen.

'When?'

'After you.'

'Right after me?' asked Richie.

'No! Not *right* after you. Years later.'

'How?'

'How did I die?' asked his mother.

'Yes!'

'Why do you want to know that?' asked Helen.

'Because I need to know!'

'I got sick and I didn't get better, okay? Is that what you want to hear?'

'No... I don't *want* to hear it,' said Richie. 'I just think it's something that you ought to be able to talk about, if that makes sense...'

'Well I don't want to talk about all that unpleasantness. I'm here, I'm dead,' shrugged Helen, 'get used to it.'

Richie was shocked. He didn't feel like he'd been in heaven long enough to settle into a routine and here was his mother, relaxing with her husband as if no time had passed. She wore the same apron that had hung on the side of the fridge - dark blue in colour - and her hair had been pushed into a familiar bun. Richie remembered Angel's words and knew this was just the ideal version of his mother, the one only he could see.

'Hello May!' said Helen as they hugged. 'Wonderful to see you again.'

'Hi Helen.'

'How have you been?'

'I'm great now. Richie and I just found each other again.'

'That's true love then,' stated Helen. 'Don't get me wrong, I didn't *dislike* Janice, but it's good to see things back to normal.'

'Mum...'

'Honestly, I'd never seen you happier than you were with May.'

Richie was torn. He didn't want to defend Janice exactly, but he wasn't enjoying the way his mother was taking sides.

'That's sweet,' said May, a polite smile creeping onto her face.

Richie rolled his eyes. 'As if I could have known that I'd see May again.'

'Well you might have! If you'd ever come to church with me,' reasoned Helen. 'You should have *tried* to be more religious Richie.'

'It didn't matter though in the end. We're both here anyway,' argued Richie.

'Well, yes. I suppose overall you were a good boy. Someone must have raised you right.'

In the background Stephen peeled himself out of his chair and changed the music to Cyndi Lauper. 'Any album I want! It's here for me,' called Stephen happily.

Helen explained that while her husband was enjoying his endless record collection she'd been fulfilling a lifelong desire to cook every recipe from her cookbooks.

'I had so many cookbooks. Do you remember Richie? They used to fill a whole bookcase. I could never throw any away.'

'Yeah I remember them.'

'I only cooked the same ten things over and over again. Now I'm trying out the rest,' said Helen.

'That's great,' said May. 'Good for you.'

'We don't *need* to eat, mind you. But it's been so nice to just imagine any ingredient you need, open the cupboard and find it waiting for you.'

'It's the same with the fridge,' added Richie. 'I tried it out before.'

Helen paced over to Stephen in time to the music, then delivered a kiss to his upturned cheek. Richie was glad to see them together, reaffirming that love can conquer any challenge: even death. It occurred to him how strange it would have been if his father had selected someone other than his mother for a soul mate, and how complicated that would have made this reunion. Frankly he didn't know anything much about his father's life before his mother entered it.

'Do you two want to stay for pud?' offered Helen, as she went on stirring her mysterious batter.

'No thanks Mum. It's good to see you but May and I have a lot of catching up to do,' replied Richie.

'You're going to love it up here kids,' said Stephen. 'It's like retirement. You've done the work and now you can just relax.'

'Sounds good,' said Richie, holding tightly onto May.

'If you want my advice, get yourself a hobby. Pick something you've always wanted to do and then do it! If you can keep yourself busy you'll be fine.'

May squeezed Richie's hand and they shared a glance. He smiled as they both remembered the powerful sexual experience they'd very recently shared. Richie hoped that could be their hobby.

'Come back and see us soon, won't you?' asked Helen.

'We will.'

They wandered over to Stephen and each took turns giving him a hug.

'It's really good to see you again Dad.'

'You too Richie. It's been too long.'

'I'm glad you're enjoying your records,' added May.

'You've never heard anything like them, honestly.'

Richie listened to Lauper as she sang *Time After Time*. The audio was truly amazing, as though it were being performed right there in the living room. It was very clean; the familiar crackle of the vinyl was missing. Richie had loved his father's collection, but only after he'd really played it all out loud, catalogued it and stored each album in a protective sleeve. By really caring for the artefacts in a deliberate and somewhat pedantic way, he had added importance to them. His father had collected them throughout his life, and then Richie had acted as their caretaker. This new system of being able to grab any twelve-inch vinyl out of thin air didn't appeal to Richie's practical side. For him, the magic was in the imperfections of the products and their history.

'Hey Dad?'

'Yeah?'

'Do you have… like… a guardian angel here in this part of heaven?' asked Richie.

'We sure do. Nice chap.'

'Is his name Angel?'

'No. Ours told us his name was Jessie. You might have a different one for your bit of heaven.'

'He did say there were lots of different parts,' shouted Helen from the kitchen. 'Pockets?'

'Yes, *pockets* of heaven,' said Stephen. 'That's right. Sounds like an Eric Clapton song or something. Why do you ask?'

'Just curious,' said Richie.

'Why? Is this Angel treating you alright?' asked Stephen.

'Oh yeah. He's fine. I was just wondering.'

The confirmation of a second guardian angel added credibility to the idea that heaven had been divided into pocket communities. Richie was still dependant on facts, despite the unbelievable magic he continued to experience. As improbable as all of this was he had no choice but to believe it, but he continued to search for a practical way of understanding it.

'I love you guys,' he said.

'Love you too!'

'Come back soon.'

'We will.'

Richie and May went back through the doorway to their place.

'That was insane,' said Richie. 'I guess it's not defective after all.'

'I wonder why it didn't work for me,' mused May.

'Maybe your Mum isn't dead yet. I mean, Angel said time moves differently up here.'

'But my Dad is definitely dead. So is Arthur…'

Richie could see that May was troubled by their absence. He held her in his arms and kissed her.

'We can ask Angel about it later, okay?' offered Richie.

'Okay. I mean… I guess they might be busy. Or they might not want to see me.'

'May, it's forever. We'll definitely see them.'

'Do you think?'

'Absolutely. We'll see everything and everyone we want. Just you wait,' said Richie.

'I've waited long enough,' she replied. 'Let's do it.'

'Where do you want to start?'

Chapter Ten

Love Letters

'It was Descartes who first argued that simple notion of consciousness. I think… therefore I am. In Latin, *cogito, ergo sum*. If you can think about your life, about the nature of it and your existence… then by that same logic you are proving that you can *have* such thoughts. That you are capable of thought…'

The lecturer had a very monotone voice, filled with soothing reverberations that had literally put Richie to sleep. He'd had a reasonably late night and was completely unprepared for this dense Philosophical exchange. The course was supposed to help fulfil the requirements of his Bachelor of Arts degree. He'd thought it would be straightforward, and hadn't counted on the pretentious lectures and unlikeable study group he'd been assigned. Every Philosophy lecture felt the same.

'Excuse me?'

Richie's eyes shot open.

'Are you still with me?' asked the lecturer, who was now standing on the precipice of his personal space bubble.

'Uh… sorry,' Richie replied, wiping his mouth on his sleeve.

His embarrassed response was met with a chorus of laughter. He'd drifted off for goodness knows how long and been caught napping, and possibly drooling.

'Shall I continue?' he asked.

Richie could smell notes of oak, possibly from the older man's body wash. 'Sorry. Yes, please continue. Sorry.'

'As I was saying…'

Richie rubbed his eyes. He felt mortified that he'd been caught like that. He could feel the lingering looks of his fellow University students. Richie debated whether or not he should stay. He'd already missed so much of the class that he'd have to listen to the lecture online anyway. Silently convincing himself, he packed his things and waited. When the lecturer was distracted and looking at an overhead slide, Richie took the opportunity to slip out undetected.

As he breathed a sigh of relief outside the auditorium he noticed a woman heading his way. She was smartly dressed in a tight-fitting blazer and three-quarter pants. She was obviously running late to the very philosophy lecture that he'd just escaped from.

'I wouldn't go in there if I were you,' advised Richie.

'No?'

'No. Professor Brand is in a mood.'

'And why do you say that?' she asked.

'Well… to be honest I fell asleep during his lecture. He doesn't seem too happy about it.'

'Was it that boring?'

'No. But I can't sit through it now. It's too embarrassing.'

'Okay. Excuse me,' she said as she tried to get past Richie.

'You're still going to go in?'

'There's still twenty minutes left.'

'But you've missed the first forty minutes.'

'So?'

'So… it's not worth it now. You should… come with me and get a drink instead.' It was a bold proposition, and he was pleased with his delivery of it.

She offered a cautious smile. 'Should I now?'

'Yes. I'm Richie by the way.'

'I'm May.'

'Nice to meet you.'

'If we got a drink… would it be alcoholic? Or just like… a milkshake or something?' she asked with a pout.

'I think we should start with milkshakes… I'll have a caramel one… and then if we like each other… maybe you'll let me take you out for an alcoholic one at the Uni Bar some night.' Richie could feel himself perspiring. Asking people out was never something he'd excelled at.

'Okay. Lead the way,' replied May as she linked her arm into his. 'I'll have strawberry, I think.'

'Good choice.' Richie couldn't believe his luck. May was beautiful. He couldn't stop himself from smiling.

'So, you're a fan of Elvis?' she asked, indicating towards his shirt. He'd elected to wear a classic Viva Las Vegas number that featured a photograph of Elvis in concert.

'Yeah. Are you?'

'Sure. Just the classics I guess. I'm not a super fan, but I appreciate that he conquered the music scene while he was alive.'

'He influenced so many great artists,' explained Richie.

'Are you a musician?'

'Me? No.'

'Just a big fan of Elvis?'

'A big fan. I'm easy to buy for.'

May laughed. 'I'm imagining a whole room full of memorabilia.'

'Not a *whole* room… I'm not obsessed or anything. My Dad just got me into Elvis at a young age.'

'So what are you studying?' asked May.

'Arts.'

'And what are you going to do after University?'

'I have no idea. How about you?'

'Well, I'm doing a Bachelor of Psychology. I plan on doing work experience at my Aunt's mental health practice. I want to help people with depression and other debilitating illnesses.'

'You've really thought that far ahead? To the point where you know what you're going to specialise in?' asked Richie.

'Yes, of course. You have to have a plan,' she stated.

'Well, you'd also *planned* to go to that lecture… which you were late for I might add…'

'True.'

'And then you ditched the lecture in favour of drinks with me.'

'Right. But the way I see it,' said May, 'you have to start with a plan in order to have something to deviate from.'

'You sound like you've got it all worked out.'

'Some of it, sure.'

The two sat down at a busy on-campus diner, where they proceeded to wait fifteen minutes for service. Neither party minded initially, as they spent the time enraptured by one another.

Twenty minutes later they'd started to become concerned about catching a staff member's eye. 'These milkshakes had better be worth it,' said May.

'Maybe they have a cow back there.'

'You think that could be the hold up?'

They shared a laugh.

'This has been enough for me,' said Richie with an earnest grin. 'Even if they don't bring the milkshakes at all.'

'I guess I could always eat these sugar packets,' said May, grabbing a couple of the single use items from the console in the middle of their table.

'Or the salt and pepper ones… they've got quite a variety here actually,' he replied.

'Yes, we're *very* lucky!' laughed May.

A disgruntled young waiter took their drink order before stomping away. May placed a pile of sugar packets onto the table. They sat patiently, turning the condiments over with their fingers as they stared into each other's eyes. If they were indeed the windows to one's soul, then by all accounts May's spirit was captivating.

'You've always gone by Richie, huh? Never Richard? Rich?'

'Richie was my father's idea. He's a big music buff and he was obsessed with Ritchie Valens, Buddy Holly and The Big Bopper. Do you know them?'

'Not really. I know Buddy Holly… sort of,' replied May.

'Well after a show one night they all boarded a plane and it crashed. Don McLean sang about it in *American Pie*.'

'The day the music died, right?'

'Yeah.'

'Maybe I have heard that somewhere. Like on a quiz show or something. It seems familiar.'

'Right,' continued Richie, 'so Dad wanted to put something good back in the world and he convinced Mum to let him name me after one of the artists who lost their lives in that crash.'

'And she didn't like Buddy? Or Bopper?'

'She's a pretty easy-going lady, but no. She let him have Richie but she changed the spelling a bit. Ritchie Valens had a "t" in his name.'

'Interesting,' smirked May.

'Is it? I feel like I've been repeating that anecdote for most of my life,' chuckled Richie. 'I don't know if it's good anymore.'

'I was only asking so I know how to put you into my phone once I get your number…' May smiled at him. 'Without a "t" then.'

'Pass me your phone?' Richie was ecstatic that their conversation was so fluid and easy.

'I don't have it. I don't bring it to Uni because I'm so easily distracted.'

Richie started laughing.

'What?' demanded May.

'Same!'

'You don't have your phone on you either?'

'Nope. I never bring it to Uni.'

May took a salt packet and wrote her phone number on it. She slid it to Richie. 'You're not going to eat that, are you?'

'Not a chance.'

'And you'll call?'

'I'll call you tonight.'

The pair held hands, just as their milkshakes hit the table. They thanked their server, even though he was doing an abysmal job of securing their continued patronage.

'So, why depression specifically?'

'Sorry?' May was a little thrown by the tangent.

'You mentioned that you wanted to specialise in mental illness. I was just wondering if there was a reason,' probed Richie.

'My older brother had some issues. He's not around anymore. I never really got to know him.'

'I'm sorry.'

'No, it's okay. It was a long time ago,' said May.

'Still… it couldn't have been easy.'

'It wasn't. He was detached, if that makes any sense? He was probably on the spectrum. He was six years older than me and would never let my Mum test him for anything.'

'And he was depressed?'

'That's what my Mum always says. I don't really remember him being depressed. I was only ten or eleven.'

May fidgeted slightly in her chair. There was some pain behind her eyes at the memory.

'What was his name?'

'Arthur.'

The vision ended abruptly when May let go of Richie's wrist.

'Oh my God. I have to fix things with Arthur. I need to see him again.'

'You will. Next time we see Angel we'll ask him,' said Richie.

'I feel like his briefing was… well… *brief.*'

'He probably just wanted to let us reconnect.'

'You're probably right,' agreed May.

'You know, you look just the same as that day when we met outside the lecture theatre.'

'Funny that.'

'What's your secret? Some kind of nightly skin regime?' joked Richie.

'Must be good genes,' she replied.

The lovers had become lost in one another's company. They'd revisited their honeymoon, all of their favourite trips together and the jokes, trysts and sequences that had jumped to the forefront of their minds. He'd finally been able to show May the psychic moment when he'd been driving, guessed that George Michael's *Faith* would be on the radio, switched it on and been correct. She'd never fully believed him before that, and the validation felt amazing.

They'd focussed on their joyful times together, some of which May confessed she'd forgotten. It was interesting to see how each party held different moments in such high esteem. Richie had laughed as he'd remembered May's impromptu kitchen dances, and they'd both revelled in reliving that long night when they'd made fifty different cocktails from a book they'd been gifted. Richie wished he could feel the effects of the alcoholic evening, but they were only memories. He could smell the booze but couldn't taste it. None of it was quite real, even though their minds were happy to be deceived. They'd spent countless hours stroking Fitty, even though they couldn't feel the warmth of his furry body. It was still nice to spend time with him again.

'Oh, you know what else would be funny to see?' asked May.

'What?'

'Actually let me just show you. This is going to be good!'

Richie took hold of May's wrist and she transported him to the kitchen of their first home. He couldn't recall the conversation he now found himself regurgitating.

'Try it out,' spoke May as she indicated towards a pump action soap dispenser.

'Okay…'

Richie placed his hand underneath the object and doled out a blob of liquid. It was a thick and cloudy white.

'I mixed it myself. To save money I thought I would make my own hand wash. Or t least water it down a little. What do you think?' May was beaming.

'I think… it feels a bit like…'

'Semen?'

'Yeah,' said Richie.

'Looks like it too, huh?'

'Yeah. A bit.'

'I thought so too. That part was an accident. That's why I made this,' said May, as she popped a cardboard image of a hunky man over the top of the dispenser, lining the spout up to double as the figure's genitals. Richie burst out laughing and May joined him. They started crying joyfully in a moment of pure bliss.

Their shoulders danced rhythmically together. Richie, in possession of his former body laughed initially, but found retrospectively that he didn't lose control the way he had that day. He didn't like the way he could hear himself laughing, in the same way one might dislike hearing their voice recorded and played back to them. He let go of May's wrist and returned to their afterlife.

'I'd forgotten all about that,' said Richie. 'I cant believe it. I didn't think I could forget something so funny.'

'It was *so* funny,' said May, who was still chuckling. 'I was so proud of that gag. We used that hand soap thing for ages too. Until it got wet and became kind of busted. We must have thrown it out after that.'

Richie smiled at May. She was obviously happy, which made everything so much easier. The stress of his former marriage had dissolved. It felt a little strange to be separated from his boys, but having May was powerful and intoxicating. 'You're so great,' he said.

'Not so bad yourself.'

It was unclear how much time had passed during their heavenly relationship. They'd been up for days, watching massive portions of their time on Earth again, but they felt no signs of fatigue, hunger or stress. It was a pleasant blur.

'I feel like I know you better now,' said May. 'I didn't like seeing your sadness… you know… *after*.'

'After you'd died?'

'Yeah.'

'I didn't really enjoy living it either!' said Richie.

'Do you like it here?' she asked.

'Yeah. Good times, good company. It almost makes dying worth it.'

'I'm not completely used to being dead though. It still feels like a bit of a dream.'

'Same,' said Richie. 'I'm happy that I'm here, but it's unreal. I was so sure that God and heaven and all of that was just some kind of fairy tale.'

'I mean… if we're being honest I doubted there was life after death. I never would have imagined we'd be in the suburbs for example, but I'm glad.'

'Me too.'

'It's funny to watch back over our lives,' she said, caressing his arm. 'It's weird to see ourselves, knowing what we do.'

'It's sort of strange watching ourselves have sex. Like having a lifetime worth of sex tapes.'

'Of course that's where your head goes to.'

May kissed Richie deeply. It was very nice to be able to connect outside of the visions. He appreciated the gesture, and gave out an involuntary moan.

'You like that?' May asked, already knowing the answer.

'I *love* that,' he replied.

Before they could kiss again a sound rang throughout the house. It resembled an angelic choir singing harmoniously.

'Was that… the doorbell?' asked May.

The noise was repeated, an identical sound byte.

'I kind of like that,' said Richie approvingly.

'Are you expecting someone?'

Chapter Eleven

Too Much

'That's weird. We don't know anyone in the neighbourhood yet except Angel. Could it be him?' asked May.

'Maybe it's the Texans?' offered Richie. 'I've been meaning to say hello.'

'I don't hear swearing.'

In their pocket of heaven they hadn't seen any other pairs of soul mates walking around. Richie had presumed that they were all more than content within their homes, an abundance of sex, memories and food for comfort. May reminded him about the extra door, and reasoned that there was no need to leave through the front door when you could essentially teleport yourself to see your deceased friends and family.

'But neither of us felt a tingle, so it's got to be Angel,' said May.

'If it's Angel we should talk to him about why the door isn't working for you,' added Richie, adjusting his glasses. 'Let's just go and see, shall we?'

When he opened the door Richie got the shock of his afterlife. Standing before him, and now coming face to face with May for the very first time, was his second wife Janice. To Richie she looked beautiful, blonde hair bouncing effortlessly towards a flowing dress, without a single human imperfection. For a nanosecond Richie fell in love with Janice all over again. It was stunning and surreal. Their last conversation had been tense, even spiteful. That seemed a lifetime ago now. Janice just looked so calm and nonchalant, *aloof* even.

Richie inhaled sharply when he saw that she was not alone. Standing just behind her and clutching her hand was their former neighbour Dan.

'Janice?' Richie managed to say.

'Hi Richie. It's been a long time,' she replied. 'You remember Dan?'

'Hi. I'm Dan,' said his neighbour, with an outstretched hand. His jawline raised, he looked as confident as ever.

'Yes, Dan. I *remember* you.' The men shook hands briefly. Richie found the contact unsettling. The only people he'd touched since dying were May and his parents.

'Ha ha! I knew you would. Just making a joke.'

'Hi Dan!' said May, before giving him a heartfelt hug. She was thrilled to see a familiar face.

'May! How *are* you?' asked Dan happily.

'Great. Really great.'

'That's amazing. This is crazy, right?' said Dan, chuckling, indicating back out towards the empty but perfectly maintained street.

'So crazy. I mean, who would have tho-'

'Are you going to introduce us?' asked Janice, interrupting their reunion. Richie froze, not knowing how to approach the awkward presentation of his wives. This was uncharted territory. He wiped his brow and then scratched at his curly hair, even though he was not sweaty or remotely itchy.

'I recognise you Janice,' said May, interjecting and ploughing ahead with the required formalities. 'Richie's been showing me his life with you. I'm May.'

'I recognise you too,' replied Janice. 'It's nice to meet you properly May. I'm sorry you died by the way. That car crash was a tragedy.'

'Thank you,' replied May. 'That's nice of you to say.'

'You got a really raw deal,' added Janice.

'I mean… we're *all* dead. It sucks, but that's life.'

'But I guess it's all worked out for the best. You wound up with Richie in the end,' stated Janice, indicating towards him almost imperceptibly.

Janice tucked a golden curl behind her ear. She looked at Richie and May, raising an eyebrow inquisitively. The couple were suddenly under the microscope, an outside force analysing their worth as a couple.

Richie could feel the intensity of her stare. *What is she saying? Is she jealous?* Richie felt unsteady as the loves of his life collided, bursting the comfortable division he'd held onto while he was alive. It was certainly the most impossible scenario he could fathom.

'I wanted to say,' said May, fumbling around for the right words, 'you took such good care of him… when he was with you. I'm sorry he was taken when he was. The twins… your boys… were so small… that must have been difficult for you.'

'It was.'

Dan instinctively placed his hand on Janice's lower back, the two appearing very at ease. Suddenly Richie was envious, though he didn't want to be. He disliked the bond that had clearly matured between Dan and Janice after his death.

'But it looks like you managed to move on,' said Richie, who wasn't sure how to feel about Dan's arrival. He scanned his neighbour for any trace of a reaction.

'Dan was there for me after your passing. I couldn't have made it through without him.'

'Janice, I…'

'Richie… I actually go by *Jan* now. Nobody has called me Janice in ages.'

'You're Dan and Jan? Oh, how fun!' said May, who seemed the least uncomfortable out of the foursome.

'So, Dan is your soul mate?' asked Richie. 'You picked *him*?'

'Yes.'

'What about me?'

'You weren't an option,' stated Jan flatly.

'I… I mean…' He was suddenly flushed with guilt and unable to finish his sentence.

'Richie, you're with May now. You made my decision for me,' said Jan. 'It's all worked out for the best.'

'I have to say, it's going to be so funny being your neighbour again,' laughed Dan.

'You're living *here*? How is that possible?' demanded Richie, who could feel the resentment building inside him.

'Well, it's what we wanted. Angel said that we were recreating the best parts of our lives here in heaven. Do you know Angel?' asked Dan.

'Yeah *Dan*… I know Angel.'

'This will be so fun,' said May. 'We should have a dinner party sometime, not that we *need* to eat or anything… but we should get together, right?'

'That would be delightful,' said Jan.

'How were the boys? What did Brody and Charlie end up doing with their lives?' asked Richie.

'Oh, they both grew up and married lovely women. Brody actually had twin boys of his own. Charlie and his wife live out on a farm. No kids, but they always said the livestock were *like* their children.' Jan delivered the news so casually that it created a deep sadness within Richie. He'd missed every aspect of their lives. The twins didn't even know him. Even this summation of events was so disappointingly sparse. Richie couldn't tell if Jan was withholding information in order to hurt him deliberately.

'Did the two of you get married?' May asked as she clasped her hands together in front of her. Richie remembered when she used to watch reality dating shows like *The Bachelor* with the same eager expression.

'Yes. Dan and I were married on his fortieth birthday.'

'Oh that's sweet,' cooed May. 'I'm glad.'

'Wow.' Richie felt like he'd been punched in the guts, but he had to know more. The words came out of his mouth before he could stop them. 'How long were you married… before… you know… *the end*?'

'Dan passed away first, he was eighty-one. And I died three or four years later.'

Richie felt annoyed at this revelation. He and May had died young, while Jan and Dan lived into their eighties. The fact that they'd enjoyed such a long and seemingly happy marriage filled him with spite. He felt even more irritated that he could develop such emotions at all. *Shouldn't I be forgiving and able to move on from this?* Richie wondered.

'You were together a really long time,' said May.

'We were lucky,' replied Dan. 'It feels like it sped by so quickly though.'

'I know what you mean,' said May. 'I feel like… even though life was the longest thing I've ever experienced, that it was still so short.'

Dan nodded along.

'So, listen… Richie, you were a really important person in my life. I hope we can still be friends here in heaven,' said Jan.

'Sure…'

'Great. We're going to be your neighbours. Pop in any time.' Jan hugged Richie and May one by one, Dan offering a throwaway wave before they excused themselves and left. Richie watched them go, closing the door extra slowly so he could stare at them for as long as possible. He willed Jan to turn around, to shoot him a secretive look. She turned left at the bottom of the path and headed away without hesitating for a second.

'That's amazing!' said May. 'They're so happy together. I didn't think Dan would ever settle down. He was always with *so* many different women… always playing the field.'

'When he was young…'

'Yeah, right. I know I only got a snapshot of his eighty-one years but he was such a player. I just didn't imagine him married, that's all,' said May.

'Well, he did get married. Dan married *my* wife.' Richie fidgeted, picking up and then putting down a nearby umbrella. He wondered whether he'd ever need to use it.

'*I'm* your wife,' replied a dejected May.

'Right… I meant to say… he married the mother of my children,' said Richie absentmindedly. He felt trapped in the doorway now, May blocking his access to the rest of the house.

'What's *that* supposed to mean?' she folded her arms.

'Not to say that your pregnancy wasn't important… it *was*. Very important…'

'What are you talking about?' said May, shooting him a confused look.

'Your pregnancy?' It had just slipped out.

'Are you telling me I was pregnant?'

Richie couldn't believe he'd been so callous. His face dropped, the mood shifted abruptly.

'You didn't know, did you?'

'If you're asking me whether I knew if I was *pregnant*… the answer is no. How would I have known that?'

'You were.'

'I was?'

'Yes. You were pregnant when you died.'

May was suitably shocked, and the room seemed to shrink. Richie had assumed that Angel would have told her. Her hollow expression spoke volumes.

'I killed our child…'

'No… no, no, no. You didn't kill our child! It was an accident. It wasn't your fault.'

'But our baby's gone. We'll never know if it was a boy or a girl. They were never born Richie!'

He hesitated for a moment. May was clearly too overwhelmed to speak so he held her. After several silent minutes Richie continued. 'You said you didn't want to talk about the bad things. Let's focus on the positives May. We're in heaven for God's sake!'

May gasped, as if invoking the name of their host would result in some immediate wrath. Unperturbed Richie soldiered on.

'Maybe Angel can give us our child back. He said it's our heaven after all. We can customise it with a thought. We could ask him! I can go and talk to him if you like…'

His passionate speech, a gesture that might have worked once upon a time, fell on deaf ears. 'I think I need to be alone for a while,' she said conclusively.

May looked solemn, clearly affected by the new information.

'Whatever you need,' he said.

Richie would take a walk. It would be fine. They didn't have to be in each other's faces all the time. They would take a breath and get through this, just like they did when they were putting together IKEA furniture: one step at a time. As he turned towards the door, his hand on the knob, he heard the words he needed to hear.

'I love you,' May said softly.

'I love you too,' he replied without turning back around.

Richie wandered outside and into the street. He stood and faced his house. The garden seemed like it had been arranged with purpose. There were no yucca trees, or odd plants in sight. Everything appeared to be in full bloom, like something out of a gardening magazine.

As Richie turned to face Dan and Jan's place he spotted them kissing in the window and pivoted on the spot, quickening his steps in the opposite direction. *Was this really going to be the way of things? Living next door to a couple he couldn't stand?*

On the opposite side lived the Texans. *Which neighbour would be the lesser of the two evils?* No sooner had the thought entered Richie's mind he caught the eye of the American in the cowboy hat, standing in front of an outdoor barbeque grill. Seeing both neighbours in such quick succession reminded him that in fact he was surrounded. It was a slightly stressful thought.

'Oh hi there,' said Richie with a half-hearted wave.

'Howdy neighbour,' came the reply. 'I'm Austin.'

'Richie Walsh. Nice to meet you.'

'Leanne is my wife, she's upstairs doing God knows what. You have a lady in there too?' He tilted the beer in his right hand towards Richie's house.

'Yeah, May. She's my soul mate.' The words sounded strange out loud. He'd never really said them to anyone before.

'Beer?' offered Austin, indicating towards a small cooler. 'I've got all the brands.'

Richie suspected the cooler worked in the same manner as the fridge, containing any beverage Austin could dream of. 'No thank you. I'm okay.'

'Another time then. Where are you from?'

'Australia,' replied Richie.

'Shrimp on the barbie, huh?' joked Austin, nudging Richie in an all too familiar way.

'Yeah… something like that.'

'Right… listen, I'm glad I caught ya. I've been meaning to apologise…' mumbled Austin, 'for the yellin' and whatnot.'

'Oh, no. You're okay. It's a big adjustment. Being dead and all. Sometimes you have to yell,' said Richie.

'Well, I don't know how much you've heard…'

'Nothing really.'

Richie thought his drawl might have placed his origins in the southern states of America, but he wasn't sure. Austin flipped over the burgers on the grill with ease.

When he saw Richie watching him he shook his head, 'I know we don't *have* to eat… I'm not crazy. I just like cooking meat. I like drinking beer too. It was something I loved doing while I was alive. Helped me relax, you know?'

'All good man. I get it. I used to listen to music to relax.'

'You a musician?'

'No, I just had a good music collection.'

'Yeah? Maybe we can listen to some of your songs sometime,' said Austin.

'I used to collect records.'

'Records? The old black, floppy kind?'

'Yeah, those.'

'You know they've improved on the sound quality since then. Ever heard of CDs? They'll blow your mind,' laughed Austin, before necking the remainder of the bottle.

'No, I know about CDs. The records belonged to my father. It was kind of the thing we had in common, you know? The music made it easy, and we had something to talk about.'

'Yeah I get ya. For me an' my Dad it was shooting. We'd go hunting sometimes, when he wasn't too drunk.'

'Is he up here in heaven?' asked Richie.

'Don't know, don't care. Wasn't much of a father really, in the end.'

'That's too bad. You don't want to mend things? I mean, you do have forever.'

'It's a two-way street, ain't it? I don't see him knocking on my door,' said Austin.

'I guess so.'

'Yeah, sometimes you just have to let go, you know? You can't always have things your way.'

'I know what you mean,' he said, thinking about Dan and Jan. Richie was surprised that Janice was able to get under his skin again so efficiently.

'You enjoying the magic fridge?' asked Austin. 'You just think about what you want and open it up. Boom! It's there.'

'Yeah,' nodded Richie, adjusting his ineffective glasses. 'The fridge is great. My Mum is using it to prepare all the meals she never got time to make while she was alive.'

'Have you two been watching all your memories?' asked Austin. 'Holding one another's wrists and whatnot?'

'Yeah, we've been doing that.'

'That's what's got me into trouble with Leanne,' he replied.

'Did she see something she shouldn't have?'

'God damn right!'

'That's no good,' said Richie, who was intrigued but also looking for a window to end the conversation. He wanted to keep walking, perhaps complete a loop of the immediate landscape before returning to May.

'Oh, it's my own fault. Just popped into my head. Now she's pissy with me. I couldn't help it man. I remembered the time I had an affair and then BLAM, I'm reliving it, with Leanne right there by my side.' Austin shook his head before rotating the burgers again. They seemed incapable of burning.

'I'm sure she'll get over it,' offered Richie, not knowing Leanne, or whether that was even remotely true.

'I only cheated on her *once* in my life! One time. It was so long ago that I'd almost forgotten about it even. What a shitty time to remind myself, huh?'

'But you're here. That counts for something, doesn't it?' Richie gave Austin a nod. 'The two of you are in heaven, so you're good people. You must have done something right. It will all work out for the best.'

'Hope you're right.'

Richie excused himself, promising to chat again soon. He stepped onwards, unsure about his statement. He considered the world around them. Richie assumed that if there was a heaven for the good then there ought to be a hell for those who'd earned it. The yin and the yang, always in balance. If heaven was, by and large, perfection, then Richie shuddered to imagine the horrible inversion that some less fortunate individuals must endure.

It was time to talk to Angel and figure some things out.

Chapter Twelve

<u>That's All Right</u>

'I used to play lots of old video games. Like on a Mac Classic? Do you know what that is?' asked Richie.

'A computer?' posed Angel.

'Yeah. One of the early ones.'

Richie had opted to do the first of their 'therapy' sessions by himself, as May wasn't in the mood. In order to get to Angel, Richie had thought about him while holding the door handle of their mystery door. It had opened out into a purposeful round room, with a single point of entry. There were no windows, but somehow the lighting felt natural. Angel, dressed in a plain blue shirt and dark pants, had invited him to sit.

Still no shoes, Richie had noted. Angel's face had seemed neutral and cherubic to Richie, lacking any authority, but he sat down all the same. The chair was deep and had a slight recline. Even though he wasn't sure what to expect it gave the therapy a feeling of authenticity. The seat was extremely comfortable and the conversation had been flowing, with both parties contributing. Richie found confiding in Angel came easily.

'I used to play *Stuntcopter*, which was this game where you had to drop little people from a helicopter and land them in a bale of hay,' said Richie. 'You used to have to judge the speed of the cart and click the mouse at the right moment so they'd land in it.'

'And you enjoyed that game?'

'It got boring really quickly. Then I used to play *Beyond Dark Castle*. Then *Shadow Keep*. I spent so much time winning those games.'

'That is nice.'

'Games got really advanced. They got online, graphics improved. It was big business. I couldn't really keep up with it all.'

'I am pleased you have found time for the hobby again here,' said Angel.

'Yeah. Since I've been dead I've had time to think about things. I've thought about that Mac Classic, the computer that started it all for me. I wanted to see myself playing the games again. I've popped back to those memories, and they're different.'

'Different how?' asked Angel, cocking his head to one side.

'I win the games… just like I did back when I was alive, and then I don't feel the same way. Just kind of empty.'

'Richie, your experience here is your own. If one memory does not bring you any joy, why not try another?'

'Yeah but that's just it,' he said reclining, 'nothing seems quite as satisfying the second or third time around. Things get more and more watered down. Does that make sense?'

'Nobody knows how they will feel about heaven until they get here. Some people embrace it, and feel as though it is the happiest they have ever been. They almost never look back into the past. Most would rather enjoy the present.'

'But it's right there. How can they not look at it? It's like having a time machine and not using it,' argued Richie. He thought about his parents Stephen and Helen, who were definitely prime examples of souls who could enjoy the present.

'If you spend too much time dwelling on what might have been you might miss what you have *now*.'

'I know what you mean. When I was alive I bought this packet of razors, right? It came with ten ordinary blue plastic razors and one super duper razor. I kept using the ordinary ones and I saved that fancy one. Never used it. I died before I could use it. I don't know why. I don't know what I was saving it for.'

'Right. You need to try and let things like that go… the opportunities you had in life. You cannot change what has already been.'

'I don't know if I *can* let go. It wasn't that long ago that I was going to work at the Bureau of Statistics and dealing with facts on a daily basis. The fact here is that I used to save my money instead of taking weekend trips. I stayed home and gardened. I hate *gardening*!' declared Richie, shaking his head. 'Whenever I look back on the last few years of my life I just feel like I lived them wrong. I didn't get to see Charlie and Brody grow up. The sum total of my life after May was zero. Am I remembering it wrong? I don't know. So, I keep dipping back into those memories. I keep watching them and thinking about them. I can't stop myself.'

'Could we try something. Would that be okay?' asked Angel.

'Sure.' Richie wasn't opposed to trying anything to change his mindset.

'Tell me something that always annoyed you while you were alive.'

'Besides gardening?'

'Yes, besides gardening.'

'Besides Janice's mood swings?' he said jokingly.

'Something simple that you had to deal with on a regular basis,' said Angel, keeping the conversation on track.

Richie thought for a moment before answering. 'Traffic.'

'Okay, great. Why do you think you found traffic to be so awful?'

'Its crap, isn't it?' said Richie.

'You tell me,' replied Angel patiently.

'Well, you're trying to get somewhere… and there's all these cars in your way…'

'Obstacles?'

'Exactly,' said Richie. 'And there's nothing you can do. You can't go faster, you can't weave through it. Traffic just takes as long as it takes.'

Angel nodded along. 'Have you considered that your position in the line of traffic was actually better than those further behind? That where you *are* is enviable, depending on which car you are in.'

'Right… so you're saying that even though I'm not at the front of the cars at least I'm not in the back? I'm still in traffic though.'

'You are all in traffic together.'

'I guess.'

'You must concentrate on your current circumstances,' stated Angel. 'Look at the here and now.'

'Are you talking about May? Did she say something to you?'

'Why would you think that Richie?' Angel paused and smiled. He would have been an amazing poker player, as Richie struggled to decipher his expression.

'Did she say something?' he asked again, considering that she could be attending her own private sessions with Angel after all. Richie wasn't policing her movements, and the access point was a door in their shared home. He had been drifting in and out, as he visited his parents and watched memories alone.

'I will let you ask May. She is your soul mate after all.'

Richie crossed his arms in silent protest. He now felt sure that May had been seeing Angel.

'This place is designed for any self-reflection you might need,' continued Angel, as he sat on a boxy chair in the middle of the round room. It didn't look as comfortable as the recliner but Angel seemed nonplussed.

'So, how are May's sessions going?' asked Richie, tossing a lure out in the hopes of catching something informative.

'You should know that I cannot tell you what May says here, in the same way you would not want me telling her your thoughts. Do you understand?'

'Yeah…'

Richie had his answer. Clearly Angel hadn't known that May had been coming here in secret. He hadn't known to keep that information from Richie. Angel was honest to a fault. While she hadn't been lying, May had omitted that from him. Still, he saw no harm in continuing to open up to Angel, seeing as how it would remain confidential.

'I guess I've been thinking about my life, and the way it was cut short,' said Richie.

'I like to think that we die when we are supposed to.' Angel looked a little confused now.

'You *like* to think? You don't know?'

'I know enough to have faith.'

'Faith,' chuckled Richie. 'Like it's all happening by design, right?'

'Do you imagine the universe is all just random chance? Knowing what you know now? Do you think there is no plan whatsoever?' Angel leaned back and the boxy seat seemed to move with him, adjusting to his new position.

'Well, if this was the plan from the start then I don't understand it,' said Richie.

'Plans do change.'

'I missed my children growing up! I missed my life!' he exclaimed.

'That is true. It can be hard to miss out on such formative years with the ones you love. But what would you have me do? Return you to Earth and let you keep on living?'

'Is that an option?' asked Richie, suddenly curious.

The two figures paused for a beat, the round room falling momentarily silent.

'There is nothing you or I can do to change what has already unfolded,' stated Angel. 'If I sent you back to Earth and you reclaimed your life somehow, you would be relinquishing your relationship with May. Quitting. Is that the message you want to send her?'

'Don't get me wrong… I love May, even when she's upset like this. We'll get through it. You know we were doing fine until Jan and Dan showed up. Now she's right there! Why did you have to let them be our neighbours?'

'It is their heaven too. Not every decision is about you Richie,' said Angel.

'This *does* feel like it's about me though! I used to be married to her, and now she's here with someone else. While it's not easy to see her with Dan, the hard part is that I thought about picking Janice…'

'I believe she prefers to be called Jan now.'

Richie sighed and continued, 'I'm having trouble separating the feelings I have for her... *had* for her. I don't know what I'm feeling. Loving someone isn't like turning a tap on and off.'

'Jan must feel the same way about seeing you here with May,' said Angel. 'Have you considered *her* feelings?'

'But I feel like I only just died! She went on to live almost another fifty years! She's had a lifetime to move on. And she definitely has! This still feels confusing to me.'

'And it is only a feeling. You can choose to feel differently too,' offered Angel.

'I'm trying. It's just hard.'

'You have to appreciate that the bond she shares with Dan was forged over many years. They raised Charlie and Brody and were there for each other in difficult times. You are not aware of their challenges. They were human. They lived a very human existence before they died, just as you did. You have all been through it.'

'It?'

'Life.'

Richie paused to reflect. 'Why does Jan have to look so amazing?'

'People see what they want to see. Jan looks the way you see her.'

Richie rearranged himself. He found Angel spoke in riddles at times, and he didn't care to decipher his words. Richie tried to be frank. 'Do you think I made a mistake?'

'How do you mean?' asked Angel.

'Do you think I should have nominated Jan as my soul mate? Maybe if I'd chosen her then she would have chosen me too. Then we'd be the ones playing house right now.'

'But what about May? She was your first love, correct? That is what you told me.'

'That's another thing. Did you know she had no idea she was pregnant when she died? Don't you think *you* should have told her that?'

'I am not sure it is my place to divulge that information,' said Angel calmly.

'So, you just let *me* tell her?'

'Yes,' replied Angel, no emotion in his voice. 'I am not here to interfere unless it becomes necessary.'

Richie bit the inside of his cheek. The image of May's face standing there, finding out she'd been pregnant had been burned into his mind.

'How did she react?' asked Angel.

'She's heartbroken,' stated Richie. 'May had no idea. I told her I'd ask you whether we could have our child. You know? Raise it here? Is that possible?'

'That is not the way this works.'

'Well… why not? Where is our child?'

'Unborn children have a different path in the afterlife.'

'That's not really an answer, is it?'

'No.'

'Well what about Fitty?'

'Your cat?'

'Yeah. Can we have Fitty?'

'Animals have a different path in the afterlife too.'

'Seriously?'

'If you want to see your cat, all you have to do is think of him,' said Angel.

'I can *see* Fitty in memories, sure. But I can't touch him. Only the memory of me can touch him. I can't feel his warm, fuzzy body. It's not the same.'

'I am sorry you feel that way.'

'You said this was *our* heaven. You said we could make it the way we wanted,' said Richie.

'Not in this case unfortunately.'

'Well that's some bullshit. Now May is in mourning and I'm stuck next door to the happiest couple in the world.'

'I am not sure you can refer to Austin and Leanne as the *happiest* couple in the-'

'Not them! Dan and Jan.'

'Using your logic, you have had many years on Earth to mourn the death of your child and move on. May has only just learned this new information. You will need to give her time to process.'

'It's just...'

'Yes?'

'It feels like there's so much drama.'

'Richie, you chose May. You chose her on Earth in sickness and in health. You chose her again here. There must be a reason for that.'

'I guess I thought the worst thing that could happen to me had already happened,' said Richie. 'Now I'm worried that dying was just the start of my problems.'

Chapter Thirteen
Wooden Heart

Richie knocked on Jan and Dan's wooden door. He'd had to psych himself into doing it, loitering for a while beforehand, but ultimately he was facing the problem head on. Jan was a weed that he needed to pull out, before she could ruin his garden. He'd had no luck talking to May, who'd been vacillating between sessions with Angel and quiet reflection. All Richie could do was leave her alone.

'Richie. So good to see you,' said Jan with a welcoming smile. She downed the remainder of a blue coloured cocktail and set the 70's style glass down.

'Is Dan here?'

'No, he's out exploring heaven with Austin and Leanne. Have you met the neighbours on the other side of you?'

'Yeah, we've met.' *Dan had befriended Austin?* Even though they'd only spoken once Richie still saw this as a betrayal. Austin was *his* neighbour. Dan and Austin didn't even share a fence.

'Can we talk?' asked Richie.

'Of course. What's on your mind?'

From the front door it was a very short walk to the living area. Jan and Dan had a huge couch with minimalist modern art hanging above it. One image was of bright red lips, another a yellow lemon sliced in two. Everything was white, with explosions of colour here and there. He sat down next to a purple cushion while Jan settled next to a pink one.

'Well, I wanted to apologise. This is awkward. You know me Janice. I never-'

'Just Jan.'

'Right. Sorry. I never believed in anything like this. I didn't think we'd all end up in heaven.'

'Being neighbours isn't awkward Richie.'

'Look, I'm sorry I chose May. Well, not *sorry*… I mean I had to pick one of you. You know what I mean. That's just the way it works up here, and like I said I never thought that something like this could be real… but it is. It's so crazy. I still haven't quite wrapped my head around things.'

'You're rambling.'

'You were an important part of my life too. If it helps, I just wanted you to know that I really agonised over the decision.'

'Well, that makes me feel a little better,' said Jan, scrutinising him for any traces of sarcasm.

'I really did.'

'Well… good.' Jan folded her arms in front of her. It was a stance that people kept taking with him. Defensive and guarded. Jan's femininity still shone through, and Richie couldn't help but steal a glance as she crossed her long legs.

'I'm *still* agonising over it actually,' confessed Richie.

'Are you?'

'Yeah.'

'So, what made you choose her over me?'

'It's hard to explain… I mean… I never thought I'd *need* to explain it!'

'Try.'

'May died a lot earlier than I did,' reasoned Richie. 'She was waiting around in limbo for me. She'd nominated me already… I just felt like it was the right thing to do.'

'You felt pressured into choosing her?'

'Kind of.'

'Fair enough.'

'Angel hadn't really explained everything… he kind of still hasn't actually. It's like, if we don't directly ask about something then he doesn't tell us. Like did you know we can't have pets?'

'We can't?'

'No. Animals go to some other pocket of heaven or something. I don't know.'

'Dan and I asked a lot of questions when we arrived. He answered everything we could think to ask,' said Jan.

'Well, I didn't know you were coming… and I was really worried about what was going to happen to May if I didn't choose her… and I was scared.'

'Of what?' asked Jan. She absentmindedly picked up the pink cushion and held it against her chest. Her fingers caressed the material, distracting Richie.

'I wasn't sure you'd want me. We weren't exactly the happiest version of ourselves at the end of our marriage. Honestly I was scared of sitting around for fifty years… feeling like I'd made a mistake.'

'I get it. May was a sure thing,' said Jan.

'Well, not exactly a *sure* thing… I wouldn't describe it like that really,' objected Richie.

'I know, I know. I get it though.'

'Thanks for understanding.'

'This is supposed to be heaven. I don't want to hold grudges. I don't want there to be any weirdness between us,' said Jan.

'Thanks. That's really mature of you.'

'Well I am much older and wiser than you,' she said jokingly.

'That's true!'

'Apology accepted Richie.'

'Thanks Jan.'

'Let's just be those exes that can get along, and be in the same room as each other. Cool?'

'I can do that.'

'Clean slate then?' offered Jan.

'Clean slate,' he replied. 'Thanks.'

'Good,' replied Jan, putting down the pillow and dropping her arms to her sides. 'Listen, I saw how your face dropped when I told you about the boys. Maybe I could make it up to you?'

'How?'

'I wanted to show you some of the moments you missed from Charlie and Brody's life,' offered Jan.

'That would be great. Thank you.'

'Stop thanking me. It's fine. Come with me.'

Jan led him to the bedroom and lay down. It was pure white, the bed coated in silk. Richie hesitated but lay down beside her. Getting into bed with Jan elicited a strange muscle memory in him that he tried to ignore.

'I get sick of standing up during these visions. I find it's much nicer to lie down. I got told I had arthritis in my neck... among other things. So it's kind of second nature to make myself as comfortable as possible,' said Jan.

'When did that happen?'

'Oh, you know… well I suppose you *don't* know. As you get older your body fails you in unexpected ways.'

'That sucks,' said Richie.

'Don't worry about it. My body works perfectly again now.' It sounded like bragging to Richie. The image of Jan and Dan moving harmoniously in the same bed they now shared popped into his mind unbidden. Perhaps this visit was a bad idea. Lying next to each other made the innocent conversation seem more intimate than it should have been.

'Grab my wrist,' she commanded.

Richie obeyed, coiling his fingers around Jan's wrist. He was transported to a soccer match. Janice had been standing on the sideline in the memory, which was where Richie now found himself. The first thing that hit him was the noise. This group of cheering parents was a jarring new sound against the previous vacuum of heavenly silence.

'There's Brody,' said Jan pointing. 'And Charlie's playing goalkeeper.'

Richie watched as Brody wove the ball through six opposition players with ease. He then thumped it into the back of the net, scoring a skilful goal. Richie was filled with pride, even if Brody's hair was longer than he would have liked. Charlie gave his brother a supportive yell, then brushed his hair out of his eyes. It had become blonde like his mothers, but was equally shaggy.

'Brody was a natural soccer player. Very intuitive. They played on the same team for years until Charlie lost interest. Then they got really into *Dungeons and Dragons* for a while.'

It was a glorious day, and it made Richie nostalgic for his life. The level of detail was breathtaking, from the grass to the sky. He knew that he'd taken it all for granted when he was alive. He wondered whether he would have been the kind of father that sat on the sidelines, watching the boys. Maybe he would have set up a net in their backyard and played a little two on one. Perhaps if he'd been alive to play soccer with them Brody would have stayed interested. *Why couldn't he stop focusing on what might have been?*

Out of the corner of his eye Richie spied a familiar face. His least favourite neighbour Dan was strolling along, really taking in the sunshine as he made his approach. Upon arrival he started to kiss Jan passionately as the other parents stared. Things were unfolding as they must have on that resplendent day. The ease with which Dan placed his leather-gloved hands onto Jan's torso was too much to bear. Richie's close proximity to the embrace made it very uncomfortable for him, and even though he knew it was impossible he was sure that Dan could sense him, idling beside them.

'Show me something else?' pleaded Richie.

'Sorry, I forgot that happened,' said Jan. 'Ummm…'

The scene was replaced with one from a Christmas morning. The twins appeared to be about five years old and they were opening presents beneath a beautiful green tree. When he was alive Richie had insisted on purchasing an artificial tree, which he saw as a sound financial investment. The tree had been dragged out of the attic every year, without fail. This was not that faithful plastic tree.

'You got rid of my tree?' he asked.

'Richie you're here to see the boys, remember?'

The Christmas pine that filled the lounge room was so plump with needles that they were scattered beneath it. It smelled different to Richie. He had to admit that it smelled like a real Christmas. Jan was sitting next to Dan on the sofa as the boys unwrapped *Transformers* and immediately started playing with them. Charlie held one of the *Dinobots* while Brody attempted to convert *Hot Rod* from his vehicle form to his robot one.

'They look so happy,' said Richie.

'They were good boys. And they grew up into good men.'

'Would you show me what they were like as adults? Maybe graduations? Or their wedding days?'

'I think that's enough for today,' said Jan.

The memories disappeared around them and Richie stared at the ceiling. Seeing the twins as children had dredged up something within him and it was obvious to Jan.

'What's the matter?' she asked.

'May was pregnant when she died.'

'Fuck off.'

'She was.'

'What? You never told me that.'

'Well, I'm telling you now. Clean slate and all that,' replied Richie.

'Is May okay?' asked Jan.

'She's processing it. She's only just found out.'

'Really?'

'Yeah.'

'What happened to her baby?'

'We don't know. Angel said that unborn babies have some other kind of path or something.'

'I should go and talk to her,' announced Jan, standing up from the bed.

'No, that's okay. You don't need to. May just needs to be alone right now.' Richie felt silly lying down on his own, so he sat up quickly.

Jan knitted her eyebrows. 'Is... that why you're over here?'

'What do you mean?'

'Is that why you came over here just now? Are you fighting with May?'

'We're not *fighting*,' said Richie defensively.

'Are you sure about that?'

'She wanted to be alone.'

'There you go. I'm your second choice yet again,' snapped Jan.

'It's not like that.' Richie scooted to the edge of the bed, his feet landing onto the soft white floor.

'Alright. If you say so,' shrugged Jan. She sat down beside him and looked at him intently.

'May will be fine,' said Richie, hoping he was right. 'I'm sure she just needs some space.'

'And is there anything you need? It must be hard for you. Reopening wounds all over again.' Jan tilted her head, exposing her neck and creating an eye-line towards her cleavage. She threw one arm onto his back and stroked him sympathetically.

Suddenly Richie was looking at Jan with lust in his eyes. The two of them on a bed felt familiar, and he had an overwhelming urge to kiss her. In so many ways she still felt like *his* wife, even though Jan was paired off with Dan. He wondered whether intercourse with Jan would be as satisfying in heaven as it had been with May. Before letting his mind wander Richie was able to snap himself out of the growing fantasy.

'I… I should probably go,' he managed to say, touching his glasses with his index finger.

'Alright. If you think that's best.'

'Thank you for letting me see the boys.'

'Anytime.'

Richie left, overwhelmed with fresh guilt and confusion.

Chapter Fourteen

She's Not You

'I'm hungry,' declared Charlie.

'Then get something out of the fridge,' replied Jan.

'There's nothing *good* though.'

Jan walked into the kitchen and stood next to her son. She suggested a list of edible items and each one was declined.

'Looks like you're not hungry then.'

'Can we get takeaway?' pleaded Charlie.

'You're having pizza this weekend for your birthday. You can't have takeaway,' said Jan forcefully.

'Pleeeeease?'

'No! Have some fruit and get out of my kitchen.'

Charlie took two bananas and left the room. Jan knew that he was bringing the other to Brody. They had become addicted to the video game *Halo*, not that it looked very interesting to her, and were playing it for hours at a time. Now that they were teenagers she'd relaxed their screen time privileges, provided she didn't have to pick up their smelly laundry or migrate their cereal bowls to the dishwasher. They were good boys, and she appreciated that they contributed here and there.

As Jan ascended the stairs in search of her husband she noted how clean everything seemed. The boys would routinely mess their rooms up, but since they'd bought the Xbox the rest of the house hadn't been touched. Such was the power of their new addiction; it was holding them in place like a magnet on a fridge.

She sailed past Brody and Charlie's room at the top of the stairs. They were completely engrossed in their game, shouting at strangers on the other side of the world through their headsets. Jan passed a litany of family photos that she'd intentionally printed in black and white. She just thought they looked more timeless that way. There was only one image of her first husband Richie. It was a photograph from the end of their wedding, confetti flying in such a manner that his face was partially obscured. Jan didn't want to erase her first marriage completely, but most days it didn't enter her mind.

As she opened the door to the bedroom she was confronted with Dan's naked rear. It was gyrating up and down rhythmically. A woman's hands gripped it tightly, green nail polish clashing against his pink skin. The shock made Jan squeal.

'Oh Jesus, Jan?' Dan couldn't rotate his head back to see her without stopping the sexual act. He removed himself awkwardly and crashed onto the pillow, revealing a buxom blonde beneath him.

'Ellie?'

'Hi Jan,' came the meek reply.

Ellie was one of the women in Jan's mother's group, although they hadn't really caught up in years. Her son Andy had been friends with the twins throughout primary school, but had drifted apart as they'd grown. When children are friends the adults tend to socialise, but Andy hadn't played with her boys in ages, making this turn of events unexpected.

'You're fucking Andy's mum? What if Charlie or Brody came in here?' said Jan, her voice low and secretive.

'They're playing Halo… they're not coming in here,' argued Dan.

'But they might have! How were you going to explain that their friend's mother is naked in your bed?'

'Do the boys still play with Andy? I haven't really seen them together,' started Dan.

'No, it's a shame, isn't it?' replied Ellie.

'We should get them back together, shouldn't we?'

'I think so. They used to have so much fun.'

'Well, let's get something on the books,' said Dan.

'Andy's birthday is coming up. I could ask him whether he wants to invite Charlie and Brody.'

'That's a good place to start.'

'He wants to do laser tag. Have your boys done that?'

'They haven't! And they're really into Halo so it seems like something they'd enjoy-'

'Dan!' shouted Jan, interrupting the conversation. 'They're almost fifteen. They know what sex is...'

'I know they *know* what sex is. So what?' asked Dan.

'So how about locking the door?'

'I thought I'd locked it!'

'Well, you didn't!'

'Okay, I'm sorry,' he replied.

'If your *sons* see their *father* having *sex* with a *woman* who's not their *mother*... they might have some *questions*, don't you think?' She emphasised every other word, drilling the point home.

'I wasn't thinking. Sorry Jan.'

'I'm sorry... I should go...' Ellie had started to dress, her bra not quite supportive enough to contain her cleavage.

'No,' said Jan, 'it's okay. You stay. I'm just mad at Dan… this isn't about you Ellie.'

'Are you sure?'

'It's okay, really,' assured Jan. 'Just make sure you lock the door, okay? And try to keep it down.'

'I will babe,' said Dan.

Jan shook her head as Ellie disrobed once more and shuffled herself towards Dan. The silk sheets moved around suggestively. They started kissing as Jan stood in the doorway impatiently.

'Dan?' she said.

'What?'

'Come and lock the door!' Jan's voice was more authoritative now.

'Sorry! Sorry!' A naked Dan jumped up and met his wife in the entryway.

'Dinner in an hour?' asked Jan.

'Absolutely.'

They kissed, albeit not as passionately as she would have liked. Jan closed the door and listened to it lock. She started back towards the kitchen, checking on the twins on her way down. A few steps away from the kitchen island she toppled, losing her balance. Jan felt faint, but managed to return to her feet.

With that stumble the vision ended. One by one Dan, Austin and Leanne let go of Jan's wrist as their surroundings morphed back.

'You've got to tell me how you did that!' shouted Austin. 'Had y'all broken up or something?'

'We were married,' said Jan.

'And you just let him do *that*?' asked Leanne.

The two couples were seated on opposite sides of Jan and Dan's kitchen table. The Texans were dressed up, Austin in a black long-sleeved shirt and Leanne in her 'formal jeans' and a top. Her light brown hair had been curled and then tied up in a side ponytail. Dan was positioned snugly against Jan on the one side, while there was a noticeable gap between Austin and Leanne.

'Who was that broad?' asked Austin.

'Who? Ellie?' asked Dan.

'Yeah.'

'She was the mother of one of my son's friends. From soccer… and school. We used to chat at drop-off sometimes.'

'And you had sex with her?'

'Yes.'

'With your wife and kids right there in the house?' chimed in Leanne.

'That was an oversight. I thought Jan and the boys were still out,' explained Dan. 'I guess our little afternoon went on a bit longer than I'd anticipated.'

Leanne turned her attention to Jan. 'You fell down a little at the end there. Were you alright?'

'Yes. That was in the early days, before I knew about my MS. I was in the habit of ignoring symptoms.'

'Jesus,' Leanne said flatly.

'It was a long time ago. I'm fine now. Don't worry.'

'You two are okay with adultery? But isn't adultery a sin? You still ended up here. So, is adultery not a sin then, or what?' Austin tilted up his cowboy hat and scratched his temple.

'You cheated on *me* you shithead! Somehow your dumb ass is here too!' screeched Leanne.

'What I mean is that *they* are clearly fine with cheating… but we're *not* fine with it,' said Austin. 'It was a mistake on my part.'

'Then why did you do it?' Leanne was livid and she'd maintained this level of fury since finding out about Austin's infidelity.

'Don't get like that, I didn't fuck the blonde with the big tits, Dan did!'

'You weren't supposed to fuck anyone but me!' yelled Leanne. Her temper was flaring along with her nostrils.

'How many times are you gonna make me apologise? I'm fucking sorry! Jesus.'

'Don't take the Lord's name in vain,' said Leanne.

'You just said Jesus! When Jan was talking about falling down…'

'That was different. She had a really serious disease!'

'Sorry! *Jeebus* then. I don't know what the rules are anymore.' Austin cracked his knuckles, a habit that had followed him here. 'If these two can do what they do and still be good people then maybe you ought to forgive me,' reasoned Austin.

'I don't have to do nothing of the sort,' argued Leanne. 'If I want to be mad at you forever then I will be, understand?'

'Sounds about right.'

'To be honest we weren't always that way. It was a gradual process,' offered Jan. 'I don't think traditional marriage was good for us. And maybe it's not good for you two either.'

'Are you trying to get us to swing with you?' spat Leanne, unable to hide the disgust in her voice. Austin raised one eyebrow at the suggestion.

'That's not what I'm saying.'

'You can't just change what we had while we were alive,' said Leanne. 'It wasn't perfect but Austin and I were in love. Deep, real love.'

'I'm not suggesting you do anything extreme, but you can both do whatever you want now. You can talk to Angel and set heaven up in any way you want. Isn't that freeing?' asked Dan.

Leanne considered this for a moment. 'It's not as easy as all that. I have to take into account what Austin wants. We're 'sposed to be soul mates.'

'But you need to figure this out. It's not a paradise if all you're doing is fighting,' stated Jan.

'I want you to be happy,' said Austin. 'And I want you to forgive me for messin' up. It was ages ago babe...'

'It doesn't feel like ages ago to me,' she rebutted.

'Maybe... if you're comfortable you could share it. I mean, we're all friends here,' said Dan.

'What?'

'You want me to show Leanne my *affair*? You're about as smart as a box of rocks if you think I'm doing that.'

'Sure, why not? If it will help her move past it,' said Jan. 'Is that something you want Leanne?'

'I don't know.'

'You don't have to do anything you're not comfortable doing,' said Dan. 'Jan's just trying to help.'

'It's just an idea,' she added.

'We started watching it...' said Leanne. 'I mean, Austin showed some of it to me accidently.'

'In my experience when you find yourself in a hole the first thing to do is stop diggin'. I switched that memory off as quickly as I could!'

'Smart,' commented Dan.

'Do you want to see the rest? Maybe it will help to see it in context,' offered Jan.

'It's done. You'll never be able to change it Leanne,' said Dan. 'But you can grow from this. You both can. We're proof of that.'

'Fine.'

'I'm not sure about this y'all,' confessed Austin. 'I think it's only going to piss you off.'

'I'm already pissed off,' said Leanne.

'Piss you off *more* then!'

'It was your idea to talk to Dan and Jan about our problems. Maybe they're right. Maybe this *will* be good for us.'

'Well, I had to talk to someone,' said Austin. 'And I didn't want to tell Angel! What if he kicks us out or something?'

'You can get kicked out of heaven?' asked Leanne.

'He wouldn't do that,' said Jan reassuringly.

'You don't know that!'

'I'm glad you came over,' said Dan. 'It helps to talk these things through. This is a safe space.'

'This is just… a lot, you know?' said Leanne.

Dan placed his hand over Leanne's in a sympathetic way. 'It's okay. Everything is fine.'

Leanne nodded and took a breath. Something flickered between them. Dan's presence was clearly appreciated by Leanne, as she shot him a rare smile. He had a way of talking to the Texan that soothed her foul mood. Suddenly Austin was looking at him with suspicious eyes.

'What are you doing?' he demanded.

'What?' Dan brushed it off casually.

'I know you're not moving in on my woman, right?'

'No Austin, it's not like that. I'm just being neighbourly…'

'We've all seen how neighbourly you can be! Keep it in your pants Casanova.'

Dan lifted his hands above his head, accommodating Austin's request. 'You got it.'

'Let me see her then…' said Leanne.

'Who?'

'Let me see the whore you cheated on me with.'

'Is that really what you want?' asked Austin.

'Yeah.'

'I'll show you then, if I have to.'

'Okay.'

'Fine.'

'Fine!' Leanne succeeded in getting the last word.

Austin slapped his arm down in the middle of the table and all parties touched his wrist.

In the blink of an eye they were all seated in a dive bar somewhere in the United States. American accents competed with Billy Joel's *For the Longest Time*, as it blared from a dull red jukebox. The walls were decorated with American licence plates and most of the tables in this section featured grease stains.

'Where exactly are we?' asked Jan.

'A truck stop,' Austin replied tentatively. 'One of the ones on my route.'

'You were a truck driver?' asked Dan.

'Yessir. Long hauls out of San Antonio.'

On the table before them there was a plate of chicken bones in a basket and the remains of a pitcher of beer.

'Anything else for you love?' asked the waitress.

She was wearing a denim shirt but Austin could see a black bra peeking out at him.

'Another beer maybe?'

'You driving after this?' she enquired as she leaned over to collect his chicken bones.

'Yeah, but I don't have far to go,' replied Austin.

'I don't think I can serve you that drink. Not if you're driving honey.'

'You like me that much, huh?'

'I just don't want your stupid ass to kill someone, that's all.'

'Nobody wants that, trust me,' said Austin.

'Something tells me you should stick around for a while. Sober yourself up.'

'I ain't drunk.'

'Nonetheless,' she said with a shrug.

'What's your name?' asked Austin. He'd leaned back in his seat as he sized the woman up.

'Lib.'

'As in Libby?'

'Nobody calls me Libby, they call me Lib.'

'Is that short for Elizabeth?'

Suddenly the scene was interrupted by Leanne's angry cries. 'This random bitch? *This* is who you cheated on me with?'

'I knew this was a fucking bad idea,' Austin replied.

'Skip this shit. I don't want to see you flirting with her.'

'Really?'

'Just show me where you fucked her,' demanded Leanne.

'No!' yelled Austin. 'I think we ought to stop.'

'Show me right now or I'm done. I'm going to talk to Angel and leave. I don't care.'

Jan and Dan did not want to interfere but neither let go of Austin's wrist.

'Fine! If that's what you want. Remember that you made me do this.'

With a flash of thought from Austin they were suddenly inside a car, the scene changing effortlessly around them. Lib was positioned in front of Austin, kissing his lips from the passenger seat. It was a harsh transition for his companions who didn't have their own places in the vehicle. They were suspended, partly within the interior of the car and partly outside of it, tethered to the scene by Austin's wrist.

'You taste like chicken,' said Lib as she lightly licked her lip.

'You taste better than good too,' said Austin.

Leanne was rolling her eyes, seemingly unable to believe that this approach was working. Dan and Jan had become voyeuristic, silently observing the event.

Lib placed her hand in Austin's lap. He offered no resistance. She undid his zipper. Austin, Leanne, Dan and Jan watched it happen.

'A little help?' Lib raised an eyebrow.

Austin freed himself from his trousers, his movements now on autopilot. The waitress lowered herself down onto him, her skirt proving the perfect garment for the situation.

'Fuck this… I'm out of here,' said Leanne as she removed herself from the memory and ran for the door. The veil was once again lifted and Austin's coerced vision evaporated around the group.

'C'mon baby, don't be mad at me. Can't you just drop it already? You're 'sposed to forgive me!' Austin followed closely behind like a lost puppy.

They left the house without acknowledging their hosts, their argument continuing out into the street. When they were alone Dan stared into Jan's eyes.

'What are you looking at?' she asked.

'Perfection,' he replied, and kissed her deeply.

Chapter Fifteen

<u>Stuck on You</u>

May was in another trance. Richie felt like she'd been sitting for days, although it simultaneously seemed as if they'd only just arrived in heaven. Time was certainly feeling blurry to him, moving strangely, just as Angel had prophesised.

His partner was sitting cross-legged on the floor, apparently in a state of meditation. It didn't take him long to realise she was in her head, reliving a memory from her short life. Her eyes darted around behind her eyelids, the same way they had when she used to dream.

Richie paused, hesitant about whether or not he should clutch her wrist and join her. He likened the uninvited intrusion to reading a person's diary, which even for a soul mate would be frowned upon. *How else could he know what she was thinking?* Perhaps she would see the gesture in a positive light. That he desired to know everything about her, in order to be closer. They hadn't spoken properly since May learned about their child, gliding through their home like ships in the night. *He had to reconnect.* Richie reached out his fingers and gently touched May's delicate wrist.

He was woven deeply into a childhood memory. This version of May had the same vibrant brown eyes, packed into the small face of a child of six or seven. Her wrist flinched against the pressure of his touch. May sensed Richie was watching but she did not halt the memory or acknowledge him. Instead the two watched in silence.

'Daddy!' young May called, towards the kitchen of a modest home. She peered around the corner expectantly.

A man in a business suit charged into the room and scooped May up, dragging Richie into the air with her.

The shift in height was unsettling and Richie released his grip. His mind was sending him triggers of nausea but his body did nothing with them. May's eyes jolted open and she looked at him.

'Hi.'

'Sorry, I didn't know whether I should just… join you.'

'I don't mind,' said May.

He was pleased that his disturbance hadn't started a fight. May had always been such a sweet and understanding person. They'd rarely fought during their marriage.

'Your Dad?' asked Richie, knowing the answer.

'Yes. I just wanted to see some happier memories of him.'

Richie knew all about May's painful loss. Her father's suicide had happened right after his proposal, shaking them out of their romantic bliss.

'Have you spoken to Angel about seeing him again?'

May shook her head. 'Not yet. I don't know if I'm ready. He said no to seeing our unborn child so quickly that I'm worried that he'll just say no again. I'm just nervous about it.'

'Well, we can go together, if that helps,' offered Richie.

'Maybe.'

Richie was struck with an idea. 'Hey, grab my wrist for a second.'

'Okay.'

Richie transported May to their old bedroom. They were now sitting on a light blue quilt, joined by their cat Fitty.

'Aw, Fitty,' cooed May.

The two of them reached out and stroked him gently, mimicking the movements of Richie's avatar.

'It's good to see him,' she said.

'Yeah. I wish we could *feel* him though.'

'Yeah, his warm little body.'

May gave a half-hearted smile and stroked Richie's wrist with her thumb. 'I think the solo sessions with Angel have been good for me,' she said. 'I'm coming out the other side now. Not that I'll ever forget about what we could have had… it was just so upsetting to find out.'

'I know.'

'And you… you had to live with that. No wonder you became so depressed. In a way I'm the lucky one because I didn't know. It's all so strange to think about.'

Richie took a deep unnecessary breath. 'I've been getting a lot out the sessions with Angel too. He's easy to talk to. It's a bit distracting that he doesn't wear shoes though. It's probably just his way of staying grounded,' joked Richie, in an attempt to lighten the mood.

'Is that where you've been?' asked May, ignoring the attempt at humour.

'Well, no. I haven't seen him recently…'

May sprung to her feet, surprising Richie who ended the vision of Fitty prematurely. His soul mate now stood with her arms folded, looking like a caricature of a grumpy housewife.

'Where *have* you been?'

'I was next door.'

'Doing what?'

'Jan let me see the boys. In her memories.'

May softened. 'Oh. Of course. I didn't think about how you might be feeling about that. How did they look?'

'Like little kids… happy, I guess. They liked soccer, they liked video games. It's funny because that's exactly what I used to like.'

'That's nice,' said May.

'My death didn't seem to ruin them in any way, which is good I guess. It feels like Dan stepped into my life pretty seamlessly.'

'You can't look at it like that. Dan and Jan fell in love, the same way you and Jan fell in love after I died. You need to accept it, the same way I've had to.'

'It's messy though,' stated Richie.

'So is life.'

'You're becoming very enlightened, aren't you?' said Richie with a smile.

'I think I was always more open to enlightenment. You didn't even believe in God. Even though you took his name in vain often enough.'

'When you stub your toe, you can yell anything you like.'

'But you didn't yell just anything, you yelled God… you were always cursing God, weren't you?'

'Not *always*! I didn't stub my toes that much.'

'But you admit you did curse God from time to time.'

'Yes, but I usually followed his name with a *dammit*,' said Richie. 'That's just alliteration. I could have yelled *Cheese-Dammit* if I'd wanted to but God dammit just goes together.'

'Word association, huh?' May smiled at him.

'Something like that. Maybe I would have reconsidered taking the Lord's name in vain if I'd have known heaven was real,' said Richie.

'Well, *has* this place made a believer out of you?' asked May.

'You'd think so. But I can't shake the idea that this is all some kind of crazy dream. I keep hoping that I'm in a coma and that I'll wake up in a hospital room.'

'Hoping?'

'Maybe *hoping* isn't the right word.'

'Because you'd rather be alive than be here?' asked May.

'I'm not sure that's it *exactly*. I guess I just haven't really decided that this is real yet…'

'Well, just because *you* don't think its real, doesn't give you permission to ruin it for me.'

'I'm not trying to ruin it for anyone.'

May nodded, and then slapped him in the face. Hard.

'Ow! What was *that* for?' While the surprise attack caused no actual pain Richie reacted on instinct. He was quite shocked though.

'This *is* real. You felt that, right?'

'Obviously!'

'And you felt something when we had sex, didn't you?'

'Yes. It was, pardon the pun, *heavenly*…' Richie looked proud of himself for the wordplay.

'Then how can you doubt it? This place is a miracle. And it's our second chance. We can do anything we like.'

'Such as?'

'We could go and see Elvis in concert!'

'What are you talking about?' Richie was confused. 'They have concerts in heaven?'

'Of course they do. They must, right? If you can go and do anything then you should be able to go and see Elvis in concert. Wouldn't that be great?' asked May.

'I guess…'

'I'll see if Angel can find out. I mean, he must still perform. Maybe he doesn't play all his songs but definitely some, right?'

'I don't know,' replied Richie with a small shrug.

'Wouldn't that be amazing? Don't you want to see Elvis?'

'Uh, I guess I would like that.'

'Geez, it's just an idea,' replied May, a little defeated.

'Hey, look… I'll try and have more *faith* or whatever, okay? I will.'

May gave Richie a kiss, which led to another and then another. When they retreated to their room, more out of habit than any desire to be on a bed, Richie found he was unable to perform. This had never happened to him in life, yet here in a place that was supposed to be a reflection of their ultimate paradise Richie was saddled with the most human of issues.

'God dammit, huh?' mused May, trying to alleviate some of the embarrassment he was displaying. 'Maybe this is his way of punishing you for the blasphemy.'

'That's not funny,' commented Richie.

'Do you want to try again?'

'No.'

'Maybe later?'

'We'll see.'

May seemed disappointed and left him alone, citing that they were both just stressed and that it wasn't a big deal.

'We've got forever, remember,' she said as she walked out of the room.

Richie was annoyed, and then he felt more annoyed with the fact that he *was* annoyed in the first place. *Why did he have so much anger, depression and sadness? Why did he feel as though his human emotions had been heightened since his death?* He'd wanted to make love to May and change the narrative. He needed to move past the memory of their unborn child and create happier, newer memories. Perhaps he *should* take her to a concert. Richie felt as though jumping straight into an Elvis Presley performance might be like jumping into the deep end. *Maybe Prince? Would Michael Jackson be a better show to start with? Were those artists just lying around, waiting for other dead souls to gather? Wouldn't they just want to relax?* The whole thought process made Richie feel tired, overwhelmed and very human.

May popped her head back into the room. 'Do you want to go and talk to Angel with me?'

'Now?'

'Yeah.'

The first thought that came to mind was *couples counselling*. He imagined May telling Angel about his performance issues. It felt like a bad idea. Richie's mind was swimming with questions but he wasn't ready to discuss anything serious right now. Even though he'd offered to accompany May to her next session he declined.

She kissed him on the side of the head sympathetically. 'You're still a man you know,' said May, referencing their sexual misadventure.

That was exactly what Richie was afraid of.

Chapter Sixteen

Got a Lot O' Livin' to Do!

'May's right! You can absolutely see Elvis in concert,' said Stephen excitedly. Richie's father's enthusiasm for music was something that could always be counted on.

'You can? How do you know?'

'I've been testing the door.'

'What do you mean?' asked Richie.

'Well, you just think about the person you want to see, hold the handle and open the door. If the person you wanted to see lets you in then you're with them. The same way you can visit anybody else in heaven.'

'And you thought about Elvis Presley?'

'No, that one hasn't worked yet,' confessed Stephen. 'I did have a nice time with Albert Einstein. Lovely chap.'

'Really?'

'Yeah. I've seen a few musicians too. It's just trial and error really. Sometimes I'm listening to a song and I have a thought, about a lyric or whatever, so I figure, why not go straight to the source.'

'And you just introduce yourself? That's it?'

'Most of them seem happy to meet a fan actually. Some aren't.'

'Wow.'

'Yeah. One or two of them have invited me to come back and see them play. I think you just have to imagine them in concert... then you just go through the doorway.'

'How does that work? What if you try and go through the doorway and you're too early?'

'You might be overthinking this-'

'There are no clocks in heaven. There's no way to know what time they'll start playing.' Richie was flabbergasted. He was used to reason and order, and neither seemed present.

'Our angel… Jessie… he explained it better than me,' replied his father. 'He said that everything is sort of folded over onto itself here, so everything is happening all at once. So, in a way there's always a concert going on… and you can just go to it anytime you like. Or not, if you don't want to.'

'It doesn't make sense…'

'And you thought it would? You thought a magical afterlife filled with all of our fantasies would be something you could understand the inner workings of? Come on son… just enjoy it.'

Richie shook his head. His father was surely right; it was beyond anything they could fathom.

'I can't believe that you've been bothering dead musicians,' chuckled Richie.

'Oh, yes. Dozens of them. Who's that rapper you used to like?'

'When?'

'When you were a kid.'

'Biggie Smalls?'

'No, his friend…'

'Tupac?'

'Yes! That's it! I met him,' stated Stephen proudly.

'You did?'

'Yeah. Smart guy. Still seems a little hung up on his death.'

'Did you ask him about it?'

'No, it didn't seem like the polite thing to do. He was asking me about it though. I was going to tell him that the case was never really solved, but I couldn't quite remember all the details.'

'Why did you go and see him then?'

'Something to do,' he replied with a half-shrug.

During Stephen Walsh's life he'd never appeared to take risks. Ritchie's parents never really travelled anywhere, despite their daughter Dawn offering them discounted airfares through her work. They were straightforward people, who had accepted a straightforward retirement. Stephen seemed to be embracing everything heaven had to offer with renewed vigour.

'You're mad.'

'Nah… I just have a curious mind. Speaking of curiosities… are you and May still fighting?'

'What was it your Angel Jessie said? That it's all folded on top of itself? If you believe that then we're always fighting… and also not.' Richie grinned at his father.

'Don't be a smart arse.'

'We were never fighting. We're just both… processing things. I don't know how to explain it. We're talking to Angel about it.'

'Couples therapy, huh?'

'Sort of.'

'Right right… but shouldn't you just talk to each other?'

'We will Dad.'

'Good. Now did you want to hear some Elvis? Nothing better to cheer you up than a song from the King of Rock and Roll,' said Stephen, standing up and flicking through his albums.

'Isn't it weird,' started Richie, 'that there isn't a *Queen* of Rock and Roll?'

'Of course there is. Tina Turner was known as the Queen of Rock and Roll. Joan Jett… Suzi Quatro had a case… Stevie Nicks. There are plenty of contenders. What are you on about?'

Richie was embarrassed. He'd used that fact when talking to Angel earlier and felt clever. 'Never mind. I guess I was mistaken.'

'Your sister liked Tina Turner I think. Or was it Tina Arena?'

'I think Dawn was more of an ABBA fan,' replied Richie.

'May? Are you alright?'

'Oh… I'm sorry. Yes. I'm alright.' She'd been gazing into space, thinking about things.

May blinked rapidly. She felt like a small child in the oversized recliner that she was resting in. She'd become used to these solo sessions with Angel and the freeing feeling that she enjoyed at the end of them. He was a good listener and May felt as though a problem shared was a problem halved.

'Can I ask you something?'

'Of course May.'

'It's my father…'

'What about your father?'

'Is… is he here?' she asked tentatively.

'Yes he is.'

'That's amazing.' May felt elated.

'Why did you think your father might not be in heaven?' asked Angel.

'Well, it's just… I mean, he killed himself. I thought perhaps if you took your own life it meant you'd committed a sin. I don't know.'

'There is a spectrum of reasons that a person would be denied eternal life in heaven. Your father was within acceptable limitations.'

'That's kind of vague. Are you saying he did enough good to make it here? Enough to outweigh his last act?'

'May, you will have as long as you need to find out those answers for yourself. As I said, your father is here.'

'I can't find anything out if he won't see me,' she protested. 'I've tried to use the door.'

'You will see him when the time is right.'

'Do you promise?'

'Yes. You have all the time you need.'

'I guess so.' May would have to be patient, which she hated.

'How things are progressing with Richie?'

'He's stubborn. He's not open to enjoying himself. To be honest I'm finding him very frustrating.'

'Richie had many years without you in life. There is ample research to suggest that parts of the human body replace themselves over the course of a decade. The Richie you married has had time to change, and not just physically but mentally as well.'

'That's about skin, isn't it?'

'It is about cells, I believe.'

'I'm not sure that's true.'

'Either am I.'

May looked at Angel's face but couldn't garner anything from his blank expression. He crossed and recrossed his legs, without ever seeming uncomfortable at all.

'Look... Richie is the same. I think maybe I'm the one that's different,' said May. 'If I'd known that I would die so young then I wouldn't have got married at all. I don't think I should have married Richie. I don't think there was a cosmic reason for our union. We were just two kids that thought we had all the answers.'

'I am sorry you feel that way. I am disappointed that my particular pocket of heaven is not very conducive for longevity,' said Angel. This time he looked crestfallen.

'Are you telling me that other couples in the neighbourhood are unhappy? Do you mean Austin and Leanne, or Dan and Jan?'

'I have said too much. Forgive me. To get back to the point, I will follow up about your father. It is my hope that we will be able to facilitate your reunion soon.'

'I want to see Violet too,' said May. She'd been thinking about her friend ever since she'd spotted her in the front row at her own funeral. It was the only positive that had come from Richie showing that vision to her. May wanted to know that Violet had had a good life, even if she hadn't been there to see it.

'Of course.'

'She was such a positive person. I think I could use some of that right now,' said May.

'Would you share that with me?'

'You want to *see* Violet?'

'Only if that is alright with you,' replied Angel.

'Sure.'

May held out her wrist and Angel moved forward to hold it. He perched at the side of the recliner, waiting patiently. May thought back to one of the many nights that Violet took her clubbing. She was transported to a noisy dance floor, her clothing now tragically tarty. *Why had she thought that a skirt that short was a good idea?* It had definitely attracted attention, now that May thought about it. Violet wore a figure-hugging pleather dress that exposed both of her shoulders and a slice of leg.

'Wooooooo!' yelled Violet happily.

They were inside *Rainbows*, a famously inclusive club that welcomed all comers. The main issue with the location was that it was undersized, so if you weren't there early you often spent the night waiting in line outside. May looked over to Angel, who seemed astounded by the loud music and strobing lights. Before them danced Violet, tall and bronzed. She'd tied her blonde hair in pigtails and doused the majority of her exposed skin with glitter for the occasion.

'Yeah! Yeah!' screamed Violet as the music changed. She pointed at the DJ with approval, and danced as wildly as possible in the huddled space.

May was on the wooden dance floor too, although her energy could never match her friends. Violet moved as if possessed. When they finally took a break it was to order more drinks.

'See any cute guys?' asked Violet between sips of her tequila.

'For you or for me?' asked May.

'Either! Both!'

May felt a little self-conscious that Angel was watching this exchange. May had almost forgotten that there was a time before Richie, a time when she was alone and naïve when it came to matters of the heart.

'We weren't… I mean, we didn't go out looking for guys like this very often,' she said to Angel.

'Why not? This looks like a lot of fun to me.'

Violet insisted on dancing again, which drew some unexpected attention.

'Hey!' An auburn haired girl with a pixie cut was shouting at Violet.

'Hey yourself!' she replied.

'Are you having fun?' the stranger asked. She was attempting to match Violet's intensity but failing to keep up with her seemingly limitless energy. May noticed her oversized belt buckle. There was something happening between them on the dance floor. This attractive stranger was repositioning herself between them, hustling May out of the picture. Violet danced obliviously.

'I'm Uma,' the woman said loudly, competing with the music.

'Violet!'

'You wanna get out of here?' asked Uma, getting closer to Violet.

'Oh my God! That's so sweet. I'm not gay,' replied Violet.

'Not even curious?'

Uma tentatively kissed Violet on the mouth, causing May to stop dancing. She was now officially the third wheel.

'You're beautiful. Did you know that?' asked Uma.

'Thanks for that. I'm so flattered, but I'm just trying to have a good time with my friend.'

Uma looked disappointed. Sensing that she was letting her down Violet gave the stranger a quick, friendly kiss on the mouth.

'She's out there for you!' May was speechless at the gesture, but Uma seemed to appreciate it.

'Have a nice night,' said Uma with a smile.

At the end of the evening Violet was bouncing along, befriending each person in the taxi line. May watched from the back, shaking her head at the shenanigans. As Violet's new friends reached the front of the queue she'd make a big show of opening the door and hugging them. They all left with a grin on their face, a feeling of contentment and varying amounts of glitter on their clothes.

'She's one of a kind,' said May as she ended the vision, returning herself to the recliner in Angel's chamber. May smiled, trying not to cry as the rambunctious scene from her life was replaced with relative silence. 'When we used to hang out Violet was always the centre of attention. But then she'd turn it around and make me feel so special. Like I was the only one that mattered. She was my best friend.'

Angel smiled. 'The moment Violet arrives I will let you know.'

'Thank you.'

Chapter Seventeen

I'll Remember You

Richie lay on the bed for a long time, testing the faux cotton material between his fingers. It wasn't *really* cotton. It wasn't really anything and it bothered him that he couldn't explain the magic behind it. Richie couldn't stop thinking about Dan and the way he'd inserted himself into his old life. Like a bird that swooped into his nest and took it over.

Tupac Shakur was right to dwell on his passing. Dying is a life-changing event, which you ought to be hung up on. Richie hated that he'd died so young, and had started wondering about his own death. *What had killed him anyway?*

He had to know.

He'd promised May that they'd only focus on the positives, and not the ugly moments of life, but Richie needed to see how his life had ended. Not knowing was like lifting the needle before a record could finish its natural rotation. Richie thought back to that fateful morning, the day Janice had suggested they have another child. This was it; he was now determined to find out his cause of death.

Richie started to review the day he'd died with fresh eyes.

He'd made his excuses and left to help Dan. He'd wandered over to his neighbour's place. As his avatar stood in front of the ladder at Dan's door Richie heard a grinding sound that he couldn't immediately identify. He looked up in the direction of the noise, while his past self remained oblivious. As his head tilted upwards a long ceramic tile slid off the roof and struck Richie's head with enough force to knock him down.

Things seemed to slow down as the tile split apart against the earth. He hadn't heard it at all the first time around. Richie toppled backwards, striking the back of his head into a sharp rock. The two separate impacts were both equally responsible for the internal bleeding that proceeded to claim Richie's life. His mind went blank, the scene blurred and the last thing he saw before the memory ended was a line of yucca trees, shivering against a light breeze.

Richie immediately watched it again. And then a third time. That God damned *tile*. *How could he have been killed by a roof tile?* It was a statistical anomaly. More people died getting crushed by vending machines than struck by roof tiles. Richie was suddenly struck again, this time by a thought he was unable to ignore.

Richie wondered whether Dan might have killed him.

It felt like a definite possibility. Far more likely than a random tile doing the job. He marvelled that he hadn't asked himself that question earlier. The tile that had struck the side of his head on that auspicious morning had come out of nowhere. If – and it was a big if - Dan had seen him approaching then he might have coordinated the attack. *Was he capable of such a brutal and calculated move?*

Richie could only watch the vision from his own point of view. He was unable to see what Dan was doing on the roof and his memory of the event ended when he was knocked to the ground. The more Richie re-watched, the more it felt like the yuccas were mocking him. There was nothing new to be gleaned from this.

He attempted to shake the idea but it lingered like a scent in the air. Surely Dan wouldn't have been able to enter heaven if he'd murdered someone. *But what if he'd committed murder and then had such a profoundly selfless life that the good outweighed the bad?* Richie tried to bury the notion as ludicrous but the seed had been planted.

Maybe he shouldn't have watched his death. Richie paced the room trying to calm down. *Why couldn't he perform with May?* It was so depressing. All he could think about was that just next-door

Dan was enjoying Jan's body. There was no way *he* was having performance issues. Nobody in heaven or on Earth was having more tremendous intercourse than Dan was having in Richie's mind right now. He needed to think about something else. *Anything else.* Richie collapsed into a chair and stared at the ceiling. He thought about the moment he'd proposed to Janice and the memory enveloped him.

They were driving back from a trip to the beach when they'd stopped at a roadside attraction. It was the site of a former castle that had crumbled and been left in ruins. Richie and Janice had walked through many stone arches before they had reached the remains of the back wall. The old rocks had been lashed by the ocean breeze for decades and were faded. Richie had wanted to propose at the beach, but the weather had been so bad that they'd opted to stay away and avoid the chilly wind. He'd thought it a bit underwhelming to propose to her in the safety of their beach house. Janice believed in signs, so if nature itself seemed against their union perhaps she'd feel inclined to say no. Here, amongst the debris, she looked so unexpectedly beautiful as she stood by the cliffs. Janice looked back at Richie and smiled, her hair still windswept beneath her beanie.

There was no right time, only the right person, he'd thought.

Without May he'd been sure that Janice was his only remaining hope for companionship. The moment was ripe and he'd had the ring in his pocket for the majority of the trip.

Richie had decided to just go for it.

He'd told her that she was his princess and asked her to marry him. She'd accepted the ring with a casual nod. While re-watching the moment for a second time Richie considered that Janice's reaction had been less emotional than he'd remembered. She looked a bit stunned. Janice seemed to take the ring and inspect it before a smile crept onto her face.

During the course of their relationship Janice hadn't expected a proposal, even going so far as to tell Richie she didn't need one.

The delight and surprise of suddenly being engaged to one another had led them to have sex right there in the ruins of the castle. It was isolated, hidden from the wind and road well enough that nobody could see them.

Richie watched himself intently, familiar dimples forming on his cheeks. It was one of the most memorable sexual experiences of his life. Richie was transfixed. He was so engaged in reliving that day with Janice that Richie failed to register May's hand resting on his left wrist. By the time he'd noticed - it was too late.

Shit.

Richie could tell that he'd been caught. The private memory ended abruptly and May stared at him, disdain coursing through her.

'Looking for some inspiration, were you?'

Richie didn't have a satisfactory answer.

May recoiled, clenching her fists towards her stomach. Richie felt like he'd been caught watching pornography, except this was far worse. He'd been caught reminiscing about another woman by his supposed soul mate. Richie didn't know what to say, so he stood up and left the house. It was cowardly and he knew it, but the alternative was a fight. He wasn't prepared to fight with May, because he wasn't prepared to lose her.

Without any real direction Richie decided on a whim to go and see Jan. Maybe she would let him see their children again. Maybe May would calm down on her own.

Jan opened the door and let Richie in without a thought. Dan was once again absent, and she was happy for the company.

Jan fetched herself a Tom Collins, which was provided at the speed of thought. Richie initially declined a drink before reconsidering.

'Did the kids ever ask about me?' he wondered, trying desperately to distract himself from the situation with May.

'We talked about you from time to time.'

'I feel terrible,' said Richie. 'It's only hitting me now that I missed their entire lives. I missed being married to you. It was all over so fast. We had some good times though.' Richie thought back to the castle ruins, still fresh in his mind. He finished his drink.

'I look back on it all very fondly too. You never forget your first husband,' said Jan with a wink. She was savouring her beverage, sipping it incrementally.

'I don't know what's wrong with me. When you die… all your fears and problems are supposed to die with you. But they don't, because they're all in your head.'

'What are you worrying about? This is supposed to be heaven,' she said.

'I just can't turn my mind off.'

They settled down on the silky bed as they had before. Richie held her wrist, ready to be shown the faces of his twin boys. Instead he found himself watching the same scene of the two of them having sex beside the castle remains, this time from Jan's perspective.

'Are you… showing me this?' he asked, confused for a moment as to whether they were now viewing his memories or hers. Jan's face in the vision now seemed filled with pleasure.

'Yes.'

'Why?'

'Because it was such a beautiful moment. You'd just proposed, and then we'd had such an amazing time.' There was a glint in Jan's eyes that gave Richie a rush. If he could blush or perspire he'd be doing both. 'That was easily the best sex we'd ever had,' said Jan, mirroring his feelings about that day.

'Do you think so?'

'Definitely.'

'I agree.'

'But being together seems to be so much *more* in heaven. More layered. Have you found that?' asked Jan.

'Yes...'

'It's indescribable,' stated Jan. 'Do you know how it feels to go from being an old woman to *this*?'

'Young?'

'My body works again. It's incredibly liberating. I know you didn't get to grow old but... things had changed. Now, my body's at it's peak,' announced Jan.

'Huh...' Richie didn't know what to say. Jan *did* look at her peak, but it felt like stating the obvious. They both watched the extremely sexual scene playing out around them. Then suddenly they were staring at each other with renewed interest, the tension rocketing them into new yet familiar territory. Jan tucked her blonde hair behind her ears.

'We shouldn't do this,' said Richie quietly.

'Shouldn't do what?' she asked with a knowing grin.

Before he knew it they were kissing. Their embrace was heightened by the soundtrack of their love making, the past still playing in the background all around them. Even though each touch from Jan felt amazing, and his body was responding to her in a way that it hadn't with May, Richie managed to stop himself.

'No, I can't. We shouldn't... *I* shouldn't.'

'You can do whatever you want. And I think we should. Let's just get it over with.'

'I might really regret this... but... I can't do that to May.'

'Richie, this is heaven. Stop thinking. We can have everything. It's like a buffet-'

'May is my soul mate. I chose her,' he said firmly, trying to convince himself as much as Jan.

'That was before you knew I was with Dan, wasn't it?'

'Yes.'

'You're jealous of Dan, aren't you? I can tell,' declared Jan. 'You were jealous of him in life and now you're jealous of him in death. You want me... am I wrong?'

'I'm jealous of the fact that he got to live the rest of *my* life! That was supposed to be my time. Dan raised *my* boys... he slept with *my* wife. That he might have-' Richie stopped himself short of accusing Dan of murder. He collected himself and continued. 'Did you move into his house or did he move into ours?'

'He moved in with me and the boys.'

'Exactly. Do you remember the day I died?' asked Richie.

'Of course.'

'You told me you wanted to have another baby.'

'I remember Richie. What's your point?'

'Why didn't you press Dan for another baby? If that's what you really wanted.'

'I think it was a passing thought. I didn't want more children after you died,' announced Jan.

'Why not?'

'The boys were enough.'

'So, if I'd lived… and we'd decided to have another baby…'

'That might have been a mistake,' said Jan.

'Wow.'

'What's wrong with you? What's going on?'

'I'm just having a lot of feelings about the fact that I died,' said Richie. 'Tupac is still hung up on his death, and so am I.'

'What?'

'Nothing, don't worry about it. I'm just saying that we should all be looking back at our lives. They were so much more real than this place could ever be.'

'You're still thinking about the day you died? That was *one* day! Haven't you had time to deal with it by now?'

'No! I feel like I died and then almost straight away you and Dan showed up.'

'I suppose Angel keeps saying that time moves differently here,' reasoned Jan. 'To me it feels like the day you died was so long ago. Fifty years at least. I thought you would have processed all of this.'

'I'm just feeling conflicted. I'm sorry. Part of me would love to be with you again,' said Richie.

'So? Let's do it then. Like I said, I haven't been with you in fifty years. I want to.'

'But what about Dan? And May?'

'It's not a big deal. We used to be married too, remember? This is heaven. Like I said, we can do whatever we want to.'

'I didn't think I'd ever have to choose between you.' Richie sighed, resigning himself to his decision. 'You were both so important to me.'

'You sound like a broken record.'

'Don't say that.'

Jan nodded and furrowed her forehead. 'I think you made your choice. You do what's right for you. I'm here if you change your mind, okay? Maybe you should go back to May now.' She looked disappointed, which made him feel even worse somehow.

Richie departed, but he didn't go home. He walked down the street and found a picturesque park. The sky was a cloudless blue, and the lack of birds made him feel as though he was on a film set. Everything looked phoney.

Why didn't anyone else care?

And why had he kissed Jan?

He'd promised May honesty, so he had to tell her, didn't he? She'd seen Richie replaying such intimate moments with Jan, and then he'd run off to spend time with her. It looked premeditated.

Even if he hadn't fully betrayed her yet, how long could he resist?

The question of whether he'd made a mistake by choosing May as his soul mate haunted him. *Did he want to be with Jan?* A part of him definitely did.

Richie sat down on a wooden bench at the park. It was very comfortable, which defied his expectations. The truth was he'd rushed his decision. If he were working at the Bureau of Statistics he would have collected more data. He wished he'd taken his time and watched more of his memories when he'd first arrived.

Was it too late?

Richie clutched his wrist. He pictured a memory in his mind, something from long ago. He remembered the first time he'd tried to shave and without notice he was back in that moment. Reflected in the mirror stood an awkward teenager that hadn't quite grown into himself. Richie knew this phase of his life well. These were formative years, just before he and May would meet. He kept watching.

The answers weren't in heaven; therefore they must be in the past. He needed more data. Richie would happily re-live his life, this time knowing the ending. It would be like listening to a record for the second time and hearing the nuances he'd missed the first time around.

Richie concentrated, locked in his own mind, repeating his life as a voyeur. He knew it was selfish but he needed to do this before he could talk to May.

Chapter Eighteen

That's Someone You Never Forget

May held a plate of food. She wasn't hungry and nothing in front of her seemed appetising but she'd needed something to do with her hands. People usually ate at a funeral for comfort, perhaps to normalise things again in the wake of a death. The service had been long and full of speeches. May's relatives were distraught. The loss of a son, especially the eldest of a family was rightfully upsetting. Everyone was saying that he'd died too young, but May knew better. The choice to die was his and he'd had enough, whether other people thought so or not.

Her brother Arthur had killed himself by slicing his wrists in the bathtub. May had looked back on that moment and in hindsight reflected that Arthur never took baths, only showers. She'd wished that she'd been more observant and questioned her brother's mood towards the end.

May was only ten years old. Of course she hadn't known what her brother was about to do. At that age she hadn't even known it was an option.

May's parents Adam and Fatimah were crushed and their lack of involvement in the funeral confirmed it. She'd never seen her mother so detached from the world around her. The arrangements had been made by May's Aunt and in line with Malaysian traditions the funeral was booked for the next day. Nobody had time to process Arthur's death. Everyone's faces were raw with tears, especially May's.

This was the first person she'd ever lost through death. Her turtle had died the year before but by her own admission she was never really a fan of it. Arthur had been her only sibling. They were close for most of her life, confiding in each other and teaming up against their parents. He would sneak her treats. He had been her closest ally. She was suddenly an only child, abandoned by someone she thought would always be there.

'Arthur was only fourteen' she explained as the funeral faded from view.

'Fourteen years is better than nothing,' stated Angel, letting go of her wrist.

'I miss him. I miss my parents too.'

'That is understandable.'

'Why aren't my mother or father seeing me? Or Arthur? Every time I try to go to them the door doesn't work.'

'The doors will only function if they are unlocked on both sides,' said Angel.

'Are you saying that nobody *wants* to see me? Is it really that simple? I know they're dead.'

'A reunion cannot be forced. If your loved ones are unwilling then I will not be able to facilitate one. I am sorry that this is so complicated.'

May put her head in her hands. She'd watched countless hours of her father Adam, her mother Fatimah and her brother Arthur since being in heaven. It wasn't enough. The memories, vivid though they were, couldn't hold a candle to the real thing. She sighed, prompting Angel to speak.

'How are you feeling May?'

'Can't you tell?' she replied.

'Actually I find it quite difficult to gauge a mood. In this place the focus is generally on the positive, and that affects the way emotions are perceived. If you are feeling negative it is typically harder to distinguish, due to the way I see you.'

'And how do you see me?' asked May.

'You are a loving, kind and patient woman. You are an exemplary member of the human race,' stated Angel.

'Ha. Do you want to be my soul mate then?'

'While that is a tempting offer, that role has been filled. I would just like to know how you are at the moment?'

'I'm fine now. I'm never going to be the same, but I can accept the fact that my baby died when I died. It happened. I didn't know… you know? It's hard to digest but it is what it is. I guess I'm a little lonely…'

'That is normal when you spend so much time alone.'

'Very funny. Are you going to tell me where Richie is?'

'He is here, in heaven.'

'He doesn't seem to be,' said May. 'Why doesn't he come home?'

'While it is generally not my place to interfere I believe he is giving you space.'

'Did he tell you that?'

'No.'

'Ugh. I can't see my parents, I can't see Arthur and now Richie's gone missing? I don't *really* want space,' said May.

'Then why did you ask for something you did not want?' asked a confused Angel.

'I want Richie to just start kissing me and not stop until I'm smiling again. I want to move on. I need him here.'

'Then he has clearly misunderstood.'

'Clearly! You know that's the main difference between men and women.'

'What is?'

'Communication! But Richie's never been great at talking. He's got such a logical mind, always presenting facts and drawing conclusions. I should have realised that heaven would break his brain.'

'I can assure you that his brain is most definitely intact.'

'It's an expression.'

'Oh. I see.'

'You don't really *get* expressions do you?'

'I understand some, however unlike you I did not spend my existence trying to master an ever-evolving language. It changes quite constantly on Earth, forever adding and subtracting words as the human race sees fit.'

'You've been watching for a long time up here, huh?'

'Long enough to understand some things,' said Angel.

'Is there a meaning of life?' asked May.

'Only if you find one yourself.'

'That's what I was afraid of. The only things that matter are the things you put importance on. For whatever reason I've stopped mattering to everyone that I love.'

'Things do change.'

'That doesn't make me feel any better, if I'm being honest.'

'There is an expression that might apply here. You feel as though you are in a dark place, in the middle of a crisis, yes?'

'Yes.'

'They say that when you are going through hell… you ought to keep going. Do you understand?'

'Yes,' replied May. 'This too shall pass.'

'That is right,' said Angel happily.

'I never thought I'd be sitting down with an angel, comparing heaven to hell.'

'Life is full of surprises.'

'You know, I didn't think that talking about my problems would solve anything.'

'And have you been pleasantly surprised?'

'No. I was right. Talking to you is a waste of time,' said May, crossing her arms. 'You can't give me my baby, you can't tell me where Richie is and you can't help me see my family. What's the point of you?'

Angel was clearly shaken but remained stoic.

'You give me *expressions*?' she continued. 'That's meant to help me? I'm at the end of my rope. How's that for an expression? I'm supposed to be in heaven. This *is* heaven, right?'

'It is-'

'Bullshit! This fucking sucks. What's the point of picking a soul mate if he just pisses off whenever he feels like it? What's the point of being able to live forever if you can't even speak to the ones you love? Tell me!'

'I understand that this is not a position you are comfortable with. Leave it with me and I promise to get you some answers. Please May, try to be patient,' said Angel.

'Thanks for nothing.'

May stood and walked back through the doorway to her residence. Angel didn't say a word to stop her.

This therapy now felt like a waste of time. If she was going to live forever like this things were going to have to change.

Enough was enough.

Chapter Nineteen

<u>Burning Love</u>

Richie opened his eyes.

The park looked exactly the same. Twenty odd years worth of memories had flown by and not a single tree had grown around him. He hadn't intended to watch quite so much. The sky was as impossibly blue as ever and Richie was still alone on the wooden bench. Hesitantly he got up and walked back to his home. He was not looking forward to the fight that awaited him. Richie knew he shouldn't be feeling this way. His search should have yielded answers. Watching his life back had not swayed him one way or the other, but he'd made a commitment to May and he'd decided it was best to honour it.

Richie crept into the bedroom, hoping to find May so enthralled with a memory that he could catch a glimpse of her state of mind. Instead Richie was confronted with a much more heartbreaking scene.

May was writhing in a fit of ecstasy beneath none other than Dan. Her bare leg was wrapped around him, toes pointing upwards.

Richie couldn't believe it. He stood in the doorway for a moment, unsure whether to intervene. Dan bounced happily above her, his muscular rear end moving rhythmically. Neither of them had noticed Richie, and they continued their heavenly agenda.

He walked out of the house and went straight next-door.

If Dan was going to screw May then he should feel no guilt in doing the same thing with Jan. She was happy to see him and welcomed him with open legs.

'He's *awful* now. I just don't know what I ever saw in him in the first place.'

'Come on. You can't think like that,' said Dan, rubbing his large hand along Leanne's arm sympathetically.

'Austin isn't even sorry. He's only sorry he got caught.' Her words were full of bitterness.

'It's not good to hold onto resentment. Your life was really just a blip in the scheme of your existence. You get a new life here in heaven. Don't let Austin ruin it.'

'Shouldn't we be speaking to Angel about this stuff? I mean… no offence,' said Leanne, 'I like talking to you Dan, but if I have a problem with my stupid… *dumbass*, lying other half… maybe I should talk to him.'

'I think that's a good idea. Next time you talk to Angel you should definitely let him know what Austin did. Where is he anyway?'

'Angel or Austin?'

'Austin,' replied Dan.

'Who knows?'

Dan had found Leanne alone on her porch. He'd seen her vacant expression and felt compelled to talk to her, to help if he could. Once while he was alive he'd seen a troubled woman sitting alone by the ocean. Dan had engaged with her and through their conversation she'd revealed that she'd come to the beach with the intention of drowning herself. He'd never forgotten the power of words. Dan was a problem solver, and he enjoyed a challenge like the one Austin and Leanne presented.

He'd found a wonderful inner peace since dying. Dan felt blessed to be with Jan in such an indescribable place. He wanted everyone around him to feel even one tenth of his quotient of joy.

'I can't believe how well y'all are doing,' said Leanne.

'Why is that?'

'We died first, you know. I thought Austin and I were perfect on Earth but you and Jan seem to have figured heaven out.'

'We have disagreements, just like anyone.'

'But you get over it. I can't believe she let you sleep with that blonde,' exclaimed Leanne.

'Ellie.'

'Yeah, that's the one.'

'Jan has had her share of fun too. We've made a lot of compromises over time and we've just figured out how we want things to be.'

'So… do you think Jan would care if you stepped out of your marriage again?' she asked, resting her left hand suggestively onto his leg.

'Leanne…'

'I've been thinking about it and I feel like this might be the only way I can get over it. If I sleep with you then maybe Austin and I can call it even…'

'It's not that simple.'

'Yeah it is,' she said, withdrawing her hand. 'And it's gotta be you. You're already open to this kinda thing Dan. And nobody's gonna get hurt this way.'

'I think you should probably talk to Angel. I'll be here too…
but I don't want to start something that will hurt Austin,' said Dan
as he stood up, ready to depart.

'You know how we saw you and Ellie… how you showed us
that day from your memories?' asked Leanne.

'Yeah.'

'I keep thinking about it.'

'Leanne, this kind of lifestyle… it's not for everyone.'

'You never know until you try.'

Dan saw a look on Leanne's face that he knew well. She had a
fierce determination that meant she would do whatever it took to
bed him. Ultimately Dan liked being the object of affection. He
used to have trouble declining these kinds of advances, but now
with maturity he found it easy. He already had everything he
wanted and there was no point in being greedy.

'I'll think about it Leanne,' said Dan, in order to end the
conversation. 'But it's not polite to have two extramarital affairs at
once. It's not fair to your main partner.'

'Good manners, huh?'

'That's right.'

When they were finished Richie's moral pendulum swung
intensely back into place. He suddenly felt like less of a man.

'We shouldn't have done that,' said Richie, suffering remorse
for their tryst and his very human fallibility.

'Why not? It was fun,' replied Jan. 'You've gotten better at that.'

'It's heaven. It's not real. Everything is enhanced!' cried Richie.

'I mean… it's been a while but it felt the same size to me.'

'That's not what I meant.'

'You're saying that it's impossible to have bad sex in heaven, is that it?' asked Jan. 'Sounds like a good thing.'

Richie just shook his head. Jan looked relaxed as she lay on the most comfortable bed Richie had ever felt. *Why was everything better in their house?*

'I have to tell you something. You're not going to like it,' he declared.

'What?'

'Dan was sleeping with May.'

'When?'

'Just now. I went over there and I saw them together. I'm sorry.'

'So?' Jan didn't seem fazed by the revelation.

'He's cheating on you! May's cheating on me. They're meant to be *our* soul mates.'

'It's alright. Dan and I have always had a very open relationship when we were alive. It feels appropriate to continue that here. We've already discussed it. It's fine.'

'Are you serious?'

'Yes Richie.'

'Were you going to tell me? Or just let Dan ruin my relationship with May? We *don't* have the same arrangement as you two...'

'You can hardly act so righteous when you came over here and did exactly the same thing,' said Jan.

'So, you and Dan had an open relationship?'

'Yes.'

'An open *marriage*?'

'Yes.'

'That pisses me off even more!'

'Why?'

'Because you and I never had an open relationship. Dan got to have you as well as any other woman he liked!' Richie sounded shrill, jealousy clouding his once rational mind.

'You never asked!'

'I didn't even know that was a possibility!'

'Either did I! If you'd asked me I would have considered it. It was just something that Dan needed, you know?'

'No... I don't know.'

'Dan's just always had a big appetite for sex. He's such a Scorpio.'

Even though Jan didn't know about his one time bedroom problem the commentary felt personal. 'Stop it! I don't want to hear this.'

'Fine. You asked,' shrugged Jan.

Richie fumed as he wandered out into the neighbourhood. Standing in front of the house he looked at the garden. It was exactly the same combination of plants and stones that had decorated their residence in life. The only difference was that here, in this place, everything was organised, lush and verdant. Richie seethed, hating this misrepresentation. The rough edges that made life difficult were all smoothed over here in heaven.

Richie thought about talking to Angel, but wondered how honest he should be about his anxiety. The four of them might have just committed a sin by swapping partners and he didn't want to get them all kicked out of heaven for adultery. *Did the Ten Commandments apply here? Were they all being monitored? Where was Angel anyway?* He was giving them all a long leash and they were taking advantage of it.

Richie considered that if heaven was a real place then hell ought to be equally real. Those damned souls probably *only* had rough edges to contend with. After pondering his next move Richie decided he must go home to May. Their next conversation was decades overdue.

He was thankful to find her alone.

'Where have you been?'

'Just over in the park,' replied Richie.

'In the *park*?'

'Yeah, just down the street.'

'What have you been doing?'

'Watching my memories. From my life.'

'How many did you watch?' asked May.

'Almost my whole life's worth,' he replied sheepishly. Richie explained to May that he'd selected an innocuous moment from his youth as a starting point. Then he'd reasoned that if he just watched things chronologically he'd understand the sum total of his life.

'Fuck Richie.'

'I guess I didn't think it through exactly.'

'Did you just watch yourself sleep too?'

'Yes.'

'Why?'

'I just needed to see it all again. I don't know. Once I started watching I didn't want to stop. I didn't want to miss anything.'

'You just abandoned me for twenty years?'

'You wanted space to breathe… I wanted that for you,' said Richie.

'You know it didn't feel like twenty years to me. Time moves differently here, remember?'

'How much time passed for you?'

'It feels like a lifetime ago,' replied May wistfully.

'You were too busy to come and find me?' asked Richie.

'I missed you in the beginning. Eventually I accepted your absence.'

'You missed me? I find that hard to believe.'

'I missed you enough.'

'And you never came to the park?'

'Why would I look for you in the park? Why wouldn't you just tell me you were doing this? Why wouldn't you just do this at home? Honestly Richie, I don't know why you don't think things through,' said May, exasperated.

'Sorry. I'm here now.'

'What good is that?'

'Huh?'

'Richie, we need to talk,' said May.

He approached her at their dining room table. He was suddenly very aware of himself and the way he was standing. Richie adjusted his glasses and tried to keep a level head. 'What's up?'

'I wanted you to know that I slept with Dan while you were away. We've been together quite a lot.'

While her honesty was refreshing, the information was still unpleasant to hear out loud.

'Uhuh.'

'I know you know about it,' continued May. 'And I know that you slept with Janice again. I know you've been doubting our connection… I don't know *when* you started feeling this way, but I know you. I know you aren't happy.'

'Jesus.'

May shot him a look.

'Sorry,' conceded Richie. It wasn't an argument worth having, even though he felt the situation warranted a *Jesus*.

'I've been talking to Dan and Jan. We've made a decision.'

'*You've* made a decision? The *three* of you?'

'Yes. The three of us.'

'Go on…'

'We want to explore a bit of a trade. Not forever or anything. I'd like to spend some time here with Dan, and Jan would like you to move in with her during that time.'

'Why do you want to be with Dan?'

'When we were alive I was always fascinated by Dan. I never did anything with him when we were together, don't worry about that… but Richie, you were the only man I'd ever had sex with. In retrospect I feel like I've missed out on something.'

'I can't believe I'm hearing this.'

'But you're feeling the same way! You've been wondering if you should have picked Jan. So why don't you just find out? See if the grass is greener for yourself. It's fine, really.'

Richie thought of the almost artificially perfect lawn outside. He thought about the fact that Jan's bed *was* somehow softer. *Did he belong over there?*

'This is a lot to take in,' he said.

'Well you don't seem capable of making this decision, so we all got together and made it for you. You're welcome.'

Richie exhaled, even though there was no reason to do so.

'Jan can show you everything that happened with Brody and Charlie,' added May. 'This might just make us better partners in the end.'

'Like Dan and Jan are?'

'Richie… don't start…'

'Why does it have to be Dan?' he asked.

'He's a good person. You should give him a chance.'

'You're asking me to do something I would never do.'

'Be with Jan? You've done that lots of times… recently too,' said May.

'That's not what I mean… you're twisting things…'

'I'm only asking you to trust me,' stated May. 'I'll come back to you. I know you'll come back to me, right?'

'Yes. Of course.' Richie wanted both women but he didn't want to admit that. There wasn't an elegant solution to satisfy his craving. The truth was that this venture could have unexpected side effects. *What if May started to have feelings for Dan? What if he felt the same way about Jan?* It was a dangerous path to take.

'Can we try this Richie?'

'It's a bad idea.'

'Leaving me all alone for like… twenty years was a bad idea.'

'Well this is another bad idea…'

'I'm feeling like I missed out on my life,' said May. 'I'm feeling like I was young and… it's not that I have any regrets or anything, but you had so much more time. Maybe you and I would have grown old together if I hadn't died… but maybe we wouldn't have.'

'Don't do that,' pleaded Richie. 'You're watering down what we were.'

'I'm just saying that if this is heaven then we should get to do whatever we want and not feel awful about it. You want to be with Jan, don't you?'

'Yes,' he replied with a sigh.

'And I don't want to make you feel any shame about that, okay?'

'Okay.'

May was sounding like Dan, with his carefree philosophy. He'd swept in and brainwashed Janice after his death and now the same power of suggestion had worked on May. Richie had made a huge mistake leaving her alone. He didn't like it but he could see which way things were going.

'If it's alright with you,' said May, 'I want to spend more time with Dan, or whoever-'

'Or *whoever*?' Richie interrupted.

'Heaven is a big place. I just don't want to miss out again.'

Despite all the claims of the vastness of heaven, Richie was yet to step outside of their pocket. He had planned to explore eventually, maybe take in some of these fabled concerts, but wanted to resolve the relationship crisis directly first. Richie found the idea of endless possibilities to be overwhelming. Heaven didn't have as many rules as he thought it should.

'It's hard to hear you say this. You're supposed to be *my* soul mate,' he chided.

'And you're supposed to be mine.'

'We were husband and wife, remember?'

'I remember Richie… til death do us part. We died. We parted.'

'You don't need to remind me,' he said.

'Look, I know fidelity is implied,' said May, 'but I think if we can agree on this then we can still be happy. Jan and Dan seem open to the experience. Can you try to be?'

Richie knew that he was still viewing the idea of their relationship through the prism of his human experience. Perhaps he was wrong about everything. The concept of marriage and monogamy were just constructs after all. *Could Dan and Jan have been right? Had they just been more enlightened?* Maybe this wasn't frowned upon at all, but embraced. In heaven anything goes.

'If you need this, then I'm okay with it.'

'I think you need it too Richie.'

'Maybe.'

'You've built me up in your mind, you know. I'm just another person,' she said.

'You're *my* person.'

'And I always will be,' said May. 'But I'm not the only wife you have up here. You and Jan have unfinished business.'

'I guess.'

'I didn't think I'd have to convince you like this!' laughed May. 'You have my blessing. Be with her if you want. I'll still love you no matter what. You were the love of my life.'

'*Were?*'

'You *are* the love of my life. Always will be,' said May, correcting herself.

'I just don't want Dan to become the love of your afterlife.'

'That's funny. He could never replace you.'

Richie immediately remembered how easily Dan had substituted for him in life and felt like he'd been punched in the gut.

'So, you'll spend some time with Dan, and I'll explore things with Jan… and then what?'

'Then we'll go back to the way things were. You and me.'

'You promise?'

'Of course,' replied May. 'This is temporary.'

Richie was still feeling horrible about the twins. He'd felt more guilt about abandoning them through death than he did about sleeping with Jan in heaven. He agreed to the terms, knowing that he'd have the opportunity to see his boys again. He didn't want to mention them directly, as he feared steering the conversation back to lost children would trigger his soul mate all over again.

'What were you doing while you waited for me to die?' asked Richie.

'What do you mean?'

'In the fifteen or so years between your death on Earth and my death on Earth… what were you doing here in heaven?'

'I spoke to Angel.'

'For fifteen years?'

'No. For me it felt more like fifteen minutes,' stated May.

'It did?'

'Yes. I had enough time to come to terms with my death and to nominate you as my soul mate. Then you turned up like magic.'

Richie's head was spinning. One of the main reasons he'd chosen May over Jan was because he'd imagined her pining alone for the equivalent of a decade. In reality she'd barely had to wait at all. This irrational grievance bothered him more than he cared to say. Angel had mentioned that time didn't move the same way in heaven, but realising the truth of that statement didn't make him feel any better.

'Fine, let's swap,' said Richie. 'I'm ready.'

'Thank you. I know that this will give us both some clarity.'

Chapter Twenty

<u>Finders Keepers, Losers Weepers</u>

'Would you like to talk?'

'Do I have to?'

'No, but this is a safe space if you feel inclined to,' said Angel.

'I mean… I just don't know what we would talk about.'

'In my limited experience of these sessions I find that subjects are most comfortable speaking about their lives.'

'But that's all over with. I'm dead.'

'Yes, that is true.'

'Did you die too?'

'No,' said Angel. 'I never had a traditional life on Earth.'

'Then what makes you so qualified, huh? You're not a shrink. You've never lived.'

'I am the only one here. What have you got to lose?'

'Okay… look… I know what you want me to do, but I can't do it. I can't choose a soul mate.'

'I assure you that you can. Nominating a soul mate is a simple process,' replied Angel.

'But I don't want to.'

'By design, heaven is built to support pairs of souls. If you do not select another, then I will have to get creative with our next step.'

May's father Adam had been deceased for a decent amount of time and despite Angel's frequent requests he refused to commence the nomination process. They were at an impasse.

'You can't make me choose.'

'You are right, I cannot make you choose. I would never force you to be paired with another. I only ask you to do so for the sake of your daughter May.'

'Why? What's wrong with May?'

'She needs her father.'

'Is she okay?'

'She is in no pain or danger. It is her emotional state which is concerning. That, and the fact that she tries to see you periodically without success.'

'What do you tell her?'

'Nothing. It is not my place to interfere,' said Angel. 'Will you see her?'

'Yes... I'll see her,' Adam replied.

'Will you tell May the truth?'

'It's time.'

'I think that would be for the best.'

'So do I.'

'I will not pressure you further regarding your soul mate until after you see your daughter,' said Angel.

'I appreciate that. Thank you.'

The four of them met in Dan and Jan's living room for a kind of symbolic passing of the baton. It was an unusual situation to say the least.

'So, Richie moves in here? Is everyone happy with that?' asked May.

They all looked at Richie, who did not object.

'Thanks for agreeing to this,' said Dan. 'If I'm being honest - and I think we all should be - I've always liked May. I was heartbroken when she died.'

'Awww. I liked you too Dan. It was lovely being your neighbour in life,' May replied.

Richie remembered the time Dan told him he'd been visiting May's grave. This arrangement was some kind of unfinished business for them as well. May was just some notch on his belt.

'You two have fun,' said Jan.

Dan made sure to shake Richie's hand before they left together to play house in what was meant to be *his* house.

'Take good care of my soul mate,' Dan said with a smile.

'You too...'

In a way it was exactly what Richie had wanted. He had nothing to complain about. May was being very cool about his desire to be with Jan, which made Richie wonder why this scenario didn't make him feel happier. The idea that May had only had to wait the equivalent of fifteen minutes for him to arrive was grating at him. It wasn't fair that of the four of them he was the only one who'd bothered to mourn properly. Jan had moved on with Dan and he'd been forgotten, barely mentioned to Charlie and Brody.

Richie had become frustrated with May and was now more than happy to have a break from her. She hadn't spoken to *him* about their unborn child either, only Angel. The whole topic felt very unresolved. It felt like she was blaming him for it, or at least blaming him for not telling her about it earlier. There was no good time to bring it up! Either way, there was an element of punishment to the swapping of wives. May wanted to sleep with Dan, and Richie was being forced to accept that.

What May didn't realise was that Richie was equally attracted to Jan. This version of his second wife was free from everything that had distracted her on Earth. There were no commitments, restrictions or children to prevent them from engaging in the incessant pleasure that he'd wished for during their marriage. As soon as Richie and Jan were alone, that's exactly what they did.

She engulfed him, dazzling him to the point that he wasn't thinking about May anymore. Jan's body was perfect and they made love tenaciously.

'Was Dan a good husband?' asked Richie, as they lay together, pretzeled in the aftermath of their latest routine.

'Do you mean… was he better than *you*?' asked Jan.

'Not exactly. I can't ask you that because I'm struggling with that same question myself. It's like trying to choose a favourite child.'

'Well, not *exactly*…' said Jan.

'No… I mean… I can't compare you and May because you were both so different. I loved you in different ways and at different points in my life. It's apples and oranges,' declared Richie.

'It's all still fruit though. That reminds me!'

Jan untangled herself from him and slipped away. She returned with two melon-based drinks.

'I guess what I'm asking Jan… is whether Dan was a good guy to you. You were together for a long time, much longer than you and I were. Did Dan treat you well?'

'Yes. He was a good father to the boys and he was always upfront with me. He took care of me. We had a good marriage.'

'Then how can you listen to him complimenting May like that? He's saying how attracted he was to her during his life… right in front of you.'

'She is attractive!' Jan sipped her green drink.

'Weren't you jealous?'

'I'd never met May. That's something from when Dan lived next door to you. That's like me being upset with you for having a crush on Cindy Crawford when you were a teenager. It's before my time,' argued Jan.

'But aren't we supposed to pair off? Isn't that why Angel made us choose someone to be with?'

'We have paired off. Right now I'm paired with you,' said Jan. 'Maybe next you can pair off with Dan.'

'Hilarious. You know what I mean.'

'If you'd like to try that I'm sure he'd be game. Nobody would mind.'

'I'd mind! I don't want to… *do* things with Dan!'

'Right. But *if* you wanted to… May would be fine with it. So you have to be fine with her being with Dan, and so do I.'

'You're so open-minded all of a sudden, aren't you?'

'If what we're doing is wrong don't you think Angel would intervene?' asked Jan. 'Don't be bitter Richie, it's starting to get tired.'

'I'm not bitter… it's just… don't you think that it's morally grey?'

'No. Dan and I had an open marriage, remember? We were let into heaven despite that. It's fine.'

'But-'

'Just drop it, okay?'

Richie was trying to go with the flow. He didn't want it to bother him but it lingered. In a way he was being allowed to have May *and* Janice, under the condition that while he was with one the other would be kept company by Dan. While he wished it could be someone else he did his best to distract himself with the most wonderful version of his second wife. Jan looked flawless to him, almost offputtingly so.

'How old do you look to Dan?' asked Richie.

'What do you mean?'

'Well you died in your eighties. What age do you look when he looks at you?'

'I never thought to ask,' replied Jan. 'How old do I look to you?'

'You look exactly like you did when we got married,' he replied. 'Maybe better.'

'You look the same. We're all just seeing our loved ones the way we want to remember them.'

'How old does Dan look? Is he forty? Like when you married him?' asked Richie.

'No. He's much younger than that. Maybe early thirties? From around the time I met him…'

As she spoke Richie started to wonder what Jan looked like as an old woman. Perhaps he'd ask her to show him a memory later so he would know. Suddenly there was silence as Jan froze. She set down her empty glass and stared at Richie.

'What is it?' he asked.

'It's… I'm getting a sensation that someone wants to see me.'

'Through the door? Like a visitor?'

'Two visitors.'

Richie was hoping that it was their offsiders, and that May had changed her mind. Maybe Dan had been filled with jealousy over that fact that he'd been with Jan, unlikely as that seemed.

'Who is it?'

Before Jan could answer two voices called out from the other room.

'Hello? Anybody home?'

They left the bedroom together and headed towards the door. Richie found himself staring at the grown up faces of Brody and Charlie.

Chapter Twenty-One

Don't Cry Daddy

'Brody? Charlie? I can't believe it.' Jan pushed past Richie to embrace her boys. They each said hello to their mother, looking a little confused as to why she was with Richie.

He stood to the side, completely dumbstruck. The twin boys didn't have his trademark curls, or his European complexion. Richie's dimpled smile fell away. They didn't seem to resemble him at all.

Brody and Charlie looked like Dan. They looked *just* like Dan. The boys had his jawline and his face. The twins weren't his.

Richie realised that he'd never seen the boys any older than children and now he knew the reason. Jan had been keeping this bombshell from him. Richie suddenly felt like his whole life with Janice had been built on a lie.

'Jan… is there something you want to tell me?'

'Jesus… yes. I've wanted to tell you for a long time.'

'So tell me…'

'I think you know the truth now,' said Jan.

'I need to hear you say it.'

'Charlie and Brody are not your boys.'

Richie felt sick at the revelation. The twins were now standing back, allowing this confrontation to play out. They seemed calm, as if they had always known who their father was. Perhaps Jan had told them while they were alive. It seemed so obvious now.

'Really? You had an affair with Dan?'

'It was so long ago.'

'It might feel like half a century ago to you, but that was only a few years ago to me!'

'Please know that I wanted to tell you. I only slept with Dan that one time. I didn't know I was pregnant until it was too late. You know me. I was never going to have an abortion.'

'You bitch!' Richie was enraged.

'Hey, watch your language,' said Charlie.

'Show me!'

'Show you?'

'Show me the one time you slept with Dan! Show me how it happened.'

'No! And don't do this in front of the boys.'

'I can't believe this,' said Richie.

'Dan and I had a connection but I shouldn't have slept with him while we were married. That was wrong and I'm sorry. Look at me Richie, I'm *sorry*.'

'So it *was* while we were married? Apology *not* accepted.'

'Of course it was while we were married. The twins were born two years into our marriage…'

'Did *you* know about this?' Richie asked Charlie. 'Did *you*?' he said, turning to Brody.

'Yeah,' replied Charlie.

'Mum told us,' said Brody. 'When we were older.'

'After you were dead Dan was there for me. He just made things easier. Maybe we were supposed to be together in life as well as in death. I've thought about this a lot. I think I was always fated to meet Dan. He was my destiny. I just didn't know it yet.'

'Do you know how hurtful this is to me?' asked Richie.

'It's not like that Richie. I appreciate what we had too. Without our marriage I never would have met Dan.'

'You make me sound like a stepping stone.'

'Don't do that.'

'Is he bothering you?' asked Brody, stepping in. 'Do you want us to make him leave?'

'No honey, it's okay,' replied Jan.

'Did Dan know that the twins were his?' Richie's voice broke slightly, his emotions betraying him.

'Yes.'

'The whole time?'

'Yes.'

'Were you ever going to tell *me*? While I was alive I mean.'

'Yes Richie, I was planning on telling you. Of course I was. I couldn't contain that much negative energy. I wanted to be with you… at least I *thought* I did. I was young and I clearly hadn't figured out how to be really open and honest.'

'Is that why you wanted to have another baby? To keep me on the hook? To keep me around?'

'No. Not exactly. Yes… I'd been feeling guilty about the boys. Yes, I wanted to give you a child of your own…'

'You lied to me. You might have only made one mistake, but it was such a big one. This is a real game changer Jan-*ice*!' he said, emphasizing the end of her name as a form of rebellion.

Richie turned to Charlie and Brody, finding vacant looks on their faces. 'Do either of you remember me? I raised you for the first two years of your life. Do you remember me at all?'

The twins shook their heads.

'Grab my wrist… I'll show you…' pleaded Richie, holding his arm out in front of him.

'Richie…'

'Come on. I'll show you both.'

Neither of the boys took him up on the offer. Instead Charlie spoke to Jan, 'Where's Dad?'

'He's around. You can see him soon.'

'*I* was your Dad,' said Richie. 'I was your Dad first. Don't you get it?'

'After you died I had to rewrite history a little,' said Jan. 'As Brody said, I did tell them the truth about Dan. They didn't really remember you all that well, which made it easier for Dan to be their father.'

'I put you on a pedestal. I thought I'd actually made a mistake by choosing May over you! You don't want me in your life. Clearly! You actually erased me so that the boys wouldn't get confused. How could you do that to me?'

'To be honest, I didn't think I'd ever see you again. It was easier to try and forget you. It was what we all needed,' said Jan.

Richie could be angry at the situation but it was hard to poke holes in that logic. He had felt exactly the same way when he'd married Jan. He'd never expected to see May again. He'd tried to put May in the back of his mind. It wasn't what he'd wanted, but it was what he'd needed to move on.

The boys hugged their mother and he was cast aside. Unwelcome in their family huddle. As they reminisced together Richie felt out of place, so he left.

He went next door wearing the loss of his sons on his face. Richie had to tell May that he didn't want to be with Jan anymore. He didn't want to be neighbours. Richie didn't want to see either of them ever again. He hoped that Angel could send them to another pocket of heaven. Richie didn't want to deal with the drama anymore. He burst through the front door, angry that he'd been so gullible for so long.

'May?'

'Up here!'

Richie entered the bedroom to find Dan and May sitting side by side on matching blue yoga mats. They appeared to be meditating, and kept their eyes closed despite his arrival.

'May, I'm done with this,' proclaimed Richie. 'I'm done with this little swapping experiment.'

'You've barely even given it a chance,' she protested, eyes still closed.

'It's been long enough.'

'Are you alright Richie?' asked Dan.

'No, I'm not alright. I just found out about the twins.'

Dan and May both opened their eyes.

'What about them?' asked May, who was now the only one out of the loop.

'Dan here is their father, not me.'

May straightened up, looking somewhat confused.

'It's true. I'm sorry Richie,' said Dan. 'I was waiting for Jan to tell you. I didn't feel like it was my place to say. I know this must be hard. Come on… let's talk it out.'

'Charlie and Brody?' asked May quizzically.

'Yes, they're Dan's kids.'

'Oh wow.' she said. 'That fucking sucks.'

'Yeah.'

'So you slept with Jan while they were married?' asked May, turning the spotlight onto Dan.

'I slept with a lot of people while Jan and I were married.'

'Dan!'

'Look… yes, we did. But it wasn't just a fling or anything. It meant a lot to us both,' stated Dan. 'I always hoped that one day we'd have this moment, as men, to talk about it. The truth is that Jan told me they were probably my boys when she fell pregnant. She loved you Richie, which is why she stayed with you. I'm sorry. It shouldn't have happened but once it did I tried my best not to interfere. I wanted to tell you, so many times. I'm so sorry Richie.'

Richie hated that Dan was so earnest with his apology, more so than Jan had been.

'They're here,' stated Richie. 'They're asking for you.'

'The twins are here?' Dan seemed excited at the prospect of seeing his offspring. There was a lifetime of love spilling out from behind his eyes. There was no point in being bitter; Dan was their father. There was no point in acting righteous; Richie couldn't change anything.

'Yeah. They're over at Jan's. You should go and say hi.'

Dan kneeled, kissed May goodbye on the hand like some kind of wooing suitor, and left on a mission to see his boys.

'Are you okay?' asked May.

'I will be.'

'You're not going to disappear on some memory quest for another twenty years are you?'

'No… no need for that,' he replied.

May hopped up and gave Richie a hug. 'Hey, guess what?'

'What?'

'Violet died. She came to see me.'

'Who?'

'Violet? She was one of my best friends?'

'Did I ever meet her?' asked Richie.

'Yes! She was wearing green at our wedding? She helped me with the train of my dress.'

Richie couldn't recall her face.

'You don't remember Violet? She and I were very close,' said May.

'I can't picture her right now. She died?'

'Yes… she died of cancer,' reported May.

'That sucks.'

'She came to see me while you were away. We're going to hang out again. Do you want to come with me? Maybe refresh your memory?' she offered.

'Will Dan be there?' asked Richie.

'No, but Violet will probably bring her soul mate.'

Richie felt like May had missed the real question he'd been asking, so he doubled down. 'Are you having fun with *Dan* then?'

'He's showing me all these films from the future. Like he'll just start remembering the opening titles and then I'll grab his wrist and suddenly we're watching a film! It's so good because I've got no idea what I'm about to see. You remember how I hated seeing a movie when all the best bits were in the trailer?'

'Great.'

'What is it?'

'I'm pissed off,' replied Richie.

'About me watching movies with Dan?'

'No… I'm mad about Jan sleeping with Dan. Or… *Dan* sleeping with her…'

'You're not going to hold a grudge about this are you?' asked May. 'It was a long time ago.'

'Uh yeah, I was thinking I might. Janice slept with our neighbour when we were married. Not long after we were married by the way! I'm pissed off about it!'

'People make mistakes,' said May.

'I've just found out about this! Can't I be upset for a minute?'

'Yes, but what's a minute in the scheme of things?' She stroked his arms in an attempt to soothe him.

'Sixty seconds, I guess,' said Richie.

'But a minute in heaven is different, isn't it?'

'I don't even know anymore.'

'Everything is different here. And being married is such a flexible construct. We're tethered together for eternity. I want you to be happy. How about you do your best to get past this? You need to let things go. Everything's already happened anyway.'

'Why should I? They robbed me of my children. You of all people should know how that feels.'

'You don't need to remind me.'

'Sorry.'

'Maybe you should try to let it go because you love me?'

May was right, of course. And he did love her. He'd made the right choice choosing May after all. He hated Jan. She was a liar.

Richie decided that he'd entered into something much more special with May. Their bond was forever and he would love her and only her from now on.

'Are you done with Dan then?' he asked.

'Not yet. I'm actually enjoying his optimistic outlook.'

'But I'm done with Jan.'

'I'm afraid you'll just have to be patient with me.'

'But I want to come back. I want to live here with you again.'

'You're welcome to move back in, but you need to understand that I'm learning a lot from Dan. He's showing me world events that happened long after our deaths. Cultural shifts, musical trends, natural disasters… heaps of stuff. It's really interesting.'

'And you're screwing him?'

'Sex is such an infinitesimal part of our existence. Why can't you see that?'

'Who talks like that?' Richie was half-laughing at the statement.

'Dan. And I guess I do too.'

'You never used to.'

'People change,' said May.

'I guess I'm just used to how things were when we were alive.'

'You're not just a man anymore. You can evolve past this if you want to. I don't want to grow without you.'

'I need some air,' stated Richie.

'No you don't. We don't need to breathe anymore!'

'It's an expression!' shouted Richie, as he slammed the front door behind him. It didn't make a sound, failing to punctuate the start of a fresh disagreement.

Richie confronted Jan only to find out that she was also sick of the swap.

'We're not a good fit, are we?' said Jan nonchalantly. She'd been sampling drinks again; a cluster of empty glasses lined the kitchen table.

'Right…'

'I mean, don't get me wrong… I loved you when I was thirty two… but I don't think my brain was done growing.'

'What?'

'I don't think I knew what I actually wanted.'

'You didn't love me?' asked Richie.

'Not like I love Dan.'

'That's really insulting, do you know that?'

'Yeah… sorry I guess.'

'Well… *fuck.*' Richie didn't know what to say. It was all becoming overwhelming. His whole world was spinning around him like a whirlpool, getting closer and closer to the inevitable drain.

Richie was now forced to walk around the abyss of heaven knowing that neither of his earthly loves wanted to see him at that particular moment. Heaven was feeling very overrated.

Chapter Twenty-Two

Hound Dog

Austin and Leanne sat uncomfortably in two single seats. Neither of them spoke, but their body language conveyed their ongoing aggression. Things weren't going well, and they'd mutually decided that the only one who could help was Angel. Both parties were nervous about the outcome of their session, fearing that their inability to get along could have serious ramifications to their residency. Austin's leg bounced uncontrollably.

'Leanne would you care to get us started?' asked Angel.

'Well, Austin cheated on me.'

'One time… and it was a BJ, not sex,' clarified Austin.

'That's just as bad!'

'No, it's not! I didn't even offer to do anything to her when it was done. If you'd stayed 'n watched my side of the story then you would've known that.'

'Leanne, I would like you to imagine your existence here in heaven without Austin. If he were not present would you be more or less content?'

'Where would he be?'

'Now you've gone and done it,' grumbled Austin, his true fear now out in the open. 'You're going to get me kicked out! Buddy, I'm not the only one who's playing around.'

'I do not wish to remove you Austin,' stated Angel. 'And none of the behaviour from your lives or your afterlives concerns me. My role as the facilitator here is to determine that the souls in heaven are paired off with their ideal counterpart. I seek harmony. I am merely asking you if you two still consider yourselves compatible.'

'Well I'm sure Austin wishes he'd picked that waitress,' said Leanne spitefully. 'That's why he was thinking 'bout her so much!'

'At least she wouldn't have put me through this horse shit.' Austin turned his attention to Angel, 'I've apologised… I've even given her time. Do you want me to pick flowers from the garden? Do you need me to beg? I don't know what she wants from me!'

'What do you want?' Angel asked Leanne.

'I don't know anymore. All I know is… it's not you Austin,' she replied.

Austin's face dropped. He knew nothing he could say would change how Leanne felt. 'Well, shit,' sighed Austin. 'What the hell do we do now?'

'Love me tender, love me sweet… never let me go. You have made my life complete… and I love you so…'

May couldn't believe it. They were standing in front of the real soul of Elvis Presley. The King looked unreal, and he was performing one of Richie's favourite songs. May had heard it countless times on vinyl, whenever her husband had felt the desire to hear from his idol. In retrospect Richie had often played Elvis songs on the weekend, and especially when it rained.

But Richie, the one person that would appreciate the gravity of this moment, was absent. May had asked and he'd declined, perhaps still harbouring some anger about the trading of spouses.

Angel stood beside her while they waited. They'd passed through the doorway together, imagining Elvis on stage as they did. To May's surprise they had arrived at a heavenly concert already in progress. There was a sea of faces but somehow there was no pushing or shoving to get to the front. They all had an amazing view without needing to move a muscle. Heaven seemed flexible enough to accommodate everything.

'He's going to meet us here? You're sure?' asked May.

'Positive.'

'Love me tender, love me true… all my dreams fulfil. For my darling, I love you… and I always will…'

Elvis was clearly in peak physical condition, now with the greatest lung capacity he'd ever experienced. When May had watched him in old videos she'd noticed how sweaty Elvis would get during performances. Here she was surprised at how effortless his singing truly was. Everyone here was seeing Elvis as they wanted to see him.

'May?'

She turned around and everything stopped. Here, after what seemed like an eternity, May was finally face to face with her father Adam.

'Dad?'

The two fell straight into a hug. May started crying, and when she looked up she noticed that he was crying too.

'Oh May, it's so good to see you.'

'You too. I've missed you so much.'

They embraced again. May suddenly felt complete, as if the puzzle of her life had finally been solved.

'Are you here alone?' he asked. 'Did you bring a soul mate?' He looked over to Angel, who shook his head solemnly.

'No… my soul mate isn't here,' replied May. 'It's Richie. I married him.'

'Oh yes, I remember. Of course, of course. You two were going to get married before I died.'

They'd danced around it long enough. May wept as she hugged her father again. She had felt lonely and powerless for so long, desperate for an explanation.

'Dad… I'm so sorry that… I mean, I don't know why you killed yourself… but if it was about my getting married to Richie, or if it was something I said…'

'You think I *killed* myself?' Adam was confused.

'Didn't you?'

'Of course not. I wanted to walk you down the aisle.'

'Then what happened?'

'I'll show you,' her father said, as he held out his wrist.

May anxiously took the limb, a little scared of what she was about to see. Angel did not approach, sensing the memory was for their eyes only.

There it was. The fake jade dragon was sitting on the coffee table, undisturbed. They were back in the apartment that her parents shared. May's mother Fatimah was parked at the small living room table while her father stood in the kitchen, plunging his coffee. Adam poured a cup and walked over to the glass balcony doors. He didn't see it coming, but May did.

'Dad, look out!' she squealed. It was useless of course, as the scene was set in stone.

Fatimah moved like lightning, barrelling towards him and timing the hit perfectly. His momentum moving towards the edge of the balcony meant that when she intentionally collided with him, Adam couldn't stop himself from falling over the edge. He dropped the mug of hot liquid as he tried to catch himself to no avail. May screamed as she experienced the fall first hand, stopping only when her father ended the vision.

Oh my God.

She remembered her mother's unusually forceful grip that day. It had never occurred to her that he could have been pushed. There had been no sign of the broken coffee mug, or of a struggle. May's mother must have cleaned it all up and hidden the only evidence of a struggle.

'Oh Dad… I'm sorry.'

'Don't be. You didn't do anything. I've had time to come to terms with this.'

May turned to Angel. 'My mother isn't here, is she?'

'No. Neither Fatimah nor your brother Arthur are in heaven.'

'But why?' she said, returning her attention to her father. 'Why did she push you?'

'I don't know. I've had a lifetime to work it out and the best I can figure is that she was sick of me. Maybe she snapped. Maybe she wanted to scare me. I truly wish I could tell you… but it doesn't matter anymore. It's done.'

'That's it? It doesn't bother you?' asked May.

'Sometimes, sure. But I can't hold a grudge. We spent decades together. Sometimes you wake up and realise the person next to you is a stranger. I just wish she'd filed for divorce like a normal person instead of murdering me.'

Elvis had started singing *A Little Less Conversation*, and was grinding away when May noticed another familiar face. It was Violet and she was dancing happily on the stage with the King of Rock and Roll. Nobody seemed to mind. It was the most ballsy move May had ever seen.

Violet sensed May and a huge smile formed on her face. She threw her arms up and hurled herself into the crowd. The concert patrons instinctively carried her as she crowd surfed her way back towards May.

'You made it!'

'Violet!'

May would never tire of hugging her loved ones, and happily they all felt the same way. Angel and May's father waited patiently for as long as the friends needed.

'I'm so happy,' said Violet.

'Me too.'

'Do you remember my Dad?' asked May.

'Of course.' Violet hugged him. 'Hi!'

As the group were reunited Elvis concluded his performance. 'Thank you! Thank you very much,' he said, heading away from the stage. The roars were deafening.

'This is so fantastic. Richie would have loved it,' May told Angel.

'There will be other concerts,' said Angel.

'Maybe.'

As the crowd dispersed a longhaired woman wandered over. She wore light blue overalls and a tight white T-shirt. She smiled at the group, pulled her brown hair away from her face and took Violet's hand.

'Hi babe,' said Violet, before turning her attention to May, Adam and Angel. 'This is my soul mate Penelope.'

Everyone greeted each other.

'I had no idea,' said May earnestly.

'Either did I to be honest, but when I met Penelope it just felt right. After I was diagnosed with cancer she was even more amazing. She just oozes love, and it had never been like that with anyone else.'

'That's great. I'm glad you were so loved,' said May.

'I'm the lucky one,' said Penelope. 'I mean… have you *met* Violet?'

They laughed. The moment felt bittersweet but May was happy to have her father and her friend back. If only she could repair things so easily with the man she'd elected to spend eternity with.

Chapter Twenty-Three

Big Love, Big Heartache

His father Stephen was parked in the same recliner, listening to the same records over and over again. Richie had tried to tell him about some new music, materialising albums and artists that had emerged after his death. His father was a true creature of habit, finding reasons to dislike every musician that was suggested. Talking about music could only distract Richie briefly, as he couldn't stop thinking about his soul mate.

'I'm having more problems with May,' announced Richie, when the conversation reached a natural break.

'You are?' his mother Helen called from the kitchen. 'That's no good.'

'Are you *still* going on about this?' asked his father.

'Yes!'

'Maybe you should find a hobby or something.'

'No, this is important,' said Richie.

'Well, what's the big problem?' asked Stephen.

'It's hard. It's not supposed to be this hard, is it?'

'It's as hard as you make it,' replied his father.

'I don't get it. May's supposed to be the love of my life,' stated Richie.

'And you're meant to be hers.'

'Right. Except she's left me alone to rot.'

'To rot?' queried his mother.

'To *fester* then. Happy?'

'Let's get real, shall we?' Stephen Walsh turned off his record player mid-song. He must have moved his chair closer as he no longer needed to stand up to access it.

'Great, let's do that. I thought May was supposed to be my true love.'

'Love fades,' stated Stephen, folding his arms.

'Love *fades*?'

'If I was a rational man I would have left your mother long ago.'

'What?'

'Your mother farts in her sleep.'

'Dad!' Richie wanted honesty but his father had selected a strange jumping off point.

'It's true. Helen farts, often quite loudly mind you, when she's asleep.'

'Oh, like you've never passed wind in the bed…' called Helen from the kitchen. His mother was still working her way through her collection of cookbooks, currently on page seventy-two of her *Women's Weekly Children's Birthday Cake Book*. Robert the Robot's chocolate eyes stared back at Richie from the bench.

'I'm just saying that love fades over time,' decreed Stephen.

'Are you saying that you don't love Mum?'

'Of course I do! She knows I love her, but it isn't the all-consuming love that you're drowning May in.'

'I don't think I'm doing that,' replied Richie.

'You're always going all in. You feel too much son. If you pour your love out like that you'll use it up. You've got to dole out your love over a lifetime, or in our case an *after*-lifetime. You can't be in one other's pockets all the time. It can be exhausting.'

'You know what *The Beatles* said Dad,' said Richie. 'Love is all you need.'

'They also sang *I wanna hold your hand*. They knew the value of going slowly too,' said Stephen. 'You don't need to be in such a rush. You've got forever to figure it out.'

'If I can just interrupt for a minute,' said Helen, entering the room. 'Your father is no peach either.'

'Okay, okay. I don't want to start a whole thing,' Stephen said, trying to placate her. 'Now that we're in heaven she doesn't fart at all. Is that what you want me to tell the boy?'

'Did you know that in our thirty-six years of marriage that your father's socks *always* had holes?' asked Helen.

'They didn't *always* have holes…'

'They were mismatched too! Because you're colour-blind!'

'Well, I might have been colour-blind then but I'm not anymore,' announced Stephen. He turned to Richie, 'You know some of my album covers look quite a bit different with their real colours.'

'Do you know *why* his socks always had holes?' continued Helen. Richie shook his head. 'They got holey because he'd never clip his toenails!'

'This is the first I'm hearing about it.' Richie's father moaned.

While they weren't raising their voices in anger Richie wasn't used to hearing his parents bicker like this.

'You need to pick your battles,' continued his mother. 'Don't sweat the small stuff.'

'Did you know your mother used to *smoke* when we first met?'

'I had no idea,' replied Richie.

'It's true,' said Helen sheepishly.

'That *was* worth fighting about. I didn't want your mother to get lung cancer.'

'He's my big softie,' Richie's mum said with a smile.

'The point is, we agree. Your mother and I have found a way to coexist and have reached an understanding about the way we live.'

'We might not be very adventurous, but it works for us,' added Helen.

'And one day if we decide to start going to heavenly concerts and mingling with the neighbours then we'll do that *together*,' added Stephen.

Richie nodded along, feeling like he was back at University in the middle of a complicated Philosophy lecture.

'Look… son. You've started to act like *The Durutti Column*.'

'The who?'

'No, not *The Who*. *The Durutti Column*. They were also an English band,' chuckled Stephen.

'And how am I acting like them?' asked Richie.

'They put out an album in 1979 called *The Return of The Durutti Column* and they covered it in rough sandpaper.'

'Why did they do a stupid thing like that?'

'They wanted to scratch up and destroy the records on either side of theirs. You know, when you store the records upright? They were prone to chaos I suppose,' stated Stephen. 'The point is you're being abrasive too. You're rubbing people up the wrong way and it's going to ruin your relationships.'

'Dad?'

'Yeah?'

'Why do you love vinyl records so much?' asked Richie. It had occurred to him that this simple question was one he'd never thought to ask.

'Well, when you listen to an artist like Bob Dylan or Cat Stevens,' started Stephen, 'you're can listen to their whole life. The stuff they decided to sing about and the way they walked through the world. Cat Stevens sang about wanting to get a gun and shoot people down in 1970 but by 1985 he was on the *Peace Train*. There's an evolution happening. You can go on a journey with music.'

'Right, but that's why you love *music*. Why vinyl? One Christmas Dawn and I bought you a box set of *The Beatles*. Their complete catalogue on CD, do you remember?'

'Sure.'

'But you never listened to it. After you died we were cleaning out your office and we found it, still wrapped in plastic.'

'CD's give you the opportunity to skip songs.'

'So?'

'So, once you can skip you're in control. You can just play your favourite songs, instead of listening to the album as it was intended. I don't want to skip anything. You have to play the record as the artist intended it to be heard. Appreciate the good and the bad tracks. Take it as it comes Richie and try to enjoy it. I like vinyl because it just goes around and around like it's supposed to.'

'You could have listened to the CDs and just not skipped them. They would have been remastered, so they were better sound quality,' said Richie.

'I like what I like,' said Stephen with a smile.

'You know, after you died Dawn and I went through all your records. Some of them were in pretty bad shape.'

His father shook his head. 'Well you can't expect them to be perfect, can you? They're going to get scratched or dusty or warped. That's just the way it is.'

'I guess. I remember one of the worst ones was Pink Floyd's *The Wall*. It was all banged up. Did you play that one a lot?' asked Richie.

'Yeah. I loved that record. Do you want to hear it now?'

Stephen reached into his unlimited collection but his son stopped him.

'That's okay.'

'Did I ever tell you that I had tickets to see Pink Floyd?'

'No. Were they good?'

'I don't know. I never got there. Your grandmother died that afternoon.'

'Jesus.'

'We've spent some time together up here though,' said Stephen. 'Just being pleasant really, nothing too deep. It's nice to have her back though.'

Richie felt his mother's hand rest gently onto his shoulder.

'Are you going to try talking things over with May?' she asked.

'Yeah. It's just hard,' replied Richie.

'If it's hard… it might not be right. That's something you'll have to decide on your own. We love May,' said Helen, 'you know that?'

'I know you do.'

'At the end of the day we just want you to be happy. That's what every parent wants.'

'Thanks. I know.'

'Come here,' said Stephen, offering Richie his wrist.

'Why?'

'Stop overthinking things and just come here!' Stephen shook his head at his son, silently chiding him into obedience.

Richie took his father's forearm, eager to see whatever memory he was willing to share.

The world fell away, sending Stephen and Richie back into a modest home. His father was more vibrant and young than old photos had given him credit for. He had an untamed mop of curly hair and sideburns leading down towards a huge grin. Stevie Wonder played in the background. On the floor where he lounged there were two little kids. Richie recognised Dawn, several years older than him, bouncing around the room with a doll in each hand. Richie saw himself too, seated shirtless in an oversized cloth nappy.

'That's me,' he exclaimed.

'Sure is.'

'Why are you showing me this?' asked Richie.

'Keep watching…'

Richie observed as his sister left the room, crashing into furniture on her way. Little Richie looked forlorn at her departure, causing him to move. The infant forced himself upwards, using his father's knee for assistance. Stephen's face was still as he watched his son shift his torso and take two clear baby steps.

'Helen!' called his father's voice.

'What is it?'

Richie watched his mother enter the room, bursting with life. Helen smiled at her son as he continued to make tentative moves. She looked great, her hair longer than Richie had ever seen.

'I'll grab the camera!' she squealed, racing away again. Their son had fallen back onto his rear by the time she'd returned.

'You were both so young,' said Richie.

'We were all young once,' his father replied.

'So, why did you want me to see this Dad?'

'Because,' said Stephen with a wholesome smile, 'just like everything else in life you have to put one foot in front of the other if you want to get somewhere.'

'One step at a time, huh?'

'Absolutely. And try to smile once in a while. It will do you a world of good.'

In his mind Richie visualised the unique gates of Graceland, with their outlines of The King surrounded by musical notes. He'd only been to the home of Elvis Presley once during his life, years after May's death. He'd made the pilgrimage at the insistence of his sister Dawn, and the trip had been integral to his healing.

He wanted to go somewhere easy, to a place that brought him joy. During the twenty year jaunt into his life he'd mentally bookmarked a couple of 'happy places' and decided to go whenever he was in need of cheering up. Remembering that sunny day in Memphis, Tennessee brought a pleasant smile to Richie's face. He was looking forward to walking around the manor again and being in a place that he considered sacred ground. Richie was amazed at the life Elvis had built for himself. He envied the importance of The King.

The white lion statues that guarded the exterior seemed to stare through him. He wondered whether the white benches that they seemed to guard got any use, as it looked like groups were ferried straight past them every day. Richie had spent that warm July day looking through all kinds of Elvis memorabilia at the visitor's centre across the street. Records, movie posters and props, collectables, clothes, cars and even the famous plane that had chartered The King during his life. The only remaining sight to behold was the home where the great man had lived, and allegedly died. He walked past the monolithic white pillars and into the mansion.

Within the house a path was clearly marked. Tourists like Richie could make their way through the manor but there were many restricted areas. While he had been infinitely curious that day, Richie had stayed within the lines.

The living room was brighter than Richie remembered. All white sofas and carpet made the room feel sterile. The cushions on the fifteen-foot custom made sofa had no definition and were likely never used for their actual purpose anymore, just like the benches out the front. Richie admired the stain-glass windows as he made his way along the designated route past the jungle room.

In Elvis Presley's lounge room there was a huge U-shaped sofa, coated in decorative pillows. A white monkey statue sat on the coffee table and three classic television sets played on a loop.

'Check out that setup babe. *Three* TV sets!'

'Shit yeah! The King was as stylish as they come.'

It was a familiar voice that Richie hadn't noticed before. He turned to see where the statement had come from. Several feet away stood Austin and Leanne, dressed in matching red cowboy hats.

'Austin! Leanne!' When he'd lived this moment the first time Richie had no context for who these strangers were. He'd ignored their chatter, if he'd heard it at all. Only now did it click. As his avatar continued to tour the residence Richie strained to hear the Texans conversation.

'Do you think we could ever own three televisions?' asked Leanne.

'Now where the heck are we gonna keep 'em? We'd need *three* trailers first,' replied Austin with a laugh.

'That's why I love you. You're so smart!' stated Leanne happily.

'Love you too butterbean.'

They were out of earshot now, and Richie was heading away towards the rear of the property. He calculated the chances of them being at Graceland at the same time as impossibly small. *Had Austin and Leanne been allocated to their pocket of heaven randomly, or was there significance to their presence?*

In the meditation garden, the final resting place of Elvis Aaron Presley was covered in flowers. Richie felt badly for his parents and twin brother, whose gravestones were not decorated at all. This man's life had been celebrated every day since his death. When Richie had come here the first time after May's passing he'd realised he wanted to live again. He'd found inspiration here in Graceland, wanting to re-join the world and emerge from his sorrow. He'd wanted to leave a legacy.

Now he viewed the site for the museum it was. Everything was stuck in time, frozen forever as a shrine to Elvis. Richie had been stuck too, unwilling to accept his fate.

That was about to change. With all of the drama of Charlie and Brody's true parentage and the swapping of wives, Richie had momentarily forgotten about the tile. His life had ended prematurely and it was time to find out if Dan was responsible. He needed to know whether he'd been murdered.

Chapter Twenty-Four

A Little Less Conversation

The dinner party had been May's suggestion. None of them needed to eat for sustenance but the idea was that a familiar setting, with an activity they were all used to might normalise things again. May had catered the event with a dish known as *Fool's Gold*. It was a delicacy made famous by Elvis Presley, consisting of a hollowed out loaf of bread containing a pound of bacon, a jar of peanut butter and a jar of jam. It was something that would have been disgusting to serve in real life, but May was trying to placate Richie. He hadn't acknowledged the ridiculous sandwich but she knew he would see it as a peace offering. He'd quietly had several servings. Charlie and Brody had been invited, but declined - opting instead to meet Gandhi - resulting in it being just the four of them in attendance.

Dan had insisted they all try some of his famous butter chicken, claiming it was a family recipe. Richie was sceptical about its origins. There was no way to know without digging into Dan's memories. It tasted fine, but by no means famous. He imagined Dan thinking of the dish, and then reaching into a magic fridge for it.

Richie was still struggling with their new arrangement. Dan and May were still living in his place, and Jan had been spending all of her time with the twins. Richie was glad the boys weren't attending. He couldn't look at them, feeling only disappointment that they were Dan's. He was lonely, which was not an emotional state that he thought he ought to feel in such a supposedly wondrous place.

Austin and Leanne had disappeared, leaving no clues as to whether they were moved out of heaven, relocated to some other pocket or kicked out entirely. It was unsettling and nobody wanted to ask Angel about it. Their guardian had always played his cards close to his chest, so his silence on the topic wasn't out of the ordinary. The Texans were certainly badly matched, but Richie was now sure that nothing in heaven was as good as it seemed. Partners could be mismatched, relationships could be tainted. Nothing was sacred.

He'd had plenty of time to think, and during that time he'd concocted a plan. It had been weighing on his mind that if Dan knew about the twins, then it was in his best interests to 'get rid' of Richie. His neighbour had a motive and an opportunity.

What other explanation could there be? It was hard to ignore that after his death Dan had enjoyed a brand-new life and seamlessly slipped into a new family. *His* family. Richie was now convinced that Dan had killed him and subsequently stolen his life. It was all he could think about. It was unfair.

Now he just had to prove it.

'And that's how we got the swimming pool,' said Jan, finishing her story.

'It took a few weeks before we even checked your lottery ticket Richie,' added Dan.

'That's crazy!' said May. 'Aw, you're so unlucky honey. That you won the lottery right after your death.'

Richie was quietly fuming. He couldn't believe that his final lottery attempt had been successful and that he hadn't been able to enjoy it.

'How much did you win in the end?' asked May.

'One hundred and twelve thousand dollars,' reported Jan. 'It went a long way actually.'

'Well, that and Richie's life insurance,' added Dan.

'That was supposed to be for Janice,' said Richie. He tried to remain calm. The plan depended on it.

'Oh, Richie?'

'Yes May?'

'I forgot to tell you… Dan and I went to see my father.'

'You did?'

May nodded happily. 'It was incredible. I saw him at the concert-'

'That was the Elvis concert, right?' asked Jan.

'Yeah, that's the one.'

Richie remained silent, feeling out of the loop.

'So, I saw him at the concert with Violet and Penelope-'

'Who's Penelope?' asked Richie.

'Violet's soul mate.'

'Oh.'

'Anyway,' continued May, 'Angel placed my Dad on his own for now.'

'Because he doesn't have a soul mate?' asked Jan.

'Right. As you know my mother was responsible for his death…'

'Horrible business,' said Dan.

'Truly,' added Jan.

'Anyway, so he's by himself for now and Dan and I went to see him. I was able to show him so many parts of my life that he'd missed, like my wedding. We cried and cried. It was incredible to give him closure like that,' said May.

Dan nodded, enjoying the moment.

'You went with Dan?' asked Richie. 'I told you *I* wanted to take you to see your father.'

'Oh, don't be like that,' said Jan, bringing a glass of absinthe to her lips.

'I just happened to go with Dan this time… it's not a big deal,' replied May. 'Next time, yeah?'

'Uhuh.' It felt like a big deal to Richie but he let it go. May wasn't going to side with him anymore, not yet. But Richie knew everything would change by the end of the dinner party.

As the group were enjoying a calorie free dessert menu he decided to initiate his plan to expose Dan. 'I'd like to propose a game,' said Richie, as he tried to be nonchalant. The time for vindication was at hand.

May, Jan and Dan all stared at him expectantly.

'I think we should share some memories from our time on Earth.'

'What a lovely idea,' said May.

'What did you have in mind?' asked Jan.

'Our final memories. Our deaths,' said Richie.

'What?' May's enthusiasm changed to uncertainty. She still had uncomfortable memories of seeing her funeral.

'Why would you want to watch your death?' asked Dan hesitantly.

'Not just *my* death,' said Richie, 'all of our deaths.' He remembered his own demise quite clearly, having replayed it many times. The plan was to see it from a fresh perspective.

'Really?' Jan sounded sceptical.

'I don't know about you,' continued Richie, 'but I've been struggling with this transition. I know I've been… *difficult* to be around. I keep feeling anxious and emotional. I thought if we each watched ourselves die… just once… that maybe I could get some closure on the whole thing. Life, I mean.'

May looked over at Jan and Dan, as if deferring to them for the ultimate decision.

'Like how you gave your father closure,' stated Richie to May.

They each nodded slowly but did not speak up.

'Did you *not* want to see what happened to me?' asked Richie, pressing the issue further. He locked eyes with Dan, silently accusing him.

'Richie…' Jan scolded him with her tone.

'Look, I don't have anything to hide if that's what you're saying,' said Dan, who was sensing something untoward happening.

'If you've got nothing to hide then you won't mind showing me what happened that day. I've seen it from my point of view, but I'd like to see it from yours,' said Richie firmly.

'What do you think you'll see?' asked May.

'Probably nothing,' said Jan.

'*Definitely* nothing,' stated Dan.

'Look, Angel thought it might be therapeutic. We discussed it in our sessions.' Although this last part was a lie Richie believed it might just put him over the top.

'I'd be more than happy to watch together,' said Dan. 'If that's what you need.'

'Great.'

'I believe in healing, and if I can help you on your journey then that's what I'll do,' continued Dan, monologuing for an imaginary audience.

'Uh… great thanks,' said Richie.

This bold reaction was exactly what Richie had hoped for. He was finally going to see the full picture and find out the truth about that day. He couldn't wait to expose Dan to May and Jan.

May volunteered to go first, mostly to get it out of the way. Richie, Jan and Dan sat in a circle on the floor like obedient school children. They connected their bodies, linked to guarantee that they'd each be able to view May's final memory.

They were transported to the interior of her car as she zipped down a road at night. May looked tired, her dark hair dishevelled.

One headlight was noticeably dimmer than the other, which affected visibility somewhat. It was a snug fit in the hatchback, with parts of them floating both inside and outside, but nobody was uncomfortable. They were only there to watch. The vehicle hit a bump, launching May and the attached trio into the air slightly. Richie was suddenly nervous. While selfishly questioning whether or not Dan had anything to do with his own death, he had failed to consider whether he actually wanted to relive May's. Losing her had destroyed him, and here he'd invited it to happen again. Richie sat patiently, about to lose his wife and unable to do a thing.

There was a chirpy noise, and May received a text message. Dan angled his neck to read it.

'It's from you,' he said, looking over at Richie.

'Me?'

'Yeah. It's about picking up some milk.'

Richie had no memory of texting his wife on the night of her death, but the evidence was right in front of him.

May sighed and started to turn the steering wheel. She was doubling back as she'd passed the grocery store already. From out of nowhere a car without headlights on smashed into them with such force that in his shock Richie let go of May's wrist. It was an act of self-preservation. He was detached from the memory for a moment and able to breathe.

Whoa.

The smashing noise had been so loud and sudden. Dan, Jan and May all looked like zombies as they sat in silence, still inside the memory. Richie grabbed May's wrist and jumped back in. He returned to the scene and had a front row seat to her death. May was concussed and bleeding, the images around them blurring before fading to black.

'Geez. That was so much more visceral than I remember,' said May. 'It's so strange to watch your own death when you know it's coming. I still jumped though! You know, like when you're watching a scary movie and you know something's going to pop out at you? It was just like that!'

'A tragedy,' said Dan, offering May a compassionate furrow of his brow.

'Kind of a morbid thing to watch,' stated Jan, clearly objecting to the experience.

Richie looked at May, who seemed unchanged.

'But that was very brave of you,' said Jan, turning to May. 'Thank you for sharing it with us.'

'That's okay. I didn't mind so much actually. I thought it might depress me but Angel was right, that was pretty therapeutic.'

Richie said nothing as he tried to supress his true feelings about the memory. It was horrible, but he refused to acknowledge it. If he showed any doubt then perhaps Dan and Jan would refuse to continue, and he couldn't risk that.

'Does anyone want anything else to eat?' asked Jan, who had been playing hostess.

Everyone had indulged at the start of the dinner party but now, following the death of May none of them had an appetite.

'Who's going next?' asked Richie, trying to keep things moving in the right direction.

It was bizarre to see the future but it was a scene that Richie recognised straight away. It was the backyard of the home that he'd originally purchased with May before he'd married Jan. There were no yuccas in the rear of the house, which pleased him. They'd been removed and it looked very tidy. It wasn't a deep space, but it was roomy enough for a washing line and a small shed. The night sky was clear with the exception of a plane flying overhead.

There were two great shocks to be had. The first was seeing Jan as an old woman. She seemed impossibly frail, hunched and wrinkled. The most recognisable part of her was her eyes. The second shock was the fact that she was in a wheelchair. Jan shook slightly as she navigated the chair onto the wooden deck. It was a futuristic looking version of a wheelchair, but it was still just a cushioned chair with wheels.

This was the evening that Jan died.

'After Dan died I decided to move back into the old place,' announced Jan to the group. 'It was actually a lovely spot to live out my final years. Full of memories. I didn't have to modify anything really. I just added a ramp at the front.'

'We'd been trying to travel,' added Dan. 'Once the boys were older we were basically retired, so we just tried to enjoy our retirement. We rented out our place and saw the world. When we came back we lived in an apartment in the city for a while.'

'Sounds nice,' said May.

'It was nice,' said Jan. 'It was just easy to have a home base nearer to the airport with the amount of flights we took. Then, as I said, after Dan passed away I wanted to be settled again. So when the young couple renting our place moved out, I moved back in. I wasn't usually alone like this. I had a carer. Sometimes the boys visited.'

Richie wanted to ask what ailment Jan had suffered from. It seemed like once again May and Dan knew more than him. Jan had outlived him by half a century, meaning she would have enjoyed many advances in modern medicine. Perhaps whatever it was could be held at bay. Richie thought it was strange to see an old woman staying up so late. He'd always imagined that the elderly became tired earlier than most.

Jan wheeled out to the end of the deck and was looking into the distance at the cityscape. Richie could see some kind of laser light show in progress and some faint music that he didn't recognise.

'Wait for it...' said Jan.

'I'm nervous,' said May. 'Is something going to jump out at us?'

'No, but brace yourself...'

As she held the low railing the deck creaked and then collapsed in one awful motion. For a moment Richie thought that the additional weight of the group had caused the structure to break, before he remembered that they were effectively apparitions. The wheelchair bounced away and Jan's ageing body was pinned beneath a section of wood. She moaned in agony. A cloud of dust particles danced around them. Jan struggled against the debris but soon passed out, dying from her internal injuries. The scene dipped to black as Jan's life ended.

'Jesus!' exclaimed May when the vision concluded. 'Sorry.' She hadn't meant to take the Lord's name in vain.

'I know what you mean. You really feel it when it's *your* death,' said Jan.

'I guess its good that the deck didn't collapse and kill your tenants!' exclaimed May, trying to find a silver lining.

'That would have been awful,' said Jan, shaking her head.

'Right, my turn then?' said Dan. 'Unless you wanted to Richie?'

'No, go for it.' Richie adjusted his glasses.

The four braced themselves as Dan recalled his demise. They were shown a bustling city block where an impossibly virile Dan was walking down the street. He'd kept his hairline but it had transitioned to a complimentary shade of grey. Richie hated how attractive he still was. He was sure that Dan was wearing the latest futuristic fashions. The simple one-piece garment looked like it might have been made of hemp.

'You look great!' stated May.

'Thanks,' replied Dan.

The world seemed in a rush as it zipped around before them. Richie noticed the men looked like futuristic gentlemen with matching hemp material and hats, some with fitted black leggings beneath their three quarter pants. The women in the street were all in identical matching attire, unique only by the variety of vibrant colours. It was as though all the ladies had agreed upon a uniform but the hue was interchangeable.

'Hi Dan!' said one woman.

'Hello!' he replied.

Dan greeted several more friends on his walk.

The walls of the city buildings were littered with holographic advertisements for products like 'Ferm' and 'Gyropock.' Richie didn't recognise the tube-shaped products or the people endorsing them. The advertisements were all in black and white, which he found unsettling.

'This is so cool,' said May.

'The world keeps changing, huh?' said Dan.

'It certainly does.'

As they turned a corner they were startled to see a fire had engulfed one of the buildings. There was a huge commotion underway as fire fighters were evacuating office workers and escorting them across the street to safety. Dan looked up at the high rise, and saw a mass of debris that had started breaking away from the building. It appeared as if the concrete was about to slide and drop, onto the people below. A woman carrying a baby was oblivious to her impending doom, and the crew of fire fighters were too preoccupied to notice.

'Get out of the way!' called Dan. 'Move!'

It was no use. The noise of the crowd filled the air with confusion and she couldn't heed his warnings. The woman started fussing over her baby, jostling him on the spot. Dan, ever the man of action, ran towards the impending danger. Richie, Jan and May were dragged along too, getting a front row seat to his bravery. Dan's desperate shouting continued and soon he was standing beside the woman, steering her out of harm's way. Richie looked up and clocked the debris, now tumbling through the air above them. Dan saw it in his periphery and in one heroic movement he shoved the woman away. The debris landed on Dan and the world around them went dark.

'That was exhilarating,' said Jan as she cuddled up to her soul mate.

'What happened to the woman?' asked May, when they had returned to the dinner party.

'She survived,' said Jan. 'The baby was unharmed. Dan saved them both. They gave him a medal of bravery, posthumously of course. I had to accept it on his behalf.'

'As I recall that building hurt like hell,' said Dan with a chuckle.

'It's weird reliving it, isn't it?' Jan gave him a kiss.

'Yeah it's odd.'

'Thanks for sharing that,' said May, who still looked a little shaken by the experience.

'They made a movie about Dan a couple of years later. It was pretty good,' declared Jan.

'Did they?' asked Dan.

'I never told you about that? Oh, I'll have to let you hold my wrist while I remember watching it so you can see it! You'll love it,' decided Jan.

'And then there was one,' said May as she glanced over at Richie.

'I'm ready.'

Richie's moment of truth had arrived. They were all linked once more, swarming around his wrist. The party waited as Richie took a completely unnecessary breath. Suddenly they were in it.

'Can you water the garden afterwards?' called Janice, standing in the doorway of their home.

'Sure,' replied Richie as he headed to the door.

'Look how good you looked Jan,' said May.

'I know! That's *after* two kids too.'

The memory moved with Richie at its centre. Past the garden and its brownish plants, which he ignored. Past the yuccas. This time, with the benefit of hindsight Richie was staring at the roof of Dan's house. As they travelled closer he kept a close watch, hoping to spot his neighbour. Dan remained elusive.

They approached the ladder and Richie's voice called out on autopilot. 'Dan?' There was no answer. 'Dan? It's Richie from next door...'

He knew the tile was in transit, he could hear it sliding. Richie scrunched up his nose as the ceramic rectangle struck him, causing him to fall against the rocks below. As he succumbed to his injuries the four were zapped back to their dinner party.

'Wow. I had no idea,' said Jan. 'That was rough.'

'Was that... helpful to see?' asked May.

'Helpful?' Richie was confused.

'Yeah… therapeutic? Like Angel said it might be?'

'No. I need to see it again.'

'Richie? You can't be serious,' scoffed Jan. 'Nobody wants to watch you die again. That's not what we agreed to.'

'Why?' asked May, who took a more concerned position. 'What are you looking for?'

'I need to see it from Dan's point of view,' said Richie.

'What do you expect to see?' asked Dan.

'I think you know.'

'You think *I* dropped the tile on you, is that what you're hinting at?'

Richie didn't hesitate, 'Yes.'

May and Jan were speechless, the latter's mouth now ajar.

'Seriously?' said Dan. He'd started using his hands as he spoke, moving them about as though he were a motivational speaker. 'We were *neighbours* Richie. I thought we were friends.'

'We weren't friends,' said Richie.

'I thought we were adult male friends. Men that don't share all of their emotions, sure… but we were supposed to have each other's backs.'

'Right. Let's see what happened then… *friend*.' There was something different about Richie's eyes. He hadn't blinked during the entire exchange.

'I wouldn't do that to you,' stated Dan. 'You know that.'

'You slept with my wife. What else have you lied to me about.'

'Yes, I slept with Jan. That doesn't mean I killed you Richie.'

'Then show me. Prove it.'

'You don't have to do that Dan,' said May. 'Richie, what's gotten into you?'

'You said you didn't have anything to hide,' started Richie, 'and I *want* to believe you…'

'You don't trust *Dan*?' screeched Jan. 'It's *Dan*, for crying out loud.'

'I wouldn't do that,' said Dan defensively.

'So that tile just came loose? I died in a freak accident, did I? I refuse to believe that. It's fine for you Dan… you were a hero. I just got hit in the head on a Sunday morning.'

'It's done. Our lives are over. We have to move on,' said Dan.

'Stop trying to get out of this,' said Richie.

'I'm not trying to get out of it.'

'I can't move on unless you show me that you didn't kill me. I need to know.'

'Richie! Honestly…' Jan was losing it now, reminding Richie of her temperament during their last few months of marriage.

'No, it's alright,' said Dan calmly. 'I'll show him.'

'You really shouldn't have to,' said May.

'No… I do. I clearly do. I have to show him or he'll never believe me.'

Dan offered Richie his wrist and he accepted it gladly.

'When this is over I'd like you to apologise to me,' stated Dan.

'We'll see who owes who an apology,' retorted Richie.

May and Jan stood back, neither electing to review Richie's death from a fresh angle. The men re-watched the scene at the door, this time from Dan's viewpoint.

'I'd like to help… I would,' Richie said half-heartedly, 'but the twins are being a handful at the moment. You understand.'

'Sure, sure, no worries,' replied Dan.

Dan migrated back into his front yard with Richie along for the ride. He watched as his neighbour put headphones in his ears and started playing soft rock. They moved up a ladder and onto Dan's roof as he straddled the highest point of his home. He now wore a white singlet, his dirt-stained checked shirt happily tied around his middle. Dan went about his business, oblivious to the world around him. Richie scanned below, stretching himself away from his guide's wrist as much as he could without letting go. There was no sign of his living self, and no sinister plan in progress. A few minutes later Richie watched as a single tile slid unassisted and launched itself away from the roof. He heard the same fatal noise when it struck his skull. Richie listened to the sound of his body collapsing out of view. Dan was nowhere near it. Richie's death had been completely random, not a well executed murder.

'Are you alright?' asked May upon their return.

'I…' Richie was lost in his thoughts.

'I didn't have a hand in Richie's death,' announced Dan to the ladies. 'Like I said.'

'I knew it,' said Jan mockingly. 'See?'

This result was underwhelming to Richie. His life had ended in such a banal way. There was no legacy from his time on Earth. He wondered what kind of God would allow that to happen to someone. Richie became infuriated and immediately started lashing out.

'You took everything from me!' Richie yelled at Dan.

'Listen man, I wanted to be friends. I tried to be nice to you. You have always had some shitty problem with me.'

'You fucked my wife! You got her pregnant with twins! And then you… the *two* of you, just fucking let me die. How long did you wait, huh? Before you jumped back into bed together?'

'Calm down. There's no need for that kind of language,' said May. 'We can talk this out.'

'Richie, you were dead. It could have happened at any time. It was an accident and I'm sorry. I shouldn't have slept with Jan either. It happened so long ago that I guess we've both forgiven ourselves for it,' said Dan. 'But we should apologise to you too. It was wrong.'

'We *have* apologised!' shouted Jan.

'It's just a bit too late, isn't it?' Richie shouted back.

'So, you're not going to accept my apology?' Dan stretched out his hand, beckoning for Richie to shake it. 'Can't we just let bygones be bygones?'

He looked at May, once so unspoiled in his eyes. Richie glanced at Jan, whose face was sour and contorted. Neither woman loved him anymore. Dan had turned them both against him, one move at a time. The game was over and Richie had been declared the loser.

'You son of a bitch!'

Richie scrambled awkwardly at Dan. The element of surprise worked in his favour and the two tumbled to the floor, Dan in a state of shock. Suddenly finding himself on top of his opponent Richie aggressively pinned Dan's arm with his knee.

'What are you doing!' shrieked Jan, although neither of the wives tried to break up the scuffle.

'Richie! Let me up,' commanded Dan, in a deep voice.

He was so cocky, even in defeat. Richie refused to ease up. The idea of a fistfight in heaven seemed preposterous yet here they were, unable to settle their differences without one. Dan reached his right hand up and tried to free himself, only to be met with a ready block from Richie. Dan's arms were now pinned by a knee and a hand. Richie found himself in the fortunate position of having an unrestricted limb. Without thinking he wrapped his fingers around Dan's neck.

'Richie! That's enough!' May was sounding more and more like Jan.

Dan made some unintelligible sounds as he tried unsuccessfully to squirm out of the assault. Richie wasn't sure how this would end, but he didn't care. He certainly couldn't kill Dan again, as they were all sufficiently deceased already. Dan didn't need to breathe, and so he wasn't hurting him, merely subduing him temporarily. They didn't seem capable of inflicting physical pain either. It didn't matter. Choking his enemy felt fantastic. Richie felt powerful for the first time in his afterlife.

Then something unexpected happened.

The dinner party disappeared around the men and Richie found himself swimming in Dan's memories. He was confused but soon put two and two together. His left hand was curled around Dan's wrist.

Richie was now at the mercy of whatever memory came to Dan's mind.

Chapter Twenty-Five
Devil in Disguise

'Come here babe,' said Dan, as he lay shirtless at the head of the bed. His body was propped up by pillows. Richie sat helplessly nearby, ever the voyeur, trapped in the vision and refusing to release Dan from his grip.

A tattooed woman in her mid-twenties came out of the bathroom. She wore only underwear, her enhanced breasts pointing effortlessly forward. Richie noted that both of her arms were heavily inked, as was one side of her neck. He felt like an intruder, but he refused to release Dan.

'You ready to go again?' the voluptuous woman asked, climbing towards Dan. Her eyes were cat-like, as were her slinky movements.

'I was just feeling lonely,' said Dan.

'You miss your wife?'

'No. She'll be back next week.'

The visualisation of Dan reached past Richie and took two pills out of the top drawer of the bedside table. He put them on his tongue and raised his eyebrows. The woman French-kissed him, before proudly sticking out her own tongue. She'd managed to procure one of the pills during the frenzied movement, leaving the other for Dan. They consumed them before he removed the final piece of fabric from her body. They swam in the sheets, connecting at regular intervals.

Richie tightened his grip on Dan's neck and the scene changed.

Suddenly Dan was passionately kissing another woman with ample cleavage. They were on a park bench near a lake. It looked like mid-morning and there was nobody else around.

'Oh Ellie, I'm so sorry about Zach,' said Dan, in between embraces.

'It's his loss...'

Ellie knelt down in front of Dan and unzipped his pants. Richie instinctively looked away as Ellie fellated Dan enthusiastically. After several minutes Richie felt pressure against his torso. Dan was trying to distract him with these memories so he could escape. Richie could also sense more limbs, perhaps belonging to May or Jan, tapping him. The actions felt distant and he was able to ignore them. Dan's tactics increased as he forced Richie to witness each and every tawdry sexual encounter that crossed his mind.

A redhead in nurses scrubs.

A brunette peeling off her Lycra workout gear.

A blonde in a spa bath with nipple clamps.

A purple haired woman inexplicably dressed in steampunk cosplay gear.

Librarians, Ski Instructors, joggers, walkers, train companions.

Richie had to endure countless thrusts, bodies slapping together, hand jobs, blowjobs, cunnilingus, anal and so many collected orgasms replayed one after the other. It was hard to stay focussed. But with everything Dan threw at him, Richie held on. The men remained in their standoff.

One night stand after one night stand, sometimes two women at a time, happily gave themselves to Dan. It felt like they were lined up to get into his bed like cars in traffic, patiently waiting for their turn at the front.

Richie screamed in frustration and the scene changed, like someone shaking clean an Etch-A-Sketch.

Dan couldn't speak, but he must have realised that his tactics were failing. He'd upgraded his assault from the equivalent of ground troops to metaphorical nuclear weapons.

When the dust had settled Richie was looking at Janice and Dan. The setting was soon after they'd moved in together. Richie knew instinctively that this was the moment they'd had their affair. This event had culminated in Jan's pregnancy. He'd wanted to see it before, but not anymore. Richie was fuming.

'We shouldn't…' said Jan, catching her breath.

'Okay… you're right. It's just that when I saw you I knew. It was like destiny or something.'

Jan had always believed in fate, and this line of reasoning seemed to be just enough to tempt her into continuing.

'Destiny? You believe in that sort of thing?'

'Of course,' replied Dan. 'I read my horoscope every morning. Our lives aren't just random chance. There's a reason that you were brought into my life. Something cosmic.'

'I'm with Richie though… we only *just* moved in together.'

'I know that… but I think there's something here… something bigger than both of us. I think maybe we met in a past life. Maybe you're my soul mate.'

'You're crazy,' said Janice, blushing red. She was enraptured with the attention.

'I don't think I am,' he replied and kissed her. 'You moved in next to me. I think that might be a sign.'

Janice seemed more passionate with Dan than she'd ever been with him. Watching her yearn for this man was too much.

Richie let go of Dan's wrist for a moment and saw the women staring at them. Jan's eyes were full of hate while May looked extremely disappointed.

He pressed back onto Dan's wrist and experienced Jan and Dan's first sexual encounter from an uncomfortably close proximity. There was no turning back now. Richie was committed to seeing this through to the end, no matter what Dan did. In that moment Richie wouldn't let go.

'Is it straight?'

'Looks good to me,' replied Dan.

'Thanks for coming out to the farm. We're really glad you and Mum could be here.' Charlie smiled. He looked so grown up in a suit and tie.

'We wouldn't have missed this for the world,' said Dan.

'I love you Dad.'

'Love you too Charlie.'

The men hugged. Richie could smell Charlie's aftershave, which was a pungent sandalwood concoction.

'You ready to do this?' asked Dan.

'Absolutely.'

Charlie and Dan walked out of a barn and into a nearby field. At the top of the paddock was an arch made of flowers. Dan led his son past rows of wedding guests, who were seated on long custom-made log seats. Richie didn't recognise any of the faces until they reached the front row.

There sat Jan, resplendent in pink. She had a walking stick beside her but was sitting up straight. To her right was a woman who must have been Brody's wife. She had two identical twin boys with her that must have been about six or seven. Brody was wearing the same grey suit as Charlie. He waited patiently at the archway. Dan shook his son's hand and sat down next to Jan. Richie could see shades of Dan in his grandchildren's faces. His genetic material lived on.

Nearby a harp was played and a young woman made her way to Charlie. She looked so pleased, as if this was the height of everything she wanted. There was no need for bridesmaids or groomsmen, it was just this young couple. The bride's face told the tale: she was hopelessly in love. Richie couldn't remember if May or Jan had looked at him with such elation. He didn't think so.

'Do you Charlie Jonathan McKellen take this woman to be your lawfully wedded wife? To have and to hold in sickness and in health?'

'I do.'

Dan slipped his arm around Jan. Richie cringed at the word *McKellen*. It was Dan's last name. His boys were part of the McKellen clan now.

'And do you Cora Annabelle Whittaker take this man to be your husband, in sickness and in health for as long as you both shall live?'

'I do.'

The marriage was sealed with a kiss and a huge celebratory cheer. Charlie turned around and hugged Brody while Cora spoke to some friends. Dan looked so proud of his sons.

This moment felt far worse than seeing the display of Dan's sex life. This was more personal and painful to Richie. Not only did Dan not kill him, he'd had the better life.

Richie didn't have to wait very long before the scene changed. It took a moment for him to realise where they were.

It was May.

It was heaven.

How?

Dan was reliving a moment here in heaven. Dan was lying in bed with May, cupping her head with his hand. Richie didn't even know this was possible. How was Dan reviewing a memory from heaven? The data of their afterlife was being stored and catalogued as well. This event must have been during the wife swap, when Richie had moved in with Jan. May stared lovingly at him, directly at him. But the love wasn't for Richie, it was for Dan. He'd encroached on Richie's heaven in exactly the same way he'd encroached on Richie's life.

'This has been so great,' said May.

'Thank you for saying that,' Dan's voice replied.

'You've really helped.'

'I'm glad.'

The memory ended and Dan refused to show him anything else. There was no context for their words. The lack of clarity infuriated Richie. He blinked and the dinner party came back into focus.

With no more distractions Richie was forced to acknowledge May and Jan were staring at him. There was no love in their eyes.

There was no hope for reconciliation. He'd lost them and he knew it.

'Aaaaaarrrgh!' Richie squeezed with all of his might as he tried to kill Dan all over again.

Chapter Twenty-Six

If I Can Dream

It was pointless.

Richie couldn't kill Dan and there was no way to change anything. He released his grip and started to weep.

'What a waste of time,' said Jan. She had been sipping white wine during the scuffle.

'What was that about? You know Dan didn't kill you,' offered May. She was the only one who was at all sympathetic. Dan and Jan retreated to the safety of the living room, putting some space between them.

'He ruined my life,' said Richie matter-of-factly.

'No, he didn't.'

'He was an opportunist! He waited around and stole everything from me.'

'Richie. When I died do you know who I was thinking about?' asked May.

'No.'

'You. I was so upset that I'd never see you again. And here we are. Do you know how lucky we are to have this?' May placed a hand on Richie's shoulder. 'I'm not mad that you married Janice. I'm glad you were able to find happiness again.'

'That's not the same thing. I mourned for you. I thought about killing myself...' Richie sobbed.

'I'm glad you didn't,' said May, 'or we wouldn't be together right now.' She was thinking about her brother Arthur and his absence from heaven due to suicide.

'Me too.'

Dan seemed to have recovered, and he and Jan re-entered the room.

'Jan mourned for you too,' said Dan. 'You asked me how long we waited before getting together? About two years. She loved you more than you know.'

'Is that true? You waited two years?' asked Richie, wiping his nose out of habit.

'Yes.' Janice looked sorrowful as she thought back on it. 'I'm not going to relive that for you Richie. It was a heartbreaking time. And it was private. Mourning is something you do by yourself.' For the first time Richie recognised that he may have been selfish.

'I know it hasn't been easy,' said Dan. 'Nothing in life prepares you for dying.'

'All of you are handling this so well. You're all so wise and spiritual. Aren't you mad? Don't you wish you were still alive?' asked Richie.

'No!' said Jan. 'Have you ever stopped to this about whether growing old was a good thing? Your body gets worse you know. It fails you in ways you can't imagine. In some ways dying young is a blessing.'

'We had our time. I'm thankful for it,' said May. 'Even if it was less time than I thought I'd get... I got to spend it with you. Can't you see that?'

'You're supposed to be making up for it here, in heaven,' scolded Jan. 'You have all the time you want now!'

'I know you'd convinced yourself that I'd murdered you,' said Dan. 'Aren't you at least glad I *didn't*?'

'Not really. This feels even more empty.' Richie had stopped crying. He now looked like a man that had no fight left.

There was a knock on the door. May opened it to reveal Angel.

'Can I come in?'

'Of course,' replied May.

Angel approached the group, his face awash with disappointment. His bare feet stopped directly in front of Richie.

'Are you finished with your outburst?' asked Angel.

'My outburst?'

'You strangled Dan. Why did you do that? It is very unbecoming behaviour.'

Richie didn't have a decent answer. 'I was angry,' he mumbled.

'We should be mad with *you* Richie! You texted May out of the blue for milk. That's why she turned around and that's why she died. You're the one that booked those dodgy contractors who cut corners on that shitty deck… you killed *us*!' said Jan.

'Well… not me,' said Dan.

Richie picked himself up from the floor and stood. He hadn't considered his involvement in their deaths before. Richie had inadvertently causing May's accident. And when they'd first made minor renovations to the house, Jan had wanted to hire a more reputable company to build the deck out the back. Richie had insisted on the cheap option, which must have rusted or become structurally unsound over time. The deck collapse was partially his fault too. In trying to prove Dan had killed him, Richie had only shed light on his own accomplishments.

'You know, when I got married I thought I'd be with my wife til the day I died. I thought May would be there at my bedside as I closed my eyes for the last time. But do you know what happened? She died, all alone. *I* died alone too… all of us were alone at the end.'

'I actually had a large crowd around *me* when I died,' chimed in Dan.

'Nobody cares Dan!' called Richie.

'Richie…' Angel's expression had changed to one of pity.

'I guess what I'm trying to say is that life didn't turn out how I planned. And that's disappointing.'

'You can't plan things,' agreed May, 'Sometimes things just happen.'

'You used to be a planner, you know.'

'And look how that worked out for me,' said May.

'And it wasn't all bad,' said Richie with a smile. 'Some of it was great. I understand now why you didn't want to watch back your deaths… why you only focussed on the good parts of life. That stuff was worth remembering. I should have listened to you all.'

'Don't worry about it,' said Dan. 'These things happen.'

Richie took a breath. 'I'm… I'm *sorry* I tried to strangle you Dan.'

'Apology accepted.'

'And I'm sorry I texted you May… I'm sorry I insisted we build such a crappy deck Jan.'

They both nodded their appreciation for the gesture.

'It is time to go,' said Angel.

'What?'

'Time for you to go Richie.'

'But I apologised…'

'Yes, you did.'

'But… can't I stay?'

'No. Please say goodbye.'

'I…' Richie wasn't sure what to do.

May stepped forward and took his hands in hers. 'I'll talk to your parents. I'll make sure they're okay.'

'Thanks.'

May hugged him for a long time. When she finally let go Richie could see she'd been crying. 'I love you,' she managed, before giving him a quick kiss on the lips.

'I love you May,' he replied.

'Bye Richie. I love you too,' said Jan. 'Take care, okay?'

Richie was becoming numb, uncertain of what would happen next.

'And I love you,' added Dan. 'You're one of my best friends.'

Wordlessly Angel led Richie out of the house. Heaven was no longer a place he could stay. Dozens of thoughts presented themselves to Richie. *Was he about to be punished? Would he be banished to hell?*

When they were standing outside the house it suddenly occurred to Richie that the experiences he'd had since dying; the impotency, Dan's behaviour, the coveting of wives, his children's true parentage and the affairs were all negative. *Hadn't Angel said that heaven was supposed to be an overwhelmingly positive place?*

'Was *that* hell?' he asked. 'Was I in hell all this time?' asked Richie.

'No,' answered Angel. 'That was heaven, you just messed it up.'

'I did, didn't I?'

'I told you that everyone affects the world around them, that you see what you want to see,' said Angel. 'You have to accept that you arrived in this place with a chip on your shoulder. A grudge. You were not reasonable. You made enemies.'

'I didn't know any of this was going to happen. I expected to be worm food.'

'Richie, whatever you did or did not do in life… they would have forgiven you. You only needed to ask.'

Richie started to cry again. He sobbed for a moment but when Angel did not comfort him he composed himself. 'What is to become of me?'

'That is not for me to decide,' replied Angel.

Richie realised that the neighbourhood was far behind them now, even though they seemed like they had been standing still. 'Where are we going?'

'To see God.'

'Really? *The* God?'

'Yes.'

'The big man?' asked Richie.

'Shortly… yes.'

'What's God like?' asked Richie.

The molecules around them swirled and they were back in the therapy room for one final session. Angel sat comfortably opposite Richie as he pondered the question.

'He is exactly as you imagine him to be, which is to say he appears differently to everyone. You will see what you want to see.'

Richie removed his glasses, saw that they were spotless and decided to put them back on. 'What does he look like to you?' asked Richie.

'That is personal,' stated Angel with a secret smile.

Angel was so content and calm. He seemed all knowing too, which gave Richie a revelation.

'You're God, aren't you?' he exclaimed.

'Me?'

'Yes. I should have known from the minute we met. You're God! That makes so much sense. That's why you're always watching us, isn't it?'

'You are trying to solve heaven like a puzzle. You cannot use logic when you have such limited knowledge. Why are you jumping to conclusions again? It has only brought you misinformation and pain,' said Angel. 'I am not God.'

'Bullshit.'

'I would not lie about this.'

'Then who are you? Just a random angel that's supervising us? This is *your* pocket of heaven, huh? And you're not God?'

'I am no-one of consequence.'

'But you're an angel? Without any wings?'

'You are lashing out at me Richie. Try to stay calm. Everything is as it should be.'

'Stay calm? I just assaulted Dan. Attempted murder. I'm probably going to hell, right?'

'Why would you think that?'

'God is spiteful… I don't know. I don't know!' Richie was bursting with nervous energy. Not knowing what his punishment would be was wearing on him now. He wished he hadn't acted so foolishly. His impulsive attack had been the last straw.

'You were not a man of faith,' stated Angel. 'But you should try to be now.'

'What if you're wrong? What if there really isn't a plan? What if he evaporates me and that's that?' If it was possible to sweat in the afterlife Richie would have been perspiring profusely. He could feel himself losing his grip. Surrendering to a higher power, literally, was never something he saw for himself as an atheist.

'Do you believe he will evaporate you? Truly?'

'I guess not.'

'There is a plan for us all,' offered Angel.

'I had two chances at happiness on Earth and two chances in heaven. Like you said… I messed everything up.'

'Richie, listen to me. God works in mysterious ways. I know you believe that to be a cliché but clichés exist for a reason. Consider me for example. My mother died when she was pregnant with me. I was never born, yet I live here in heaven.'

'What?'

'I asked to supervise this particular pocket because the inhabitants are very important to me. I wanted to meet them, selfishly. You think that you don't matter? That your life amounted to nothing? You are wrong. If nothing else, your life amounted to me.'

Angel smiled. For the first time Richie noticed the dimples in his cheeks. The eyes before him were coffee-coloured like May's. The features of his face were familiar for a reason.

Angel was his son. *Had he always looked like that?* Everything before this moment seemed inconsequential suddenly. Angel's face looked different now. The truth was finally available to Richie, like a key had been turned unlocking a box of secrets.

'You're *my* son?' he asked, needing to hear confirmation.

'Yes.'

'May is your mother?'

'Correct.'

'Does she know?'

'Not yet.'

'Why don't you tell her? She'd love to meet you I'm sure,' said Richie.

'I will… but she is not ready yet.'

'I'm not sure I'm ready yet either,' confessed Richie.

'Well, whether you are ready or not we are out of time. I do not think you will be returning to the cul de sac,' said Angel, hanging his head a little.

'There's so much I want to say,' said Richie. 'I've thought about you so often, and wondered what you'd be like. I… I *love* you. I know that's crazy to say but I love you.'

'I also love you,' replied Angel.

The two men hugged for a long time. It felt as though each man needed it as much as the other.

'I hope I did not hamper your experience in heaven. I suppose that knowing you were my father forced me to be more hands off than I was with the rest of the neighbourhood.'

'You were leaving me alone on purpose?' asked Richie.

'I was afraid of saying the wrong thing and exposing myself.'

With Richie's impending departure this turn of events felt cruel. 'I don't want to go. Not after finding out the truth.'

'While our time together was short, know that I am forever changed through our meeting… Dad,' said Angel.

'You… you just called me Dad,' said Richie with a smile.

'I sure did.'

'Will you tell May? When she's ready to hear it?'

'Absolutely.'

'And will you take care of them? Dan, Jan and May?'

'I promise. And I probably owe you an apology,' said Angel.

'You do?'

'Yes. Upon reflection I have come to realise that a part of me wanted to keep you here, and make sure you and my mother were together.'

'How do you mean?' asked Richie.

'I may have influenced you to choose her over Janice, because I needed to see you two together. To know my parents and see their happiness, even if it was just for a short while,' said Angel. His words were full of hidden sorrow.

'I never thought I'd ever get to meet you… to know you,' said Richie.

'It is special for me too.'

'Now that I know the truth, I see myself in you.' Richie and Angel had the same curly hair, the same build. 'It's like I sent a part of me on ahead… to heaven.'

'It has been an honour to know you father.'

'Been? What happens now?' asked Richie. 'I was supposed to be May's soul mate and now she's alone.'

'You can leave this place knowing that I will look after May. You have got bigger things to worry about. I promise that everything will be okay,' said Angel reassuringly.

'Thank you.'

'It is time to go. God will see you now.'

Chapter Twenty-Seven

<u>Return to Sender</u>

'This is it. The end of the road.'

Angel had transported the two of them to a void. There were no clouds, or houses, no façade at all. They now stood on nothing, with more nothing stretching out in all directions.

'This is where God lives?' asked Richie.

'No, but this is where the two of you will talk.'

'Where is this place?'

'Just another part of heaven. It is a vast realm that is hard to comprehend. It would take an eternity to see it all.'

'Will you wait with me?'

Angel shook his head. 'Unfortunately, it is time to say goodbye.'

'Okay.'

'It has been my pleasure getting to know you,' said Angel.

'Same. Thank you for looking out for me. Sorry I caused so much trouble.'

'Good luck Richie. Maybe we shall see each other again sometime soon.'

'I hope so.'

They hugged again before Angel slipped away, leaving Richie alone. He felt weightless, as if he were floating; yet he could sense his feet against an invisible surface.

'Hello?' he called out to no one in particular. The sound didn't echo, rather vanishing as soon as it left Richie's mouth.

'Hey there.'

The response caused Richie to pivot on the spot. Standing a few feet away was the King of Rock and Roll himself: Elvis Presley. He wore a classic flared white jumpsuit, fashioned with countless sequins. His eyes were hidden by oversized sunglasses.

'Are you… *him?*'

'Am I Elvis?'

'No. Are you God?'

'Yes sir.'

He removed the sunglasses. The resemblance to the real Elvis Presley was impeccable.

'Why do you look like Elvis?' asked Richie.

'That's what you need man. Subconsciously I guess you see me as The King. This felt like the most appropriate way to meet you. Would you have preferred I looked liked Ritchie Valens?'

'No. I guess not.'

'Alright then.'

'What should I call you?'

'Elvis or God. Either way.' His voice was far better than any impersonator. It was pitch perfect, as close to the genuine article as possible.

'I never got to meet Elvis in heaven. I never went to see him in concert. I guess I thought there would be more time.'

'You thought you'd have forever, huh?'

'Yeah.'

'Well sir, all good things come to an end.'

'Does this have to be the end? I don't want to leave. I'm not ready.'

'I can't forgive this silly old behaviour. It's done,' replied God.

'But isn't that kind of what you do? Aren't you all about turning the other cheek?'

'Look at you. You're an expert on me, huh? You didn't really think I existed until you died.'

'That's true. Sorry about that.'

'I forgive you.'

'See! That right there! You're all about forgiveness,' said Richie. 'Please. I've only just met my son.'

'I know. I know all,' he said in his unique Memphis drawl.

'I'm sorry. I'll do whatever it takes.'

'You can't stay here Richie. You don't belong here.'

Fear flooded in as Richie realised what that meant.

'Am I going to hell?'

Elvis pulled a funny face, chuckling with a raised lip. 'No.'

'No?'

'That's right.'

'But I don't belong here? So where am I going?' asked Richie.

'You're going to be reincarnated.'

'Is that a real thing?' asked Richie.

Elvis swaggered from one leg to the other. 'Of course. All of the myths you've heard about heaven during your life are based on half remembered dreams of this place. When you read about

somebody that died for a few minutes on the operating table…
they came here. You bet they did.'

'Really?'

'Yes sir. They saw something but they can't remember all of
the details. Sometimes folks who get reincarnated a few times can
remember *more* details, but it's still hidden in the dark recesses of
the mind.'

'As?'

'What are you asking me there Rich?'

'Will I be reincarnated as… *myself* or something else?'

'Your soul will be attached to a new body. It's a fresh start.
You'll have a second chance at life.'

'So, I'll be a baby again?'

'You'll be born again, yes. You don't get born as a full grown
man, do you?'

'That's it? I just try again?' shrugged Richie. 'I won't
remember this, will I?'

'No. Probably not.'

'Then what was the point? Are you going to reincarnate May
too?'

'Yes. If she wants. May is more than likely going to spend
some time with your son Angel before she makes up her mind
about all that.'

'But I can't?'

'No. Sorry man.'

'Jesus…' Richie realised his faux pas and added, 'sorry.'

'Thank you, thank you very much,' said God with a flawless Elvis impression.

Richie reached into his pockets and felt they were full. He turned them inside out to find dozens of salt and pepper packets.

May.

Richie had no idea she'd placed them there, concluding May had slipped them in when they'd hugged.

'So, that's that. All my anxiety, everything I felt is just… done?' asked Richie.

'It will be, yes.'

'I stuffed everything up.'

'If that's true then you ought to embrace a second chance.'

'This would be like… my tenth chance,' surmised Richie.

'All the more reason to give it your all. Maybe next time you'll hit the right note.'

'But I don't want this. What if I don't want to be reincarnated?'

'Well, nobody really refuses it. And it's a one time offer.'

'It's now or never, huh?' said Richie dryly, quoting one of his favourite Elvis tracks.

'You like that record, huh?'

'Yeah it's one of my favourites.'

'Have you been listening to a lot of records here in heaven?'

Richie realised that since his death he hadn't listened to a single album. The activity he'd savoured during his life had been cast aside. Given eternity, Richie hadn't been able to enjoy it.

'Listen, you know all of that anxiety you brought up?'

'Yeah.'

'This will wipe that away,' offered God. 'You'll be the same old soul, with the same moral compass. It's up to you where that leads you. The essence of you… that spark… will be passed on.'

'But I'm not good at starting again.'

'Nonsense. You were married twice. Even in the face of adversity you've proven that you can start again. I believe in you Richie.'

'But what if I fail?'

'You might,' declared God. 'Big deal.'

'That's not very reassuring.'

'I'm going to tell you something that I don't usually share. We've been here before. You and I.'

'We have?' asked a dumbfounded Richie.

'Of course we have,' he replied. 'You've stood there, wondering whether you should be reincarnated. I've stood here and convinced you that you should try it.'

'And I've been convinced each time?'

'Yes.'

'How many times have I been reincarnated?' asked Richie.

'Dozens.'

'Dozens? And I *keep* messing it up?'

'You're a real glass half empty kind of guy, aren't you?'

'Sorry.'

'Don't apologise. Every time I send you back you've connected with someone. You find yourself a soul mate. This time it was May. While you thought she was the answer to the question of your life the truth is that she wasn't. The yin to your yang is still out there, waiting.'

'They are?'

'Yes.'

'This is a lot to take in,' said Richie.

'I know. Nobody gets it right the first time. Not even me,' said God.

'But what if I choose the wrong person again? What if I make mistakes?'

'You *will* make mistakes. That's life. Then you'll try again. You'll live as many lives as you need to. People choose one another and get it wrong all the time. Half the couples on Earth get divorced for crying out loud. People grow and change. You might wake up one day and realise the person beside you isn't the same person you thought you were marrying. That's the way it goes. But I promise, one day everything will fall into place.'

'But… you know *everything*. Can't you just help me? Point me in the direction of my soul mate and I'll do the rest.'

'It's not about the destination,' said God, 'it's the journey. Finding love and happiness wont mean anything if you don't earn it. Did you know that Elvis Presley got a C for music in High School?'

'I didn't know that.'

'A C grade is considered a fail. Did Elvis let that stop him?' asked God, grinning from ear to ear.

'I guess not.'

'Then you shouldn't let this little setback stop you.'

'But I won't remember! I won't remember any of this!'

'Your soul will. With every trip back and forth the shape of your soul changes until one day it finds the form it's meant to hold.'

'You've got all of the answers, don't you?'

'Most of them.'

'Must be nice.'

'To know everything?'

'Yeah.'

'It's better not to know. Life is much more full of delight and surprise that way.'

Richie looked his hero Elvis Presley in the eye and knew that somewhere within his soul he would remember this moment. It was overwhelming and powerful. He would try with every fibre of his being to bottle this interaction and keep it in his heart.

'Okay,' he said. 'Reincarnate me.'

'Are you sure that's what you want? You want to be reincarnated?'

A clean slate.

The choice to try again, make better moves and be more. It was impossible to deny his desire for another go at things.

'Absolutely,' stated Richie.

'As you wish. You'll leave this place and go with Angel. He will ferry you onwards.'

'Thank you, for… *everything*… I guess.'

'You're welcome.'

Richie smiled, knowing that in a moment he'd be free of his ever-growing worries about May, Jan, Dan, Angel and the universe. He'd never see his parents or Charlie and Brody again, but that was okay. It was the way things needed to be.

Richie would happily start anew, while holding on to the feeling that somewhere deep within himself he'd met the most powerful being in existence and been blessed with another in a string of chances.

Richie was determined not to waste it. No matter how improbable the odds were that he'd find the yin to his yang, with any luck he'd one day feel what heaven ought to feel like.

It was all just another short lifetime away.

Chapter Twenty-Eight

The Wonder of You

'This is what you want?' asked Angel. 'You are quite sure?'

'Yeah. This is the only choice I have left,' replied Richie. There was a sadness in his voice that felt final. He was done fighting and ready to accept his banishment. 'I wish we had more time.'

'And yet we had more than enough,' replied Angel with a smile.

'This is all so strange.'

Angel furrowed his brow, deep in thought. 'Reincarnation is not the *only* choice…' he said quietly, before trailing off.

'What are you saying?'

'God would not have to know,' stated Angel.

'He's God! What are you talking about?'

'I can send you back.'

'Where would I go?' asked Richie.

'Leave that to me. While God is all-powerful he is not as all seeing as you would believe. That is why he tasks the management of heaven to his angels. I told you that heaven is vast. If you trust me, I can hide you.'

'But what if he finds us? Won't you be in trouble too?'

'He will not find us. Consider it a parting gift from me to you.'

Richie pondered his choices. He could either start a new life right now as a newborn or roll the dice with whatever his son wanted to try. It was an easy choice.

'Let's go,' said Richie.

'Okay. Thank you for trusting me,' Angel replied, before hugging his father tightly.

'What do I do?'

'Hold my wrist for a moment.'

Richie did as he was told. It felt like he'd been tossed by a powerful wave. Initially Richie couldn't stop reality from spinning, but when it did he found himself sitting at a familiar table.

'What are you smiling about?' demanded Janice, in a very quiet voice. She had wandered into their dining room while he'd been trying to figure out where he was.

'Janice?'

'Shhh… Charlie and Brody are asleep.' She sat down and tied her fair hair into a ponytail using a black elastic band from her wrist.

The scene was eerily familiar to Richie, having revisited his life so frequently. He looked around the room. *Was he back?*

'I want to have another baby,' said Janice.

'What?' Richie couldn't believe what he was hearing.

'Well, I wanted to go back to work… but now I don't. I've changed my mind,' said Janice. 'I think we should start trying.'

Richie paused and removed his glasses. Things were blurry without them. *He was back.* He put his glasses back on.

'You don't really want another baby,' he said.

'Yes, I do.'

'You have the twins. That's enough I think.'

'But I'd really like to try. Can you think about it at least?'

'Janice…'

'Yeah?'

'If you want another baby, why don't you talk to Dan,' said Richie flatly.

'Dan? I don't understand…'

'I know he's Charlie and Brody's father.'

'Don't be ridiculous,' said Janice, turning away from him.

'It's okay. I don't care anymore.'

Janice stared at him, unable to believe what she was hearing. 'What have you and Dan been talking about?'

'Honey, I don't love you anymore,' said Richie. 'You don't love me. I'm leaving you.'

'Are you serious? What the fuck Richie?'

Without warning Richie started laughing. Angel had sent him back to the day he'd died. He remembered *everything*. Janice looked furious, the power dynamic having shifted between them.

Suddenly Richie hopped up from his chair. He bounced towards the front door, crashing into it as he flung it open. The noise of it hitting the side of the house immediately woke the children.

As Charlie and Brody cried out for their mother, Richie paused at the edge of his property. He looked up in anticipation and held his breath. After a few moments a tile slid off the roof and cracked onto the ground below. He had avoided his death.

Standing outside in his sunken front yard Richie spotted a familiar face. Fitty was perched on the fence, soaking in the rays of the sun. He approached the feline, took a breath and picked him up. *Fitty was warm.* He shouldn't be here, but neither should Richie. They were both being given a second chance. Richie silently thanked Angel and stroked Fitty happily. He mewed with contentment and looked away, withdrawing affection.

Richie took another breath. The air tasted better here than it had in heaven. Birds flew overhead and somewhere in the distance a jackhammer pierced the earth. Everything felt right. His life would continue and he'd be able to change it. He'd divorce Janice and leave her to be with Dan. There was no sense in fighting with destiny.

As Richie returned to his living room he realised that Charlie and Brody were still crying. He turned the corner and saw Janice furiously smashing his father's record collection to pieces. She worked quickly, pulling the discs from their cases and snapping them in two. On the floor was a growing pile of useless black plastic.

Richie wasn't mad, he was grateful. He'd find new music in time.

Just outside, hidden from view stood Angel. His bare feet rubbed against the grass as he watched the scene. He saw his would-be-father's joy through the window and knew that this next phase of their adventure would bring them both what they needed.

'So, you can *change* soul mates? That's allowed?'

The angel that stood before May had introduced himself as Jessie. He had a mess of dark hair, worn long down past his shoulders. He had a tan coloured shirt and loose white pants. As he was only the second guardian angel that May had encountered she found the dress code interesting. Both of them had worn plain outfits and had bare feet. Jessie had wasted no time shaking up their little neighbourhood.

'Yes, although it is not a fact we share with everyone,' said Jessie calmly. 'Not every pairing of soul mates needs to be romantic. That kind of thinking is a very human idea. Your partner could be a friend, a teacher or someone you knew very briefly during your life. The important thing is that your soul mate left an impression on your soul.'

'Do I just pick a new one?' asked May, trying to get her head around the idea. 'That might take some thought.' She was starting to see the appeal of watching back her entire life in real time. Richie might have had it right after all. May didn't want to make a mistake and choose the wrong person.

'God foresaw that you might need a new soul mate. I would like to propose that we place you with your father Adam.'

'I'd like that.'

It was the most elegant solution. Without her mother or brother to choose from the pairing was logical. May sensed that she was the reason he'd been held in heaven after all, waiting for Richie to spit the dummy. If God knew this was all going to happen, then he'd expected Angel and Richie to disappear together. God had known that May would need her father.

Jessie led May to the magical wooden door in her heavenly residence. 'Take the handle and think of your father,' he instructed.

May did as she was asked. A moment later her father's face was smiling back at her from the other side.

'Hi May.'

'Hi Dad. I was just wondering if you wanted to move in with me? Richie's not going to be around anymore… and I could use the company.'

'Nothing would delight me more.'

He hugged his daughter and wandered into the room, closing the doorway behind him.

May turned her attention to Jessie. 'Thank you.'

'You are most welcome.'

'This is great, really… but I can't stop thinking about Richie,' confessed May.

'That is only natural.'

'Do you think he's happy? Now that he's been reincarnated…'

'Richie was not reincarnated.'

'I don't understand. If Richie wasn't reincarnated… where is he?' demanded May.

'Richie is a unique case. He represents one of the souls that we categorize as *difficult*,' said Jessie.

'You're losing me. What makes him so difficult? Is it because he assaulted Dan?' asked May.

'No, the difficulty I refer to is that Richie is unable to let go of his past. He is stuck.'

'What does that mean? Is he in limbo or something?'

'Limbo is not a different place. It is just part of this place.'

'Where is he stuck? Can I see him?'

'Unfortunately that is not possible.'

'But he's safe?'

Jessie steadied himself, squaring up his shoulders. 'During their sessions Richie informed Angel about video games. Do you know them?'

'Of course,' replied May.

'He spoke about the phenomenon of *lives*, and that within a video game you are given additional lives so that you might attempt the levels again. This concept gave Angel an idea. Richie is in another pocket of heaven, one that has been fabricated to resemble his life. He does not doubt its authenticity. He believes he has been allowed to resume living. Richie is with Angel, but he is unaware of it.'

'What? What are you talking about?'

'Richie is fine. He is better than fine.'

'You said he's with Angel?'

'Yes. For all intents and purposes Angel is now paired with Richie.'

This statement caused the conversation to momentarily stop.

'Will I ever see Richie again?' asked May after a beat.

'Of course you will. Richie was your *first* soul mate. Even if you pair off again, souls have a way of being drawn back together. Richie and Angel will spend some time together now, and when they are ready you will all see each other again.'

'I'll look forward to that,' said May confidently.

'A little belief goes a long way,' stated Jessie. 'There is often a plan, even if it does not seem obvious.'

'God's a planner, is he?' asked Adam.

'He'd have to be, wouldn't he?' suggested May.

Jessie nodded. 'It is more complicated than you could possibly imagine, with an octodecillion moving parts.'

'Is that a lot?'

'Yes.'

'That sounds pretty complicated,' said May.

'It is. That is why it is often best to just go with the flow. Live your life and trust that the bigger picture includes you, as it includes everyone.'

May smiled and took her father upstairs. She could go with the flow. Of course May would see Richie again. Their story wasn't finished yet. When Richie returned to her she'd welcome him back. May understood why he'd reacted the way the he had. It had been overwhelming for him.

Nobody is ever ready for the end.

She felt that Jessie had been wrong about one thing though. May didn't see him as a difficult case. She saw Richie as a work in progress, just like her.

'Chicken or fish?'

'I'll take the chicken,' replied Richie.

The pre-selected meal was placed before him and he gobbled it down. Comedians had joked for years that airline food was inedible but lately Richie had found that just wasn't true. He took out his travel diary and made a quick note.

Soon the passengers around him had started to fall asleep and the lights had been muted accordingly. Richie had remained upright, watching a film, when he received a tap on the shoulder. He paused the drama in front of him and removed his headphones.

'How are you doing Rich?'

Richie swivelled his head towards the aisle and smiled at his sister Dawn. She bobbed down beside him and spoke in a hushed tone so as not to disturb the others.

'I'm great. How about you?'

'You know… work,' shrugged Dawn. 'It must be nice to be on holiday. Or should I say *holidays?*'

Dawn was referring to her brother's recent addiction to flying. Richie had travelled to Egypt, Canada and Japan during the past three months. Now he was on his way to explore Europe, starting in London.

'Well, it's not everyday you win one hundred and twelve thousand dollars,' Richie chuckled quietly.

'You're really making that lotto win go a long way though.'

'I couldn't have done it without your family and friends discount Dawn. Thanks again.'

'Don't mention it. I'm glad you're finally getting some use out of it to be honest.'

'What do you mean?'

Dawn took a deep breath and continued. 'When May died and you came to stay with me I couldn't get you out of the house. You were so morose and just… hard to live with.'

'I'm sorry…'

'No, I'm sorry. You've had some really shitty luck. I'm glad to see you're turning it around.'

'Thank you.'

'I can't believe Janice let you think those twins were yours,' said Dawn, shaking her head.

'She was just scared. I understand why she did it now.'

'Look at you. So Zen and cool.'

'Life's too short to let them get to me, that's all,' stated Richie. 'Besides… Dan and Jan are actually buying my house, so I'm trying to be civil with them right now.'

'Dan and *Jan*? She's going by Jan now?'

'Yeah,' said Richie.

'Yuck. I hope you're overcharging them.'

'I am. It's a seller's market. Who knew?'

Dawn nodded in approval.

'Oh, and I'm going to sell Dad's record collection.'

'Really?'

'Yeah. When I ended things with Jan she started to break the records but there were so many she gave up pretty quickly. You know Dad. He collected hundreds. I think it's time. I've just been hoarding it all for years. I need to let it go.'

'You should keep a few,' said Dawn. 'Just some of his favourites to remember him by.'

'I'll keep them in here,' offered Richie, pointing to his chest. 'I know them off by heart.'

'God, he did play them over and over again, didn't he? I think I know them off by heart too!'

'Poor Mum.'

'So, you're going to be loaded after that. What's the plan? Are you going to buy another house somewhere?'

'No. I think I just want to keep moving for a while. See the world, you know?'

'I get it. That's why I became a flight attendant in the first place,' said Dawn. 'Even though I love being home with Derek and Mikey it's still amazing to get away once in a while and have your own life.'

'I know what you mean. I never realised how big the world was until I started exploring it.'

Dawn stood back up with the assistance of Richie's armrest. 'We're still going to spend some time together in London, right?'

'Of course. Right after we land.'

'Great. Love you.'

'Love you too sis.'

'Try and get some sleep,' said Dawn as she wandered away.

Richie knew he was too excited to sleep. There was too much to do and too much to see. Richie planned on experiencing every second of the remainder of his reinstated life.

THE END

I would like to thank my wonderful wife Tess for her support and love during the writing of this book. I appreciate you letting me bounce ideas off you. Thank you for your tolerance, helpful suggestions and enthusiasm. I love you. To my children, I hope you enjoy this book once you're old enough to read it.

To my parents: you were among the first to read this work. Thank you for the notes and ongoing encouragement.

And finally a big thanks to you, dear reader. I hope you gleaned something positive from this novel.

David Farrell

<u>**About the Author.**</u>

David Farrell lives in Melbourne with his wife and children.

He has directed two independent feature films:

The Last Resort & *The Young and the Wrestlers.*

The Last Resort, Twelve, The Glove, Dropping the Belt, Twelve More, Portals and *2 for 1* are available now on Amazon.

Many of his titles are also available as audiobooks.

You can contact him about his novels @DaveFarrell1 on Twitter.

Reviews are always appreciated

on either Amazon or Goodreads.